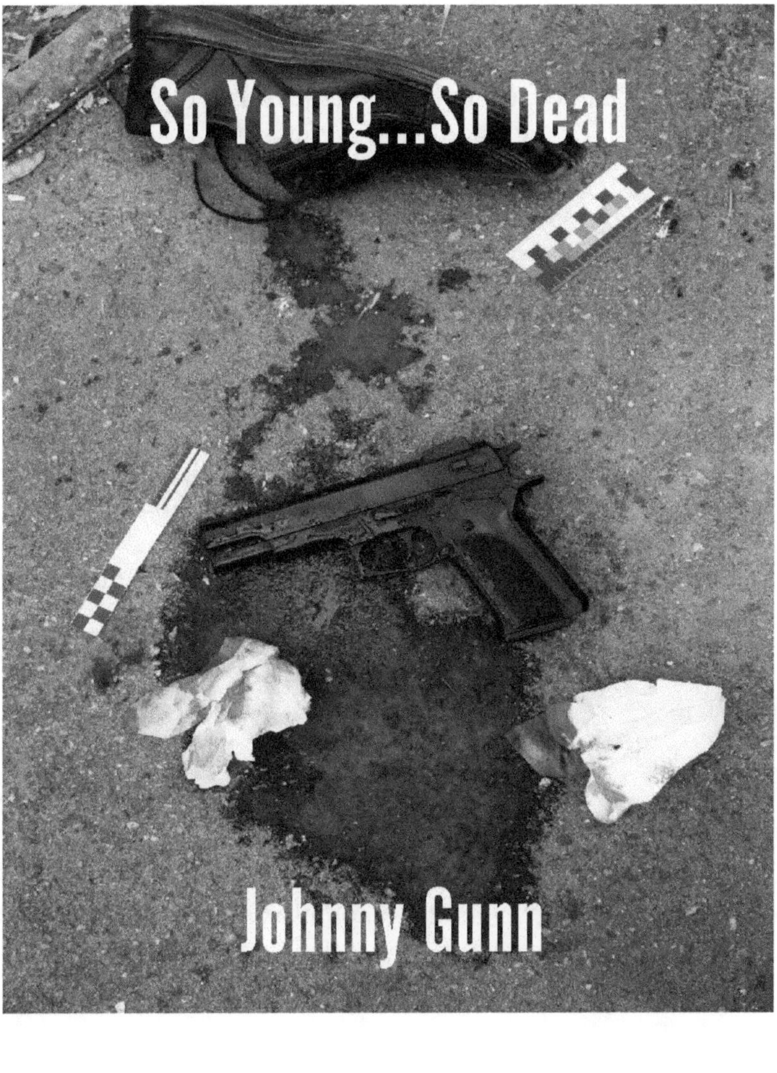

So Young...So Dead

Johnny Gunn

Cover Art:
Michelle Crocker

http://mlcdesigns4you.weebly.com/

Publisher's Note:

This is a work of fiction. All names, characters, places, and events are the work of the author's imagination.

Any resemblance to real persons, places, or events is coincidental.

Solstice Publishing - www.solsticepublishing.com

So Young ... So Dead

a novel
by Johnny Gunn

Dedication

As always, this book is dedicated to my wonderful wife, Patty. Couldn't do it without you, pretty girl.

Chapter One
Saturday night—Sunday morning, May 9-10

This should have been the beginning of the best times of her life. Instead, her naked, brutalized body, many pieces no longer connected to anything, some parts almost unrecognizable, was stretched out on a slab of cold steel, being analyzed, examined, cubic centimeter by cubic centimeter. Pacing around the room, now filled with the stench of an open human body coupled with the peculiar odor of formaldehyde, was a strong-willed detective sergeant in the county police department, considering a list of possible perpetrators, and he was drawing a blank. His mind was not completely on the matter, but to his credit, he was trying. This wasn't a young druggie, wasn't one of the few youthful offenders he knew about. This was a beautiful young girl, mutilated by God knew who, or even what.

"I know this girl, doc. This is Florida Justus. Her mother, Sandi, is all but a local whore, but this little girl hasn't ever been in trouble, that I know of. What the hell kind of person would do something like this?"

His mind was also, as usual, distracted by thoughts of another young lady, also nude, one he wished he was still with. Ken Swicker has been on the force for twelve years now, has seen many murdered, viciously defiled victims, and he would like everyone to believe this— that he has been affected by each and every one of them, in his own way. The death of little Florida Justus wasn't any different. And his list of potential suspects was narrowed to zero in his mind.

"Give me all the details, Doc. Was she raped? Did she fight back or did this start out as consensual? I want a complete report on this killing just as soon as possible. Cause of death, possible weapon used, male or female perp. I want it all, and soon." Swicker loomed over the examining table, his large frame highlighted by his flashy blazer, open collared silk shirt, and full red beard, overwhelming the coroner. It was late on Saturday night and Ken Swicker had been partying with his current squeeze Karen Carter when the call came in about a body at Holy Oak Park. As usual, he took his own sweet time getting there, then arrogantly took command of the grisly investigation.

It had started as any other Saturday night, as far as Swicker was concerned, and coming out of the shower, he said to himself, "I'll spruce up for this little bird, take her to dinner, and spend the rest of the night nestled comfortably between her legs." Swicker has never known defeat, either in the ring, on the job, or with a woman, and it never entered his mind that he wouldn't get laid tonight, or any night he wished, for that matter. Recently, there have been problems, and he hasn't been willing to face them, problems of a serious physical nature, and as he had all his life. He was looking for something or someone to blame other than himself.

He had mentioned it to his doctor, and was told his best bet would be a quick visit with a psychiatrist. Swicker blew up at the doctor and slammed all the doors on the way out, bellowing at the office nurse, "Don't give me this psychological bullshit. I can get it up anytime I want."

Why a grown man acted like a high school freshman toward a woman has probably been the subject of many psychological papers, but the fact that this behavior was somewhat prevalent had not. From wake up to dream time, Swicker's mind was on women, naked, available, and willing, and despite the fact intelligent women looked on his moves as less than appealing, he continued in his quest for more, every day. He looked on a turn down by a woman as a personal affront, and would make the woman almost an enemy. In his mind, any woman who said no to him just wasn't really worth the effort, and would probably not be the best anyway. Sergeant's stripes didn't always relate to worldly intelligence.

Swicker stood in at six feet, weighed 225 pounds, was a linebacker at State, was captain of the school's boxing team, and NCAA heavyweight champion to boot. He lifted weights daily, ran five miles every morning, and was very proud of his body. Some of his morning workouts had been postponed lately because of severe headaches brought on by the previous night's drinking. The drinking in turn was brought on by that inability to perform.

"You've been drinking quite a bit tonight, Sergeant. Are you okay?" The county pathologist could smell the liquor as soon as Swicker walked into his operating theater. Liquor and an amazing amount of aftershave lotion.

"This is a stressful job, and a couple of jolts of joy juice ease that stress. If you're inferring that I'm drunk, you're out of line. It isn't any of your damn business whether I have a drink."

"I was just concerned, Sergeant, that's all. I mean, you do usually take pretty good care of yourself." Dr. Tim Darling didn't like the man to begin with and wasn't going to take any guff off some inebriated cop.

"Of course I'm proud of my body. I work my ass off to keep myself in perfect condition, and it's just a natural thing to show it off to as many women as want to see it. How many of those fucking queers have you ever seen who really appreciate their own bodies? Sissies, that's what they are, just sissies."

"That's inappropriate, Sergeant. You don't need to talk like that to impress me, and in Vietnam, I knew a few gay soldiers who would knock you on your ass in a Saigon minute. Now stand back so I don't get high as well." A foul look came across Swicker's brow, but he did step back a little bit.

The coroner's operating theater was cold, and Swicker could feel the damp air working its way through his lightweight sport coat and thin silk shirt. Swicker tried to take on the air of a professional. "Tell me what you're seeing right now, Doc. I understand completely that we're talking preliminary, but anything I learn now could end this investigation right away." He should have known that this kind of intimidation didn't work with Dr. Darling, but he persisted. "Tell me something, damn it."

Swicker believed in intimidation, didn't like this coroner at all from the day he arrived on the job, and discovered the man simply could not be intimidated. All the bluster in the world, all the swagger and loud talking, all the menacing and threatening body language would not intimidate him.

Timothy Darling, M.D., had been the county coroner for about three years, and was never pleased when overbearing cops felt it necessary to lean over his shoulder or demand information before it was available. "I'll have some information for you in just a while, Sergeant. This isn't the time to pester me. I'll get you a report just as soon as I can." Dr. Darling didn't even bother to look up from his continuing examination as he spoke, and this too pissed Swicker off.

"Just tell me what you see right now, Doc."

"What I see, Sergeant Swicker, is a very dead little teenage girl, and if you don't get the fuck out of my operating theater you won't get a report for many more hours. Now get the hell away from me and let me do my work." Ignoring the Sergeant of Detectives, he started talking into the microphone that hung over the work area. Swicker didn't leave, but he did back up a couple of steps. Darling smiled to himself as he chalked up a personal win.

"The subject is a young female, into puberty, probably about twelve or thirteen years old. Her body has been mutilated by something with a ragged edge, something causing jagged, mutilating wounds, not clean as a sharp knife wound might.

"You can plainly see what I'm seeing, Swicker. Her genitals have been ripped open, her breasts slashed. This girl was horribly mauled. I don't know yet what exactly killed her. Everything I see could have. The back of her skull is smashed, her face has been crushed, even her eyeballs are out of their sockets. As you can plainly see, I haven't even opened her up yet, and I can't tell you any more until I perform a complete autopsy. This girl was physically destroyed, but until I get inside, I won't be able to tell you when she died, or what exactly, finally, caused her death. Now, please, get the hell out of here." He was exasperated by Swicker literally hanging over his shoulder, the breath of a lush infecting his private sanctum, and the fact this was such a young girl he had to work on made it harder.

Swicker patted the doctor on the shoulder, muttered something under his breath and went back upstairs to his office. It was 2:30 A.M. Sunday morning, May 10, he remembered, just a week before Mother's Day. Now, he had the dreadful job of finding this little girl's mother and telling her. Unfortunately, he knew Florida's mother, had arrested her twice in the last two years, once for leaving her child alone over a weekend, and once for fighting with a neighbor. Mary Beth Justus was a wild cat, and Swicker wasn't looking forward to this next duty of his.

"Could a mother actually do this to her own daughter?" His mind was reeling under the impact of that question, and he went back over the scene as he found it at Holy Oak Park. Holy Oak sits along the Sandesta River, a broad, somewhat deep body of water flowing gently to the ocean not too many miles away. The river was the centerpiece of the 150 acre park nestled in the Sandesta Valley. The river, with many tributaries feeding it, is a

9

favorite among bass fishermen in the area, and some pretty good- sized catfish are also taken each year. No one was thinking about fishing this night.

***

The little village of Sandesta is the hub of the county, and, while never incorporating as a city, sprawled along the river and nearby rolling oak covered hills, home to a widely diverse population. Current District Attorney, George Andrus, liked to say there were as many flaming liberals as there are members of the so-called moral majority. Money was obvious in many neighborhoods along the river; there were pockets of poverty, and as would be expected, a large middle class filled in the gaps. There was little separation between what would be considered the town of Sandesta, and the county's more rural setting. Most residents liked it that way, having just one government agency to deal with as far as local issues are concerned.

Most of the roads were rural, two lane affairs, meandering through ranch and farm land, past milk cows straining at the fence, trying to understand the hurry of those passing by. Artists were seen regularly, easels and paints established among the herds, canvases splashed with pictures of barns and trees and bramble bushes and fences lined with berry bushes, heavy with fruit. Rabbits and quail thrived, and of course, foxes and hawks to harry them. All found on the canvas that's Sandesta County.

In a recent newspaper interview, Andrus was quoted as saying that despite problems in other parts of the state and the nation, there was almost no racial unrest in the county. "We have black politicians, black business owners, black teachers, and of course, about twenty percent of our population is black. No, racial problems are not of a high concern here.

"One thing that does bother me is the influx of these gay artists that keep arriving. A large gay population is not

10

something we should strive for." Letters to the editor were as much in favor of what he said as opposed, and the subject was hotly discussed around the valley.

Late at night, in some of the more hidden spots along the verdant banks of the river, there are reports of men meeting men, of men and women copulating, and of teenagers learning the grand differences of their bodies, and putting those differences to use. The stretch of river Swicker was called to was one of those spots.

He had responded to the call of a dead teenager at the park, expecting to find one of the area's punks, or maybe some drugged out or boozed up kid, and instead found beautiful little Florida Justus, brutalized almost beyond recognition.

***

"My God, what kind of fiend would do this to a little girl?" He knelt next to the body, blood still fluid, not completely congealed, staining what few clothes were still clinging to her young body. Her head was smashed from the front and the back, her body ripped and torn, not cleanly, but horribly, her eyes, drooping onto her high cheeks, filling the sergeant of detectives with horror. "Any visible signs of a weapon or other person?" he asked the uniformed cops who had responded initially. "This happened just a short time ago, guys, what have we got here?" Swicker wanted facts as soon as possible. Cops knew that getting on the trail fast could lead to fast arrests. Don't let perps get too much time to create alibis and plausible stories.

"I need to get on the trail of this asshole right away, so feed me."

"Here's what we found, Swicker. There are footprints all over the river bank here, some probably made by the girl, and the others, we don't know yet. I'm having casts made of all the prints." Deputy Claude Perkins was a longtime and very thorough investigator, and Swicker knew

11

he would be on the scene. "It appears to me like this whole thing took place within about ten feet or so of where she is right now. As much blood and physical destruction as there is, it is all localized right where the body is." Perkins was using his flashlight to point out the various pools of blood, disturbed ground and brush, ripped clothing, and the scattered body parts of the dead girl. "I haven't found anything nearby that could have been used as a weapon. Those slashes and gouges were not made by a knife, Ken. Something very ugly was used for that."

"That rock near her head is probably what caved in the back of the head, but the weapon that was used on her face is different, and I don't know what it was yet."

"Is it possible she stumbled onto something else happening here, and was killed because of it?" Swicker was still horrified at the sheer violence of the scene. "I can't see this as a sex crime, can you, Claude?"

"No." Perkins was emphatic about this. He had been thinking of a possible motive since arriving, and simply wasn't able to. He was positive however about what didn't create the situation. "I've never seen this level of cruelty in any murder before, and certainly not in a sex crime. Passions exploded into rage here, and there is sadistic, ruthless brutality. This is a very young girl, just beginning to blossom into a woman, but still just a kid, and somebody, a monster, an animal in human form, went many steps beyond killing her. Look how her breasts have been almost ripped from her body, and the destruction of her genital area is past just savagery." His flashlight continued to highlight what he was talking about and Swicker turned away.

Perkins was an old hand at police work, had worked on many crimes of passion, crimes involving violence, beatings, shootings, even once had to investigate the death of a man who had been dragged behind a tractor in a field until all that was left still attached to the rope was one foot and a piece of a lower leg. "I've never seen this level of wanton cruelty in a crime involving a child. Someone either went totally mad, or hated this child. This can't be simple anger or fright. This is hate, evil hate, Swicker."

Perkins was a big man, actually larger than Swicker, and lanky in build. He was raised on a ranch in the Paradise Valley of northern Nevada, got big and strong throwing three-wire bales of hay onto the back of a truck, wrestling calves for branding and doctoring, and from two decades of serious police work. Like Swicker, Perkins worked out every day, but unlike Swicker, wasn't the least bit vain about his body.

Ken Swicker had been affected by what he has seen more than even he was willing to admit, and headed downtown. "Have all those pictures and your report on my desk in the morning Claude, and keep me up to date on anything else you find. Give me a good rundown on the plaster casts of those foot prints too, I'm going to play the prince to some asshole's Cinderella, and find some feet to match them." The coroner's meat wagon arrived as Swicker left, and he made a note to pop in on Dr. Darling right away.

"So, our mighty Sergeant of Detectives has some little chick-a-dee on the string somewhere, I see."

"Don't start, Doctor. I'm sure wherever Swicker is going is in the line of duty." The guffaws from Dr. Darling and several of the deputies nearby caused Perkins to give just a hint of a wry smile, and his bright eyes were filled with the humor of the moment. "You boys need to keep this stuff for camp fire talk. Let's be professional here," but he was smiling.

***

Springtime in the Sandesta Valley was glorious as thousands of varieties of flowers and trees came into bloom, pastures and wild grasslands turned a delightful emerald, before the summer browning, and the air was filled with fragrances of new life.

Claude Perkins could remember some of the scents from his youth, so many miles removed, so many years away. Northern Nevada in spring, way up north of Winnemucca, in a cloudbound valley, is home to this long, lean tough investigator, and he could still feel the freshness of spring, with alfalfa and grass, sagebrush and rabbit brush, cedar and dogwood exploding with color and aroma, longs for the sounds of spring among the cattle, horses, and sheep of the family ranch. He often told people here in his new home, "There is nothing like the scent of desert dust, or of spring rain splashing off desert rocks. I miss the high mountain desert, but it's true, I have found a wonderful home here." Sandesta County was about three thousand miles from Paradise Valley.

He could smell spring this late night and wanted to go home, back to his ranch, even if only for a short visit. Years in the Elko County, Nevada sheriff's office, bouncing then to stints in Texas, a wonderful assignment with DEA, and now, in Sandesta County. "I've been a cop for most of my life," he recently told George Andrus, "and I've never been in a command structure. Would I behave as Swicker? God, I hope not."

Perkins was totally absorbed in the crime scene, but was aware of another nagging thought, and he put it to voice, not particularly aimed at anyone special. "Why did it take so long to find Swicker, and where the hell is the sheriff?" He was less than pleased that the sheriff hadn't even bothered to come to the crime. "I don't understand him at all. Just another damn politician. What we need is a cop as sheriff, not some fool who wants to be governor."

A deputy piped up. "Why not you, Claude?" He just smiled, but it was a good thought.

"Before you start saluting, let's see if we can solve a crime or two. Be especially careful in gathering the evidence. This is the kind of crime that might take a long time to solve. There will be lots of forensic work, guys, so be at your best." His mind did turn over a time or two regarding being sheriff, or even sergeant of detectives, and Dr. Darling was quick to note the other deputies responded as if Perkins was the sergeant or possibly even the sheriff.

***

Sergeant Ken Swicker responded to none of the natural stimuli of spring as he began his long investigation. "I don't know why I'm doing this. Two o'clock in the morning, I'm not going to get laid, and I'm looking for the bitch who killed her kid. One of the deputies should be doing this, not me. Damn it, I'm the sergeant." Ask any of the detectives and they'd tell you, they'd solve this crime and Swicker would take full credit.

There was no one home at the Justus residence, no lights either inside or outside, and no car in the driveway. Swicker got on the radio and put out an alert to find Mary Beth Justus and inform her of her daughter's death, and to keep in mind, she could very well be a suspect.

Perkins was continuing to go over the crime scene very carefully, very slowly. He was talking out loud; it didn't matter whether to himself or to one of the uniformed officers nearby. "I've been in Sandesta County for a long time now, and I would not have believed someone this ruthless could be living here. What on earth would provoke this kind of reaction? It can't be race related, we just don't have racial problems here, and I refuse to believe this is sexually motivated. Florida was a beautiful little girl, but I don't believe I ever saw her being provocative in the least, and never saw her with any of the men in town who might take advantage of a little teenager." His thoughts trailed off as he neared the river bank, and his flashlight picked up something gleaming in the shallow water less than a foot away offshore.

"Come here, Edmonds. I need an evidence bag and some rubber gloves." He couldn't quite make out what he

15

was looking at, but he could see a piece of cloth attached to it with red stains about the same color as blood. Stepping in the cold water, he felt it go over the top of his boots, knowing full well he'd be wearing wet socks for the rest of the shift.

"Look at this. It has to have played a part in this, Edmonds. See that the patch of cloth is sampled against what Florida was wearing, and do the same with the blood. Doc, see if there might be more than one type of blood. If there's any tissue still attached, make sure we get a complete lab report on it.

"Listen to me carefully, people, there is a lot of blood here, and it is possible that we have more than one type. If this little girl was able to fight for her life, we might get lucky. I want to know blood type on every separate splash here, and I want DNA tests on everything. Somebody had to have left a clue, and we'll find it. Doc, can you help us get this to the state labs right away? This is no time to get sloppy in our investigation." His voice was smiling as he thought about how this little piece of metal could be what is needed to solve this vicious crime. Just one more example of his own professionalism.

"I'll get samples sent out first thing in the morning, Claude. I'll do the blood workups tonight, and then send everything to the state labs as well. Redundancy doesn't hurt at all. I'm glad you're thinking of DNA. That could be a big help in this."

***

Dr. Darling worked over Florida Justus for another several hours, discovering in his examination several old wounds and injuries, including what appeared to be stab wounds, slashing wounds, and broken ribs, a broken arm, and smashed nose, none related to the attack that killed her. He was voicing out loud, for benefit of his tape recorder, what he was going to include in his official report. "Young Florida has been someone's punching bag and has endured extreme physical abuse during her very few years. I wonder if this is the final chapter. It certainly points fingers at her mother. This girl has been brutalized her entire life."

After his report was written, the coroner dropped it off on Swicker's desk and went up the street for breakfast. Sausage would not be on the plate. His report sat on top of one from Claude Perkins, and another from a social worker who was familiar with the home life of Florida Justus and her mother, Mary Beth. Despite all the old wounds and injuries discovered by Dr. Darling, the social worker's report didn't mention any reports of physical child abuse in her life despite the fact the division of social services had investigated the possibility of such abuse several times.

Darling had worked in pathology for the army, had seen service in Vietnam and the Gulf, and retired as a full colonel. He had worked with death his entire career, and debated about going into private practice as a GP, but decided his background and knowledge might be better put to use in the public sector, and applied for the job of county coroner, actually referred to as pathologist, in his home town.

This quote came from the newspaper when he was appointed to the position. "I like Sandesta. There's great fresh water fishing, we're just an hour from the ocean, and there's enough wild country to make camping and hiking fun." The truth was, Dr. Darling hadn't fished or hiked in the three years he's been retired. "I guess I'm just a workaholic. But, it's good to know that all those things are available."

The good doctor was widowed during his last year in the military, and even though he had been offered that coveted general officer star, he opted to retire. His wife's death took a lot out of him, and by moving back to Sandesta, he knew he would be close to the places he and Edith knew when they courted and married. Darling was never an aggressive man, more intellectual than fighter, and told friends, "I was always a romantic, always loved Edith so deeply, and now I can feel and see all the places where we began our relationship. This is very special to me."

His thoughts included evening strolls the two had taken through Holy Oak Park and along the Sandesta River, picnics the lovers had shared on the broad lawns and under the large old oak trees; in particular, the Holy Oak, named by some obscure pioneer of the valley, probably because it was so large and imposing, as if some god had placed it there to oversee the valley and river. Arms of Zeus reaching for Olympus, he would say of the tree limbs, with a trunk large enough to fit Poseidon himself. How many times had he and Edith told of their love sitting under that tree or wading the shallow waters along the banks of the river?

It's that romanticism that was eating at Timothy Darling right now, and he couldn't get the picture of little Florida Justus out of his mind. He made another entry in his journal. "So young, and she had been so pretty. It's terrible when anyone is murdered, but when it is just a child, a baby really, it's more than I can take. She apparently never knew love, not from the way her body had been treated, and now, maybe it's better. No! Death can't be better than life, even when that life is miserable. Was there hope in her life, even if she didn't have love?" He wanted to believe there was, but he knew better.

***

The village of Sandesta, wandering in the same manner as the river, had a main shopping district, with general merchandise businesses, clothing and shoe stores, movie theaters, three large supermarkets scattered about, and several very good restaurants. Despite the village atmosphere, Sandesta County was home to almost 150,000 people, and what most of them appreciated, was the fact there was almost no such thing as a city. Rural in all its aspects, the valley didn't even have a Wal-Mart or K-Mart.

18

Sandesta County was probably the only place left without a street full of chain restaurants.

One of the good locally owned restaurants was a specialty omelet house with all the trappings of a farm kitchen, including gingham drapes and table coverings, booths and tables done in a country style, lots of leather or Naugahyde and natural wood. Walls were adorned with art work from local citizens along with photographs depicting the town's history. It had been a local's hangout for generations.

As he had done every Sunday morning for the last three years, Dr. Darling moved into the booth occupied by Stanley Lyons, the retired sheriff of Sandesta County, and a boyhood friend. "Morning Stan. Sorry I'm late, but I've been up all night. Little Florida Justus was murdered last night, and I just completed the autopsy. Stan, that little girl had been beaten and whipped her whole life, and now, she's deader'n shit, mutilated by someone who had to hate her. There are times I hate this job, Stan, I just hate it."

Lyons reached across the table and squeezed his old friend's hand. "Little Florida. I knew her pretty well, Tim. She used to help me with my yard work. She and her mother just live a block away from me. Her mother. There's a case, Tim; there's one mean and angry woman. I always suspected that little Florida suffered at her mother's hands, but she would never say so. Her bruises and cuts and scrapes always came from some kind of play, she told me. She fell off her bike more than any kid I know.

"God, Tim, maybe I could have prevented this. I should have let my police background take over. My intuition told me she was being abused, but I didn't do anything about it. How many times have I lectured others about getting involved, and now, because I didn't, some pretty little girl is dead. Jesus, Tim." His voice trailed off and his eyes moistened up. Lyons had been a good cop, a decent man, an honest and fair person, and now he was feeling a responsibility that he knew would eat at him for years.

"Don't blame yourself, Stan. Ken Swicker has the case, and I'm sure that whoever did this will come to the bar. Tell me about yourself, old friend. I'm worried about you." Lyons had called Darling the day before, just to make sure he would be at breakfast Sunday.

"There's something happening in my life that you, old friend, need to know about. I can't hold it in any longer, and you're the only person I know who can be trusted with this." He wouldn't go any further in his discussion, despite assurances from Dr. Darling that no one could possibly be listening. "I'll see you at breakfast, Tim. Just don't judge me, that's all. Please don't judge me." Tim Darling had known Stan Lyons for so many years, but couldn't remember him being this upset about anything.

One of the things that made Lyons such a fine sheriff, such a fine representative of the county, was the fact he never seemed to be agitated by events around him, was always quiet and sincere, not given to outbursts of temper or furor, able to see through problems, whether they be legal, or something more political. Stan Lyons was even-tempered, composed, in control of his passions. This conversation then was very much not his normal manner.

Stan Lyons, now sixty-six years old, was facing one of the hardest decisions of his life. He had chased criminals and evil-doers for more than forty years, but nothing frightened him as much as what he was about to do, and his longtime friend Dr. Tim Darling knew it, even if he didn't know exactly what was troubling the sheriff so much. Darling continued holding the former sheriff's hand, and Lyons let him. He needed some support, not just words, but something physical that he could use for strength.

"I've given this so much thought, Tim. I always had my doubts about myself, but I just passed them off. I simply don't have any desire to be with a woman, regardless of how attractive or seductive she might be. I always gravitate toward the good looking men, even the women movie stars aren't a turn on for me, but the leading men are."

Tim Darling winced at what was being said, and now could understand what was troubling his old friend so much. Doctors are also trained in psychology, and many of the pieces of Stan Lyons's personal life started to come into perspective. "I never could understand why you hadn't married, Stan. You were big and strong, ugly in a masculine way," and both men had to smile at that. Darling himself was often called a pretty boy, and he wanted so much to be craggy and rough as his friend was. "I remember how the girls used to almost beg you for a date, and you just shirked them off. Before I fell in love with Edith, I was often quite jealous of you." He smiled across the table at his friend, and could see visions of Edith, the one love of his life.

"I've finally reached the obvious conclusion that I'm gay, Tim. I've never been with a man, but I've wanted to. I've only been with one woman, and I hated it. It turned my stomach having that relationship so many years ago. Does this make me a bad person, Tim? I don't know what to do."

Inside, Stan Lyons had known for years he was gay, but he never did anything about it, never let on to anyone that he was different. If he couldn't bring himself to admit it to himself, this revelation to someone else, despite so many years of friendship, was devastating to him.

"I even used to pretend to ogle the pretty girls when other cops around me did." He could have gone to other towns or communities to find sexual release, but he just held it all inside, turned himself to his work, and denied himself a complete life. "I'm so empty, Tim. You had your great love, and God, was I envious of that. I dreamed of finding my own Edith, as you did, but mine was named

Edward.

"The frustrations are so hard to beat down, Tim. I've even had doctors want to treat me for depression. Of course I was depressed. All of my internal systems were looking for a sexual and fulfilling life and I was denying that I was a queer. I couldn't come out though, could I, being the elected sheriff of the district, lead investigator for the entire area, looked up to by the children, by my own force of fine police officers, by the local judiciary? Do you remember when the county Republican Central Committee came to me and asked me to run for the state senate? How could I? I came so close to moving out of Sandesta so many times.

"Just imagine what would have happened if it had been discovered that Sheriff Stanley Lyons was homosexual. Maybe I should have been more honest, but with those social standards, I would have been run out of town, shamed and vilified. Tim, you're the only person who knows my secret, and I don't know what to do about it."

His mind slipped back to that first and only time he had been with a woman, so many years ago. He was twenty-two years old, fresh out of military service, a young deputy sheriff, tall and handsome in his uniform, his nose pushed over to one side just a bit from an encounter with another soldier in Saigon, that jagged scar along the left side of his face, between his eye and ear, from a very sharp bayonet wielded by a Viet Cong.

Everything shone, his polished black leather boots and service belt, shield glistening from all the Brasso he had used, and Cindy Jackson, also twenty-two, just graduated from State with a degree in journalism. He was talking softly, more to himself than the doctor. "As girls go, Cindy was a pretty one, long legs, firm breasts, long black hair and big brown eyes. She always wore something that would emphasize those breasts with her pert nipples pointing skyward.

"Hell, all the guys at the station wanted to have sex with her except me, but of course they didn't know that part. It was Cindy who picked me, not the other way around, and I went out with her just that once, to the movies, then to the A&W for burgers.

"God, she was all over me, and I had to go along. I was almost sick when she put my hand between her legs, and when she put her hand inside my pants, I was helpless. The most beautiful girl in Sandesta wanted to fuck my brains out, Tim, and I wanted to make it with her brother." There was no gentle chuckle, just an ironic or wry smile, his mind reeling as all these thoughts returned for the millionth time.

"Tim, I shouldn't have bothered you with all this. It's my little problem, and I'll take care of it, somehow." He knew he could never face this town, these people, if they knew he was gay. "You know old friend, if word of this gets out, it will kill me, and I mean that. I'll be better off dead than to have to face all these people and tell them that I've been lying to them for forty years."

Dr. Darling squeezed Stan Lyons's hand again, withdrew his, and stared at his old friend, trying to put all this together in some way. "The idea of you killing yourself is absurd, Stan. You are one of the strongest people I know, and this kind of a personal storm is something you can work your way through.

"First of all, you're certainly not the first man to discover he's gay, and second, you'll find you have some very good and staunch friends here in Sandesta who will stand by you regardless of your sexual proclivities. Some will turn on you, to be sure, but that's when friends like me come into the picture. I am your friend, Stan, and that means I'm with you no matter the situation."

His mind returned again to Edith. "I lost my one true love, you know, and you haven't found yours yet.

We're both alone now, but we have multitudes of friends who make us happy. Let's concentrate on that for a while, and nurture what we do have."

"Thank you, Tim. I'm so alone, so lonely, but you have reminded me that I'm not really friendless. Thank you, old friend."

Chapter Two
Saturday, May 9

M ary Beth Justus was angry most of the time anymore. Angry at having to work. Angry at having to do laundry. Angry at having to raise a thirteen year old daughter without benefit of a husband. Angry, as she voiced it at every opportunity, "at the whole fucking world." When she turned thirty, and that was just a couple of months ago, she also discovered what so many others have found at that point in life's cruel cycle of growing older; her hair was starting to gray, and worse, as her anger boiled to the surface regularly, the frown marks between her eyes, furrows so deep already, increased while the lines around her mouth turned south offering everyone only the face of unmanaged fury. What could have been laugh lines at the sides of her eyes, crow's feet if you will, became disturbingly cruel and angry scowl lines.

When the guy at the service station made a comment about how he hated growing older, Sandi Justus blew up. "I'm only thirty years old, you prick. You are one bastard to say I look fifty. Fucking kid, fucking job, fucking world. I wish the whole bunch would just go away. Let me have a fucking life." She found herself screaming these thoughts, sometimes out loud when she was alone as well, sometimes just within her own head. Watching her, one could almost taste the bile.

Known by her few friends as Sandi, she had gotten pregnant the first time when she was 12, and her mother forced her to have an abortion. She didn't even have a clue what it was that made her pregnant. It was a nurse at the abortion clinic who gave her the facts of life. The real tragedy of the situation was, she didn't have a clue who the father might have been. She had been making it with the neighborhood men and boys for months because it was so much fun.

As she told that nurse, "The first time was with one of Mama's boyfriends, and it was really fun. I let anyone who wanted to put their hard on in me, and I just had a ball. It was just something to do, I guess." Her mother had never told her a thing about sex or the differences between men and women, had never had a talk that lasted more than the amount of time it took to yell at her about some chore, either to do, or that should have already been done. Mother and daughter may have shared genes, but not love.

Her second pregnancy, just a few years later, yielded Florida. Sandi had never had a childhood, never had what so many teenagers enjoy, those fleeting years of absolute terror and fun known as adolescence, had always been on the brink of mental collapse. She had been told about birth control, had been given books and pamphlets by the nurses at the abortion clinic, but one has to have had an education to read and understand such things. Sandi Justus showed up at school once in a while, but she never received an education. Sandi didn't give a damn whether Florida went to school or not, and didn't care if Florida made it with the neighborhood men and boys.

It only took Florida one solid beating to learn not to mess with one of Mama's men friends, and not to brag about any of her adventures. Sandi was finding it harder and harder to have a relationship because of her dreadful personality, and she screamed at Florida, "I don't need to hear about your fucking, either."

Those from Social Services had contact with Justus on a regular basis, but could never come up with enough evidence to take Florida from the home. They were astonished by Mary Beth's feelings about her daughter and sex. Child Protective Services field investigator Monica Rapinski, talking with Claude Perkins remembered

26

interviewing Sandi Justus several months before. "It's right there in the report, Claude." Perkins read, "I screwed every man Jack I could find at her age."

Rapinski continued, "She said as far as she was concerned, sex was the only fun a girl could have. I asked her if she meant that she condoned her little girl having sex. Even unprotected sex?" Rapinski told Perkins that Justus replied, "Hell yes. I did, why shouldn't she? You can't be that fucking dumb. Pay attention, bitch, it's the only fun a woman can have."

"When I put that in my report, my boss said to delete it. She said that Ms. Justus was having some fun at my expense. Claude, that's just not true. That woman not only let her daughter have sex anytime she wanted, she encouraged it."

Rapinski thought, *If you were to run into Sandi at the supermarket, you might think twice before saying hello.* Her passion boiled just under the surface, her eyes darted about, narrowed, fierce, looking for something or someone to devour. Although not a user, she showed every sign of one who pumps way too much speed into various veins. More than once she had to convince those in official capacities that she wasn't a user. Going over the social services interviews, one reads several times how Justus insisted she wasn't a user. "I have never used drugs. Shit, give me a man with a hard dick and some vodka or gin, and I'm happy as hell. Happy. There's a crock. Get me the fuck away from this bullshit. Florida needs to move out, and I need to get drunk." Perkins learned that all these reports have been sitting in the file at Sandesta County Health Department, never acted on.

***

It was Saturday night, and Sandi Justus was even more angry than usual, if that was possible, and coming home late, she was ready for a fight. "Fucking Jerome. Fucking beauty shop. I hate this fucking life. Florida, where

27

the hell are you? Get your ass in here, bitch." Jerome Tichner, owner of Mr. Jerome's Beauty World had kept her overtime because of a special client, and the society lady had stiffed her. "Not a fucking dime, Jerome. Your mother comes in here this morning and screws up the whole day, calling me a whore and bad mother, and now, one of your customers keeps me here an extra two hours and doesn't even say thank you, more or less give me a tip. Some day, asshole, I'm going to walk out of this shop." Jerome Tichner didn't give a hint that he wished that might happen.

More than one driver had faced her wrath as she terrorized the streets on her way home, and now she was ready to take her life's frustrations out on her daughter, one more time, but little Florida wasn't home. It was eight o'clock on a Saturday night, and Florida Justus was not available for her ritual beating at the hands of her mother, a beating as predictable as the fact that Saturday follows Friday. By the end of the week, Sandi Justus was filled with rage, and the slightest wrong, perceived or real, would lead to physical abuse for Florida, a situation that had been a part of the girl's life for as long as she could remember.

"Florida, you little bitch, you better not be out fucking somebody. You get in here now." But Sandi was screaming at an empty house, and her rage increased as that fact became clear. This has happened before, and always, Sandi eased her personal pain by heading to the neighborhood tavern and getting sloshed drunk, slovenly drunk, puking on the bar drunk, getting thrown out of the joint drunk.

"God, how many times am I going to let that woman in here?" the tavern keeper would say, but he knew she would be back, would spend her fifty dollars, would create a scene, but spend that fifty dollars, puke on the bar and break glasses, but spend that fifty dollars. There were those who left when Sandi walked in, but there were also some of the neighborhood men who stayed, knowing that one of them would take her home, and drunk or not, get laid. More than one dude had gotten a piece of Sandi's ass in the men's room, and the tavern keeper himself could remember some excursions around her panty line.

It was just another Saturday night in Sandesta County.

***

Early that fateful Saturday morning when Jennifer Tichner awakened to the yapping of her precious Pekingese bitch she called Schau-Lin, not that the name meant anything, it just sounded good, and being a frustrated poet and writer, Jennifer often said, "Words that sound good should be used." If she ever took the time to reflect on her life, she would discover frustrations far deeper than not being published; frustrations such as not being acclaimed the next voice of feminism, not having a man in her bed for the past year, having a son "who was a sissy" (her words), and an ex-husband who hadn't been seen since the day he left her off at the hospital to bring Jerome into the world. Frustrations ran deep in Jennifer Tichner, and paranoia, and jealousy, and hate. More than one person had learned the hard way not to suggest anger management, counseling, or a talk with a member of the clergy.

As can be seen in so many people who matured during the '60s, Jennifer was quite unwilling to take responsibility for any of her own actions, but was demanding that other people be perfect. This self-righteous attitude cost her son most of his friends, since not one of them was as perfect as Jennifer, and kept her in a continuous state of perplexity. Her own son didn't measure up to her high standards, as she was quick to point out regularly, and, as she told anyone who would listen, none of the literary publishers in the world measured up to her level either. In reality, Jennifer Tichner had only offered one short story to a publisher, and was sent a rejection notice.

29

This proved to her that her writing was so far superior to others in the world of fiction that she was to be considered a threat to the entire literary community, and therefore would never be published. Using that as justification, she refused from that moment on to submit any of her writing for publication. Just another victim.

Jennifer had lived in Sandesta most of her life, arriving with her parents when she was about five-years-old, and from day one voiced disapproval of the town, the valley, the county, and most of all, the people. "The intellectual level of this town is so low, there has never been a published author who called it home." Including Jennifer Tichner. Arrogance, cynicism, selfishness, and one large ego, have kept Jennifer from having many friends, and of course, she blames her lack of close friends on them, not herself. A school psychologist suggested once, many years ago, that Jennifer and Jerome attend counseling. Her reaction was to file charges against the woman, claiming civil rights violations, libel, even harassment. "To suggest I need to see a counselor is slander, personal slander, and I want that woman out of her job. My son may be mentally unstable, may even be different in other ways, but that is not a reflection of me. To even suggest I need counseling is slanderous. You are trying to say that I'm not fit as a mother. How dare you."

The school district gave thought to investigating Jennifer's charges until their attorney attempted to get a statement. She ran him off her place, screaming obscenities, and the situation evaporated. She has continued to assail the school district, however, even though her son has been out of school for more than fifteen years.

"Just look at that so-called boy I raised. He went to school here, but he sure as hell isn't educated." There was hatred in her voice anytime the subject of Jerome Tichner was broached, and that hatred had spilled into other areas of her life. She knew everyone was out to get her, to make her life miserable, and hatred that boiled from that paranoia made more than one person leave the area.

She even discussed roasting her little dog Schau-Lin when she discovered the dog was hateful toward her. "That takes the cake when my own dog is out to get me and can't get pregnant." Often the irony of her paranoia was coupled with a self-deprecating humor, biting, even personally hurtful. She gave the impression from time to time that she was aware of her mental instabilities, but often used those same instabilities to pass over what others would consider problematic.

Tichner wanted to breed the little dog. She told her attorney, "After all, she has papers longer than my arm. There's lots of money in breeding," but the dog had developed some kind of infection when she was a puppy, unknown to Jennifer, that made her unable to conceive. "Those bastards that sold me that bitch knew it. I know they did. They sold that dog to me just to watch me suffer. I want you to sue their ass off. They are trying to make me look foolish." Nothing came of that effort either, and Jennifer told anyone who would listen, "Fucking lawyers were paid off, probably."

It was Saturday morning, the sun was shining, and Jennifer Tichner rolled out of bed and muscled her way into a terrycloth robe, one that almost covered her rotund butt, let the dog out, started coffee, and found the morning paper in the bushes out front. "Bastard puts it there so the whole neighborhood can see my ass when I try to find it. I'll shoot the little bastard some day, 'cause I'm tired of complaining to the newspaper."

She would not have been surprised to find out some of the neighbors did watch her try to find her newspaper. It was quite a show, what with a very short housecoat, and nothing else between her and the world. She would not be pleased to know that the situation was rarely if ever discussed over the back fences or around the barbecues.

31

"Saturday morning, and that son of a bitch will learn just what I think." Jennifer Tichner had thought about it all night, and was continuing to mutter to herself. This will be the day to finally put Jerome in his place, get him the hell out of her life, out of her town, force him to admit he was homosexual, beat him to death to admit that he chased children. "He'll wish he'd never been born. I do." The little house shook with her stomping around, shouting and talking to herself. Schau-Lin hid under a ratty sofa, amid empty beer cans.

***

Jerome opened his beauty shop precisely at ten o'clock on Saturday mornings, and there were usually a couple of cars parked nearby with clients waiting. Called Mr. Jerome's Beauty World, the shop catered to the best of Sandesta, and even if he arrived a bit early, the open sign didn't come on, and the door wasn't unlocked until precisely ten o'clock a.m. On this Saturday morning, there were three people waiting, Carrie Jackson, a hairdresser, Mandy Cunningham, a delightfully attractive and very rich client, and Jennifer, Jerome's mother. His best cosmetologist, Sandi Justus, was of course, late. She was always late—hateful, spiteful, and late.

"I may have to let her go," he had told a friend recently. "She is more disruptive than anyone I've ever had working for me." He was still thinking these thoughts as he opened for business. "Sandi is a very good cosmetologist, but is so lacking in people skills. It's a shame too, because it means I'll probably not get to see that beautiful little daughter of hers again." Thoughts of young Florida rushed through his head, brought a swelling deep in his groin, and made him blush slightly, a sure sign he was again thinking of sex with a child.

Jerome had never been arrested for child molesting, but the Sandesta Sheriff's Office had considered him a prime suspect in more than one instance, and he had been questioned by cops in other areas as well. The question he could never ask himself, and was probably terrified of the answer he might give; did he hire Sandi Justus just so he could be close to Florida? It wouldn't have been the first time. Being homosexual was one thing; being a pedophile was another in his life.

He was also remembering his visits to psychiatrists over the years. Counseling had started when he was in school, and he continued it in his later years. His mother was never aware of that. The school hid the fact, and Jerome was smart enough to never mention it. Any mention, and Jennifer would have beat him half to death, and in her words, it would have reflected on her, not him. He needed the fulfillment brought by close contact with a child. The fulfillment he received from men was different, he told the counselors. Patient-doctor privilege had kept all his thoughts hidden all these years. Not one doctor was concerned enough about his mental stability to contact officials. He met Florida because her mother had brought her along when she applied for the opening at Mr. Jerome's.

It was true that in the legal sense of the word, Jerome Tichner had rarely resorted to forceful rape, but he was a pedophile in every possible meaning of the word, and a charming and very attractive child was prey to him, and the season was always open. He sought them out by walking by schools in the mornings, by attending softball games on weekends, by going to Holy Oak Park at every chance, hoping the young children would be swimming or sunbathing, and he hired women in his shop who had young and very attractive children. Young children danced in his every dream, every night.

He had a van painted a plain and simple dull green, and the few police reports about the van had it as gray, blue, green, even a dirty brown. Jerome Tichner had several sets of license plates and fictitious registration slips for the van. He was wanted for child molesting in several surrounding communities, but not by name, and not by very good witness descriptions.

There were only two times he had stepped over his own boundary lines, two times when molested children did not come home screaming in fear and pain, two times when missing children posters were plastered in so many surrounding counties. He had nightmares, he knows his actions would bring the death penalty, but he couldn't stay away from lively, ostentatious, pretty children.

He had asked Sandi Justus some innocuous questions, found out that she was a fine cosmetologist, and hired her on the spot. It was just a day or two later that Tichner took Florida to the amusement park located in a corner of Holy Oak Park.

And now, on this bright Saturday morning, Sandi was again late, but worse, Jerome was watching his mother come across the street, and he was facing yet another confrontation. He should be used to it by now, these confrontations with his mother. But the two are so similar, connected by imperfect genes, paranoia, and a deep desire for each other's riddance, that just the sight of her brought almost uncontrollable fear surging through his system.

Thank God there was just one customer waiting this morning, he was thinking, and he would be able to have this confrontation in the back room, not in the middle of the shop. Jennifer Tichner didn't give a damn where she was, said what was on her mind, and the humiliation and embarrassment of her son in front of his customers and staff meant nothing to her. Jerome believed she took great delight in his public humiliation; after all, he remembered, she had been doing it all his life.

One ghastly tableau stayed in his mind constantly, that of being spanked in front of his entire first grade class, his horrified teacher trying to stop Jennifer, his pants down around his ankles, his buttocks bared to the world and raspberry red from that blistering right palm, and he could still hear himself screaming for help.

He had not been able to answer a question during a celebratory parent's day in the school, and Jennifer knew he had not answered to make her look bad, that the teacher had asked a question she knew he couldn't answer to prove Jennifer was a bad mother. She certainly straightened them out.

He could still feel the sting of humiliation when Jennifer had ripped one of his prized art pieces from the school auditorium wall when he was in the fifth grade. She had ripped it into pieces in front of parents, teachers, and fellow students, telling the world it was not up to her standards, and then ridiculing some of the other works of art being displayed by other students.

When he was twelve years old, he brought a young girl home to meet Jennifer, and she told the girl she wasn't good enough for Jerome. "You're just a slut looking to move up in the world. Your family certainly isn't good enough to associate with members of the Tichner clan," and then to make the entire scene a slapstick farce, Jennifer marched the poor girl into the front yard and in a loud and obnoxious voice, told her, "Go home to the slums where you belong. Don't ever talk to Jerome again."

That story spread through the school, neighborhood, and town overnight, and Jerome was devastated by the actions and words the other children used toward him.

It was at about this time in his life, he told the examining psychiatrists, that he found he could create his own world, deep in his soul, never to be let out into the real world. A life of love and warmth, of sexual gratification with those who weren't like grown-ups, a life where he was never humiliated, never publicly embarrassed, where he, Jerome Tichner, was in control. This evolved into what he now calls his personal reality, where little children, boys and girls, bent to his will, either forcefully, or not, and where, after they were used, they were discarded, just the same as he discarded them in his dreams, even in his thoughts while awake. How many children? Jerome couldn't remember, didn't want to, actually. And now, on this Saturday morning, he faced again the specter of his own mother, come again to humiliate him, create another public indignity on his soul, insult, and disgrace him.

Chapter Three
Sunday morning, May 10

S wicker got back to his bachelor pad about five
o'clock Sunday morning, frustrated and angry, first
at not being able to track down Sandi Justus, and
second at not getting laid, and in his mind one was just as
important as the other. There was a note from the honey
he'd left several hours before. "Can't wait all night for a
quickie, Kenny. See you sometime." He tore it into shreds
and dumped it in the trash basket next to his little desk, the
desk he stored his booze in, the desk at which he now sat,
and poured a healthy straight shot of bourbon.

"Little bitch. What does she know about the stress
of running a goddamn detective division, of trying to
maintain a semblance of control. Fuck her." He was talking
out loud, and there were at least two more hefty shots of
whiskey before he headed for his bedroom, the one with the
messed up sheets, sheets that still had her particular aroma.
He thought about going back out and getting the bottle, but
didn't.

Swicker was a good cop as long as someone else
was doing the leg work, capable of using his abilities at
conceptualizing and deciphering situations, and he
believed, at understanding people and human nature. It was
the drudgery of the leg work that got him down, and there
was more than one deputy on the Sandesta force upset by
Swicker's taking credit for all their work. Swicker slipped
into bed knowing that Claude Perkins was out there busting
his ass to come up with the clues that Swicker would need
to solve a very grisly murder. He slammed his fist into the
headboard, cursing the little bird that had flown his coop.

He had been sleeping that deep sleep of those gone

to bed half soused and exhausted by long hours, visions of beautiful women dancing in his head, thoughts of conquests past, present, and hopefully, future, when the telephone jarred him back to reality. He had never outgrown his little boy thoughts about women and sex. There had never been a serious romance, only conquests and trophies, there had never been thoughts of what his partner at the time might want or need, only his desire to bed another beauty. No soul satisfying feelings, only sex, and these thoughts of conquest filled most of his waking and sleeping hours, more hours than his work as a detective sergeant in the Sandesta County Sheriff's Office.

He grabbed the phone and saw his bedside radio alarm flashing seven-thirty. "Swicker," he snarled, and heard the official voice of Deputy Sara Lane calling from the dispatch center. In his dreams he had bedded Sara many times, but in reality, she had a hard time speaking in civil terms to the man she considered nothing but a predator. Too many of her friends had found their way to Ken Swicker's bed, only to be set aside for the next warm, willing, and beautiful, young victim.

"Sergeant Swicker, this is Deputy Lane. Deputy Perkins has found Mary Beth Justus and is bringing her to the station house. He said you should be informed."

"Thanks, Sara." Swicker had never called her Deputy Lane, another sign of outrageous sexism, and Sara Lane seethed at the lack of professionalism shown to her. "Tell Claude I'm on my way."

"Someday I'm going to smack that son of a bitch right between the eyes," she fumed as she dialed Claude Perkins' extension. "Kenny baby says he's on his way," is what she wanted to say, but she was far too professional and intelligent to do that. "Sergeant Swicker is on his way, Claude. Is there anything I can do to help?" Because of Swicker, none of the women deputies were ever included in any of the investigations. Dispatch and court security was the extent of their duties, oh yes, and making coffee and cleaning the break room, and Sara Lane was among those who spoke up about what she considered serious abuses by the department. In a recent conversation with some friends, she laid it on the line.

"If Swicker had his way, we'd all line up naked for inspection each morning, he'd pick one to fuck, and the rest could mop the floors and empty the trash. I've got four years of university education, police academy training, four years on the force, and not one hour in a patrol unit or one minute on an investigation.

"You're damned right I've got resumes all over the state. Perkins and one or two other deputies will put together this whole case, give anyone with half a brain a good look at who the prime suspect should be, and why, and that asshole Swicker will take all the credit. I wish Stan Lyons hadn't retired when he did. At least he listened to us."

There was a determined swagger to his walk as Sergeant Ken Swicker entered the station house. Located in the court house annex, the investigations unit on the second level. He was wearing an open necked silk shirt with virtually brand new jeans, black and shiny cowboy boots, and was carrying a lightweight sport coat slung over his shoulder. His service revolver was holstered in black leather, attached to a black leather belt. Rather than throw on a pair of pants and shirt to get to the cop shop fast, Swicker had taken a long shower, trimmed around that prized red beard of his, and splashed cologne on his face. He was dressed as if he were about to attend a cocktail party. Claude Perkins and Sandi Justus were forced to drum their fingers for about forty-five minutes. He could have been there in ten.

Perkins had brought Justus to what was called the interrogation room, got some coffee for both, and an ashtray for the woman. She was still dressed for Saturday night at the bar—slinky black skirt, split halfway up length from the hem, and a soft yellow blouse open enough to reveal well-rounded breasts obviously not encumbered by any other piece of clothing. She lacked, or rather, she wore what makeup was left, smeared about from her recent sexual encounter. She had dressed rapidly when her lover told her there was a cop at the door asking for her. She was a contrast to Deputy Perkins's starched and pressed uniform and black leather. Perkins's creases were sharp enough to cut through an icy fog, and his leather and brass shined.

"I've got a raging hangover, Claude. Do you have a vat of aspirin handy?" It was the closest she had come to just being a person since he had picked her up, and Perkins ducked out to get her some help.

It was good old police work, investigation at the street level, that brought Perkins and Justus to the same point. Perkins had canvassed the neighborhood, and found the little bar where Sandi had been for several hours, until she went home with one of the regulars. Perkins suspected that Sandi Justus had been in the bar at the time of her daughter's murder, and had names of several patrons who might attest to that. More leg work to track them down, but first, find Sandi. The bartender thought the guy she left with lived nearby, but didn't know where exactly. He did know his name, and it took Perkins another hour to locate the guy.

There was the thing that separated Perkins from Swicker. Perkins believed in the law and how it operated. Swicker only cared whether the case could be solved. If someone's rights got stepped on, but the case was solved, that's just the way it was as far as Swicker was concerned. Perkins described his philosophy as nothing more than a sense of fair play, and a belief in the law. Because of this, he was being very careful in how he informed Sandi of her daughter's death. In his mind, she could very well end up a suspect, and this wasn't the time to foul a case.

Perkins was as calm and supportive as possible, but Sandi Justus was not a normal young mother. She just stared at the deputy when he told her about Florida's death. There were no theatrics, no screaming or crying—there was absolutely no reaction at all. Perkins' mind was working on part of this. He was thinking, "I hate this job, sometimes. I have to tell this young mother that her daughter has just been horribly mutilated and is dead. There is no easy way to do it. I just have to blurt it out, and then try to be supportive." The three just sat, Sandi's paramour stunned, afraid of what it might mean for him as well, Deputy Perkins waiting for the reaction to the news of her daughter's death, and Sandi Justus not seeming to even have heard the news.

"We have to go down to the station, Ms. Justus. There are many questions that have to be answered."

"Am I under arrest, Claude?" She asked the question matter-of-factly, as if the question might come at any time during any particular day. Perkins was taken almost off his stride.

"No, of course not. But we do have to know why your daughter was at Holy Oak Park so late at night, who she might have been with, and other information that will help us find her killer." Perkins was confused by her complete unconcern about the fact that her only daughter had just been brutally murdered. His mind kept turning over the point that someone had broken Florida's bones before, many times before according to the coroner's preliminary report, and had done other reprehensible acts of violence on the girl. His mind kept turning it over, asking, *Was it her own mother? One of her many men visitors? Did she have someone kill Florida tonight? It's as if she doesn't care.* His mind wouldn't stop, and he couldn't help thinking of his own family life back on that Nevada ranch.

He loved talking about home and did so at every

opportunity. Talking with George Andrus recently, Perkins told him, "It was as different from Sandesta as possible. Mom, dad, my brothers. Everyone working to make things as good as possible, raising hay, working cows, mending fences. Mom insisted us boys learn to cook, and I'm sure glad of that now. I did fight it though." A smile wanted to work its way to the surface as he remembered, but this was now, Sandi Justus was looking at him, and he kept seeing pictures of Florida Justus, and hearing no kind of remorse from her mother. This was now, and other than himself, no one was terribly upset by the news he brought, news that just changed this woman's entire life.

Claude Perkins was a deep thinker, contemplative, and he saw images of his own mother and tried to understand what she would be doing if some deputy came to her with news of one of her children being murdered. *How could this woman be so calm?* he thought, when he knew his own mother would be screaming in agony. Inside, he wanted to reach out and smack Sandi Justus across the face, but outside, he remained calm and reassuring, professional.

The picture was confounding at best. A young girl is desecrated, her mother doesn't seem to care; the young girl had been physically abused many times before, and there doesn't seem to be any outrage, any grief, not even any questions about whether they were positive it was Florida.

Perkins tried to explain his feelings to Sara Lane when he and Sandi Justus arrived at the court house. "What a strange woman this is. Everything she's doing, every emotion she's either showing or not showing, is telling me she murdered her own daughter last night, and yet, I can't believe she did.

"The evidence I've found so far, and there's lots of it, Sara, says Florida Justus was killed slightly before midnight last night, and people at Freddie's Place tell me

Sandi Justus was drunk at the bar from about nine o'clock until she went home with that dude sometime after one this morning. And yet, it's as if this woman doesn't care that her daughter is dead, as if she herself has rid her life of some kind of problem. A pest is gone."

"Well, try to get Sergeant Swicker. He'll want to be in on our talk."

Claude Perkins would never be allowed inside the mind of Sandi Justus, but if he had been, he would have found two very different ideas running around. Sandi Justus would never allow this thought outside her head, but the idea of not having Florida around had entered her mind more than once. The freedom of not being a mother, the idea of being a free and single person with no stupid obligations forced on her, were good thoughts. The second thought came to the surface immediately, and she told Perkins about that.

"You better find Jerome Tichner, Claude. He's been getting into Florida's pants, and he's the prick who killed her. Jerome Tichner is a pedophile, and queer as shit, Claude, and he's the one who killed Florida."

It was another pot of coffee and half a pack of cigarettes later that Detective Sergeant Ken Swicker arrived, bursting with cologne, silk, and ego. He didn't seem to understand that Sandi Justus, definitely a suspect in his mind, was also the mother of the victim. He showed no sensitivity toward her or her loss, and plunged right into a series of statements aimed at Claude Perkins, statements that could infect any possible case that might be made against the woman.

"The coroner says it was the rock to the back of the skull that killed the girl, Claude, but the other wounds were serious enough that any of them could have been fatal over a period of time. Bleeding or whatever. She was dead slightly before midnight, he says, and she hadn't been involved in any kind of physical sex, rape or otherwise, in the hours before she died." The interrogation room was small, just room enough for a table that might seat six, plain walls, one adorned with a two-way mirror, and lights directly over the table. It was a small room, but it seemed that Swicker was just now noticing that Florida's mother is at the table. He went right on with his dissertation.

"Darling says the mutilation of the body occurred after the girl was dead. That's strange to me, Claude. Somebody killed this girl by crushing her skull from behind with a rock almost as large as her head, and then mutilated the body, ripping her genitals away, tearing her breasts off, and destroying her face.

"Have you got anything else?"

Perkins was stunned by the way Swicker was completely ignoring the fact that Sandi Justus was sitting at the same table, listening to the brutalization of her daughter. He was horrified at the fact that Justus, this little girl's mother, was not horrified. His mind was on fire trying to put these pieces together. Either Swicker was trying to fill Sandi with fear and horror, or he just didn't give a damn about her feelings, and she apparently didn't have any feelings. *I can't play Swicker's game*, he said to himself. *I know that, but there has to be some way to get into Sandi Justus's head.* He looked at Sandi who was lighting yet another cigarette, and then at his sergeant.

"I found Sandi at a friend's house, Ken. She had been at that Freddie's Place bar all night. I'm not sure she understands what's happened here. I have statements coming from several patrons at the bar. It appears that Sandi was there from about nine o'clock last night until early this morning.

"I also found what could be a weapon in the river. It's down at the lab now. The boys are going to try to pick some prints off it. Dr. Darling will also follow up to see if it could have been the cause of those horrible wounds the girl suffered." He didn't mention Jerome Tichner, but Sandi did.

"I don't know if you're a good cop or not, Swicker, but you better find that bastard Jerome Tichner. He's the one, Swicker. He's the one that's been screwing my little girl, and he's the one murdered her." She was foul-mouthed mad, all the anger that had been building, then released through booze and sex, had returned. This was the first sign of emotion that the Justus woman had shown, and Perkins jumped on it.

"Tell me why you think Tichner would want to kill Florida, Sandi. Don't you work for him?"

"Yeah, I work for the bastard. He's a child molester, Claude. He's been dickin' around Florida for a couple of months now, and he's always chasing after little girls and little boys. He probably wanted a piece of ass and Florida said no, and he went into a rage and killed her. I've seen him when he loses his temper, Claude. He's the one who killed my little girl."

She was emotional, but it was anger, not loss, and Perkins saw that immediately. Swicker didn't.

"It's all right, Sandi. We'll find the bastard, it's okay." Detective Sergeant Ken Swicker for the first time showed some tenderness toward Justus. "We need to get a statement from you about where you were and who you were with last night. What was Florida doing at the park so late at night? Do you let her stay out that late, even if was Saturday night?

"Claude, will you follow up on this? I'm going to try and find our swishy little friend Tichner."

Perkins thought immediately about what Sara Lane had been talking about, and with an ironic little smile, said, "Sure, Ken. Sure I will." Perkins enjoyed seeing his sergeant stiffen a bit and changed his focus toward Sandi Justus, ignoring his sergeant. Swicker hated being called anything but "sergeant" or "sir," particularly if there were other people around, and Perkins used that little prod on

45

many occasions. It was not so much a case of not liking the man, he often told himself, but rather a case of not having much respect for him.

***

Jerome Tichner loved Sunday mornings, particularly springtime Sunday mornings, when his garden is in bloom and he could sit in the back yard amongst roses, gardenias, pansies, tulips, and other myriad and fragrant flowers, sip some elegant imported and rare coffee, even a trumpet of champagne if he was feeling especially fine, and hope some of the neighbor children would be out playing. There were times, he knew, that just watching beautiful children at play, was as much of a turn-on as being with them physically, and he savored those times. As a youngster, Sundays were no different than any other day. Just another opportunity for his mother to belittle him, or embarrass him, or publicly humiliate him. Many of his adult lifestyle peculiarities were nothing more than changes from what was to what he wished the world could be. He relished his own reality, the reality of his mind. Sunday mornings therefore have become very special, a temple within his precious reality.

Ordinarily, Jerome was not a contemplative man, but there was something about Sunday mornings in the spring, maybe the aroma of new life, the color of springtime flowers, or the gaiety of the children, or possibly, all the above, that brought on these feelings of reverie. Whatever the cause, this particular Sunday morning found Jerome in deep thought about his life, his dreams, his concepts of what the rest of his time on earth should be like. There were great white and billowy clouds meandering through a deep azure springtime sky, filling his eyes with glorious beauty. Only his eyes were full.

I'm empty, my whole life is empty. My mother calls me a pervert, and I guess in some eyes that would be correct, but it's still hurtful to hear coming from my mother. She has always worked hard at hurting me, emotionally and physically, so I shouldn't be surprised, but to barge into my own business and call me a pervert in front of employees and customers, is so painful. He was trying to put it all together. When was it he discovered that a sexual experience with a child was different from a sexual experience with a man? When in this life did he discover that grown men were more of a turn-on, more of a sexual desire, than a woman?

He knew he had never reached sexual fulfillment with an adult, only with a child, but even so, every week or so, he would end up at the Blue Lamp, a little jazz bar, and find a man who felt as he did. But he also knew he was never complete.

My business is successful, and still, I'm empty, as if my soul is a large empty bowl sitting on a large empty table; just a void. No fruit. No sweetness. No color. No love. I can bring physical release, sexual release, but I don't have any feelings, deep, emotional, gripping, grasping, feelings of love. Of belonging. Emotionally, I'm nonexistent. The closest I come to real emotion is my hatred of my mother, and there's nothing opposite to counteract that loss. I want love of something, anything, as long as it's real love. The depression had overtaken his system this Sunday morning, and the only thing that would bring him out of it, he knew, was an encounter with a child, physical or otherwise.

I wish Florida was here. I can't ever have her over here again, I know that. It was stupid to bring her here in the first place, but I wish she was here. His mind flashed on whether anyone else knew she had been there.

***

Jerome Tichner walked out to his van and drove for an hour to the coast, hoping that he might find some young and beautiful child along the beach or at one of the amusement parks along the way. He loved living near a

47

warm coast, beaches and parks to draw tourists, to draw children. Just ten minutes after he pulled out of his driveway, Ken Swicker drove in. That long shower cost him his chance to see Mr. Jerome this Sunday morning.

Swicker was on his way back to the office when he saw former sheriff Stan Lyons's car in front of Omelettes Ahoy, and realized just how hungry he was. The cafe still had some late Sunday morning customers, but Swicker had no trouble finding his former boss and headed for the table.

"Morning, Sheriff. Hi doc. Mind if I join you?" He was already settling his huge frame into the naugahyde covered seat as he spoke, and the first thing Tim Darling noticed was the heavy aroma of cologne, and wondered just what this investigator had been doing. The doctor could not understand this man at all.

This is strange. A murder investigation underway, it's not even noon, less than twelve hours since that little girl was victimized, and this galoot is smelling like Saturday night at a Saigon whorehouse, Darling was thinking to himself. Dr. Darling had never had much use for egotistical investigators in the first place, and Ken Swicker just proved his point. *Why would a man want to smell that way?* His mind wandered back to what he and Stan Lyons had been talking about earlier, and wondered what Lyons might be thinking about this jerk Swicker. He would have been surprised to learn the two men had almost identical feelings about the detective sergeant.

Lyons had hired Swicker many years ago, and the man had progressed through the ranks, using police skills and a few underhanded political moves to get those three stripes, but never making very many friends among the troops. He thought as much about making it with any pretty woman as he did about solving serious crimes, always thought more about how he looked than about an investigation, regardless of the severity of the situation, and was never willing to give credit to someone else's effort in an investigation. Everyone else's work was there to allow Swicker to solve the crime was how he viewed his position as Sergeant of Detectives.

Having Swicker join the table this particular Sunday morning would not have been high on Lyons's list of priorities, but, being the gentleman he was, he welcomed his former employee. "Hello, Ken. I'm afraid Tim and I are just about finished with our breakfast, but you're more than welcome to join us," and he slid over a bit to give the large man enough room to sit.

"Thanks for your report, doc. I have several people following up right now. Stan, you knew this family, what on earth might have happened to bring something as brutal and vicious as this attack on that girl? She was mutilated, Sheriff."

"I know, Ken. Tim told me about what happened. Her mother apparently abused her repeatedly, but as you know, a family abuser rarely kills in such a manner as what Tim described. Beat to death, yes, but usually at home, and the death is from internal injuries coming from the physical abuse.

"This is a different matter. This girl was killed in a public place, very late at night, and brutalized beyond just a physical beating. This was a mutilation, and to find the perp, Ken, you're going to have to find out why, I think. You might want to look for potential or known child molesters, possibly even serial pedophiles or serial killers. I'm kinda out of touch, you know, but I think that's where I would begin."

Swicker wanted to simply arrest Sandi Justus or Jerome Tichner and get it over with, but he had a lot more respect for Stan Lyons than Lyons had for him. He had always idolized the former sheriff, followed him around when he first began his police career, and tried to learn from him.

It had been frustrating because Lyons had the

mental powers of a giant compared to Ken Swicker, and was able to reason his way through many rough investigations and situations. Swicker always remembered it was Lyons who brought Claude Perkins to Sandesta. Was Perkins there to replace Swicker? Well, as long as Swicker had things fed to him by his department, Perkins sure as hell would be held in his place, his place being well below Swicker's.

It was Dr. Darling who broke into his thoughts. "From what I could determine, Sergeant, that girl has been sexually active for a while. That might be some place to start, you know, finding out who she's been with. Knowing her mother's background, it isn't surprising, but there are men who prey on pretty young girls, and, as Stan said, some find the greatest pleasure in racking up big scores, lots of conquests. They don't care about personal feelings, just the thrill of getting one more girl in bed." Darling took great pleasure himself with this description, knowing he was detailing the life of Ken Swicker, the only difference being the age of the victim.

He didn't dare look at Lyons. The laughter would have rocked the old cafe, and he had a hard time even looking at Ken Swicker. Swicker, of course, didn't comprehend any of it, and ordered chicken fried steak with potatoes and gravy from the curvy young waitress who leaned gently on his shoulder.

"When I brought your copy of my report to your office, Ken, I noticed a short report from child protective services. It seems they've had dealings with the Justus family in the past. You just might learn something from that report." Darling didn't go into detail that the report from child services came about from the interview Perkins had about three o'clock that morning. The waitress just kept trying to snuggle her hips into Swicker's shoulder, and Swicker's thoughts were not on a murder investigation..

Lyons looked away, disgusted. *It'll be Claude*

Perkins who solves this one, he was thinking to himself. Out loud, he said, "I think if I was investigating this, Ken, I'd check around some of the towns and counties nearby and see if they have anything similar. Then, again, just a thought, I'd see what has been happening as far as child molesters, child abusers, and serial murderers nearby. Florida was mighty pretty, even if she was very young, and it's hard to say what some men will do."

The Sandesta County Coroner jumped in. "According to a piece I just read, Ken, some women take offense when men pay attention to very young but very attractive girls, and they put the blame on flirtations by the girls themselves, not aggressiveness from the men. Several people were quoted, saying child murders in which the victim was a girl, were done by women out of fits of jealousy. My first reaction would be aggressive men, but this study says otherwise."

"Well, doc, you can contemplate that psychological shit all you want, what I know is that a girl was killed, and I'm going to find the person who did it." He didn't see Stan Lyons shake his head ever so slightly, and scowl as he drained his coffee cup. Lyons, however, caught a disdainful look from his friend Darling.

Chapter Four
Saturday—Sunday—Monday, May 9,10,11

Jennifer should have felt jubilant following the confrontation with Jerome, but instead felt nauseated, hurt, even angry. Angry at something other than a perceived injustice, which was what generally led to her anger. This time, there was a reality behind it, and she was at a loss as to how to react.

"That dirty little bastard. I've always known he was a pervert, but to actually hear it said, right out loud. My God." She had waltzed into his shop, eyes blazing with fury, hair frazzled, no make-up, dressed in sweats that hadn't seen a washing machine in weeks, and demanded to know if he was a queer.

"Tell me now, Jerome. Do you have relations with men? Is it true, the rumors I hear? Tell me, you little creep, before I bash your fucking head in."

"Mother, not here, please." But Jennifer wasn't to be denied. She hadn't slept all night, thinking about this.

"You're a fag, aren't you? You're nothing but a sissy, a homo. What do you think that makes me, you little bastard? I'll tell you what that makes me, it makes me a bad mother, a woman who raised a queer, who couldn't even raise a man. I won't have that, Jerome, I won't have it. I'm going to drive you completely out of this town, this town I've nourished and cherished all these years, and whose citizens are now laughing behind my back because of you. They're calling me a bad mother, Jerome, and it's all because of you."

Fact was, Jennifer didn't give a damn whether Jerome was gay or not. In her mind, it was only Jennifer that counted and if Jerome being gay was a reflection on her, then she must react. If in her mind there was no reflection on her, it would have been totally ignored. If she had been asked, she would have been hard pressed to know whether or not she even knew any other gay person.

In recent years, Jennifer became more and more interested in being known as a good mother, despite so many years of working to destroy her son, the son now she felt was out to get her, to make her known to one and all as a bad mother. Her paranoia was increasing incrementally, and was about to blow.

There had always been stories circulating around Sandesta County by those who feel it's necessary to follow rumors, that young Jerome Tichner was more interested in boys than girls, and Jennifer had always reacted to those stories by pointing out that Jerome's father had abandoned him when he was just a day old, and he was simply looking for some form of male bonding.

And then she'd beat the hell out of him, or find some way to make a fool of him in a public forum. All the hurt, all the shame and disgrace of being left on the delivery table by a husband was borne by Jerome, and after so many years, she made up her mind that her pain will be suffered by him.

At first, when he realized he was drawn to men, not women, Tichner tried to talk with his mother. He got magazine articles detailing how homosexuals feel, live, respond to life, and she tore them up and threw them in his face. He got psychiatric reports explaining that homosexuality was simply another form of human sexuality and she ridiculed those, called the authors— doctors themselves— homosexual, and even wrote letters to the hospitals and clinics those people worked for, complaining about their behavior.

There was one conversation with a counselor when Jerome was seventeen that helped him more fully understand what it meant to be different. He felt he was standing on the edge of a high cliff, and no one really gave a damn if he jumped. "Jerome, I have often had dealings with gay men, helped them understand where they fit in. So many have told me they simply don't feel welcome in the world, that there is no place for them. This is changing, Jerome. All I can suggest is you read as much as you can about the gay life, and remember too, education or intelligence has no bearing on a person's sexuality. Some very intelligent people are gay. You may seem or feel different from the mainstream, but you are an individual, like all others, unique to yourself, yet there are many like you."

Eventually, beaten into the ground, denied any form of parental love, Tichner hid in the secret places of his mind, doing what he could to evade his mother at all times. But on this Saturday morning, there was no hiding. "I want you out of my town, Jerome. Do you hear me? Out of Sandesta." She was screaming right in his face, her eyes narrowed as a demon's might be, her breath as foul as he could remember, her arms waving menacingly, and he, cringing backward, hoping to get away from this horrible scene.

Run, Jerome, run, he was thinking, but there was nowhere to run. This was his shop, his employee looking on, embarrassed, intimidated, terrorized, frightened, and his customer,—*yes, his customer*, a fine bill paying customer— walking out the door, probably never to return, and his mother, screaming obscenities. It was Sandi Justus who put the finishing touches to Jerome's Saturday morning, arriving just as Jennifer was uttering the words, "out of Sandesta."

"You deviant bastard, you've been fucking Florida, haven't you? You're not satisfied with having sex with men and boys, now you're having sex with my daughter. You dirty bastard. Today is my last day here, Jerome, and if you say even one word to me, I'll kick your skinny little ass from one end of this town to the other.

"My little girl just turned thirteen, you bastard, and you've been fucking her. I know you have. I hope the cops lock you up for a hundred years and those jail bastards rape you every single day. Thirteen, Jerome, that's all she is."

Of all the things to happen, Jennifer stepped in to say something and Sandi Justus thought she was going to be sticking up for her boy. "I think..." and that's as far as she got.

"Shut up, you fat cow. He's your son and you know he's a pervert." At that Jennifer swung a mean right cross, clipping Sandi just under her left eye, but Sandi had a little more juice than Jennifer expected, and she drove her body into the older and considerably heavier woman, sending the two of them crashing to the floor, smashing the reception counter and upsetting a large vanity filled with beauty aids, mirrors, combs, gels, and hair color kits. There was a new display of expensive perfumes Jerome had put up, hoping an upcoming Mother's Day sale would help finances. The salon reeked from broken vials.

Jerome was trying to separate the two women. His hairdresser, Carrie Jackson, had run to a corner of the salon and was screaming and crying, fearing she might get involved. A solid left came from somewhere, catching Jerome in the neck, sending him sprawling when young Florida came into the shop. All she wanted was a few dollars so she could go to the movies, and found herself the center of attraction of two angry, bruised and bleeding women, and one mortified and mauled beauty parlor owner,

Her mother grabbed her, shook her unmercifully, slapped her hard across the side of her head, and demanded that she tell the truth. "Have you had sex with this fucking pervert? You tell me the truth, bitch. Have you?" Florida was shaking, biting her lip, looking down at the floor. Her head hurt, and she didn't know what was going on. She had sex with many men, and her mother never asked about it before.

"What's happening, Mom? Why are you so angry? You know how much I like having sex. Why are you so angry?" Tears were rolling down her cheeks, she was rubbing the side of her head where Sandi smacked her, and she was scared. The other woman, Jennifer, scared her too. "Who are you? Why are you angry at me? I don't even know you." Florida tried to get out of her mother's grasp, but couldn't and felt another blow across her head.

"You little bitch, you have been fucking this fairy, I know you have. You just wait until tonight, Florida, you're going to get the beating of your life. Get out of here." She turned to Jerome and his mother, then, with more anger than she had ever shown anyone other than Florida.

"I'm not the best person in the world, asshole, but I'm better than you or your fat fucking mother. If I ever see your queer face anywhere near my daughter again, I'll kill you both." A psychiatrist might say that Sandi Justus wasn't upset that her daughter was screwing some guy, but was incensed that the guy was also gay. That seemed to put her over the top.

Florida ran from the salon. Jennifer stormed out of the little shop. Jerome hid in his office for the rest of the day, Carrie Jackson spent the next several hours trying to clean up the mess from the short-lived but ferocious fight, and Sandi kicked furniture, spit on mirrors, and raged at customers coming in for appointments.

Jennifer caught up with young, frightened and crying Florida about two blocks down the main street. "I'm not angry at you, little girl. Jerome is my son, and I'm angry at him. Can we talk for a few minutes?" The two sat on a bench, under some spring blossoming trees, and Jennifer heard horror stories for more than an hour. A glorious spring morning filled with beatings, sexual encounters with men whose names the little girl didn't even know, hideous stories of a home life even Jennifer couldn't begin to understand. Florida told of her regular beatings, told of having sex since she was ten or eleven, told of having sex with Jerome many times since her mother went to work at the beauty parlor, told of cold meals, or more often, no meals, stories of more beatings, more sex.

It was the first time an adult had actually shown an interest in what Florida had to say. "That sheriff was always very nice, but he wanted me to be a tattletale. He kept wanting to get me to say things. I think you're a nice lady. I'm sorry my mother hit you." Too many times other adults had tried to pry into her life, that really mean woman from social services was always prying, trying to get her to say her mother was mean and hurt her, but Jennifer was different. Jennifer didn't try to get Florida to say bad things about her mother, instead she simply asked about her life in general, and the little girl responded, flooding Tichner with a life's story of pure hell. Jennifer Tichner wasn't discerning enough to recognize her own story in the child's, or a story her own son might tell.

"When I'm bad, my mom hits me pretty hard. Sometimes, I have to tell lies so she doesn't get in trouble. The sheriff is always trying to get me to say that my mom beats me up. I just tell him I fell off my bike.

"You're a very nice woman, Mrs. Tichner. You aren't going to get my mom in trouble, are you?"

"No, honey, I'm not mad at your mother, just my son. He's done a bad thing with you, and I don't think it's right."

"Why did you have sex with Jerome, Florida?"

"Because he is so nice. He bought me things at the park, and we go to movies and things. And, you know, he's like me. He's more like a little boy than a man. I really like him. It would be very nice if we could spend the rest of our lives together. I'd like that."

"He's not a little boy, Florida. He's a grown man and he's done bad things." Jennifer didn't allow her emotions to come to the surface, and that in itself was unusual. If she had, if she had vented her rage then, Florida would have run for her life, because Jennifer Tichner was more angry at her son than she had ever been in her life. On her way home she was planning how to rid herself of the bastard. "It will be a better world without him." Thoughts about Florida saying how much she liked him made her even angrier.

"Oh, honey, you simply don't know him, that's all. You just don't know that bastard." In her mind, she was still thinking, *How can that sweet little girl think he's a gentle little boy? I'll kill that prick, I swear I will.* Her thoughts were muddled, but she knew it wasn't jealousy about a sweet little girl enjoying the company of her son. While she hated the thought of it, she would see to it he never got another chance to be with this little baby girl. Out loud she said, "I don't know exactly how just yet, but Jerome Tichner's days being able to have sex with you are numbered, Florida. Let's take a walk, okay? I need to know more about what you two do. And maybe we can go to a movie and dinner later. Would you like that?" An adult actually wanted to spend time with her and Florida responded joyfully, even if this large woman had frightened her so just a few minutes earlier.

That was Saturday.

***

Now, it was almost two o'clock Sunday afternoon and Sandi Justus was suffering from a raging hangover, a lack of food, and arriving at a very empty home. The full ramifications of her daughter's death had not made it through the fog of inebriation, despite the long and serious grilling she had faced from Claude Perkins. She almost called out to Florida as she came through the kitchen entrance of the small house, cluttered with dirty dishes, dirty clothes, food left out, and general disorder. "God. Florida. I've been looking forward to the day she was gone, but not like this. Mutilated, ravaged, probably fucked too. God."

She fell onto her bed, a bed that had seen so many local men and boys, a bed that hadn't been made since the sheets were changed two or three weeks ago, a bed she ran to when life's dangers were overwhelming, and, fully dressed, she pulled the covers tight, pulled the pillow over her head, and cried for the first time in years, real tears, real crying. But not for Florida. Sandi was crying for herself, because all she could see or feel following the death of her daughter was how it would affect her. "The fucking funeral will cost me every dime I have, everything I've put up with from that jerk ass Jerome Tichner. Save money? Why? That pittance he pays, customers who are too tight to tip, and now, Florida, you bitch, I have to spend my last fucking dime to bury you."

***

Sandesta County Sheriff Deputy Claude Perkins was equally tired, but his fatigue was different. Perkins was stimulated by the investigation on the one hand, but exhausted by the fact he had been mentally and physically laboring for well over twenty-four hours. "I sure picked a hell of a day to go for a horseback ride. I miss being able to do that any time I want, but yesterday's ride followed by a big barbeque, and then this investigation, boy. I'm beat." He was in those middle years of life, not yet forty years old, but with the responsibility of a man with a little more age, a little more time, a little more experience. Even though he was in the best physical shape of his life, he understood he simply didn't have the endurance of a twenty-something.

If someone had told him during that afternoon get together that he would be conducting a major murder investigation, he would have passed it off and said something about only being a detective, that those kinds of investigations are conducted by the brass. He'd only be getting enough information for them to continue. It was becoming clear, slowly, that Swicker had dumped the entire process in his lap and he better make sure he was up to the situation. At least, he was thinking, there were some light moments yesterday.

Andrus and a couple of deputies and their girlfriends or wives were over for the bar-b-q. "Just how the hell big are you, Claude?"

"Well, George, back home they say I'm smaller than a mountain, but big enough to tame a mountain lion." He was giving that old Nevada buckaroo grin when he continued. "I've broke horses, roped and throwed mean steers, and had my face slapped by ninety pound girls, George. I'm more than six feet tall and weigh more than two hundred pounds, but recently, I'm thinking of shedding a few of those." All around were laughing and trying to picture this long and lanky deputy, strong as they come, but with a little boy grin and a shock of hair that wouldn't stay put with the heaviest of gear grease, getting slapped around by a pretty little girl. It was deputy Edwards who ended the conversation.

"Maybe Swicker should meet that little girl."

***

Sandy cried for about an hour, followed by a fitful sleep of another two hours, sleep in which visions of her own youth danced about in her mind; visions of her daughter, her mother; visions of a life that until today has had no meaning or direction; visions of horrible crimes, of mutilated bodies, some headless, some only heads, slashed beyond recognition, but always with a secondary vision of Florida floating through the haze, a billowy mist she could almost but not quite see through. And those things she could almost make out, faces, figures, so nebulous as to not be real, she knew were those of her daughter, returned to make her life even more of a hell. Too many times the visions of her daughter would twist and the mist would fall away, and she could only see herself. When she awoke she was more tired than when she had fallen onto the bed, and with the beginnings of twilight, she didn't know if it was morning or evening. What's more important, she screamed again, "I don't give a fuck."

***

Perkins could almost feel his muscles cry out as he put the finishing touches to his daily report in which he detailed his interview with Sandi Justus, spent several paragraphs outlining how he followed up on her alibi, and created a local file on men and women who had come in contact with law enforcement because of dealings with a child or children. Of most import—and Perkins knew Swicker wouldn't even grasp the meaning of this—he discussed the blood samples sent to various labs around the region. "I think we'll find more than one type of blood, and this case might hinge on the DNA coming from some of our evidence. Above all, in a case like this, we must keep an open mind. It is too easy to simply go by stereotype or hope." Perkins hoped above all that young Florida Justus had been able to fight back, even a little, and draw blood from her attacker.

He sat back in his chair, feet propped on the desk while his computer printer did its work, contemplating what little he knew so far. It was a small office, one used by the detective on duty, so that files had to be cleared from the desk at the end of each shift. There were no pictures on the walls, and worse, in Perkins's mind, no windows. His mind was occupied by the case, not the office.

Two names kept cropping up, and he made a point of wanting to interview both Jerome Tichner and his mother. More than one person had mentioned that Tichner had a predilection for children, boys and girls, including Florida's mother, Sandi.

The printer was spitting out the last page of Perkins's report when George Andrus, Sandesta County District Attorney, strolled into the office. His demeanor was very Southern, having been raised along the Georgia coast, near the border with Florida, and more than one adversary took his slow drawl and languid approach to life as indicative of a mental slowness. Andrus used that to his benefit and had more than one defense attorney wishing he'd never heard Andrus's name. Four years at Georgia State gave him a brilliant general education, and Harvard Law School finished the Southern gentleman. His mind was like a saber, but his public behavior gave an entirely different picture. Once grasped, a concept was held, once comprehended, that famous Georgia bulldog came to the surface.

Slight of build, George Andrus had never been one to get involved in sports, finding reading a much more enjoyable pastime. Before he was out of Steadville Junior High School, he had a personal library many would envy. Quick of mind, but personifying a typical Southern attorney, George Andrus usually had the advantage.

"Evening, Claude. Tell me about this murder. I find it hard to accept that something this heinous would happen here. We have killings, for sure, but this is grotesque. What do you know so far?" He straddled a chair alongside the investigator's desk, and sprawled his long, thin frame into, around, and across the bent wood and wicker frame. One could picture George Andrus in an illustration of a country store. He'd be the one nearest the wood stove, probably peeling an apple with a jack knife, slightly unkempt and mostly unshaved. He'd also be the one with a big old Southern grin on his face, and his hair would be tousled. Perkins was looking at the live model of that illustration right now, minus the apple and jack knife. He also was wondering why the district attorney would come to him and not his sergeant.

"Hi George. I just finished my report for Swicker. I sure wish Stan was still the sheriff. I'd feel more comfortable with this investigation. I spent several hours interviewing the girl's mother, George, and I'm convinced she's innocent of the murder, but she's certainly not innocent of the girl's death. Unfortunately, being a piss-poor mother isn't a capital crime.

"According to Dr. Darling, the girl suffered years of physical abuse, probably by her mother, but we'll never know that now, and, here's the part I really don't like, George, her mother doesn't seem to give a piece of rat shit that her daughter was killed, mutilated, ravaged. There wasn't a bit of remorse, or indication of loss. She never asked to see the body, she didn't seem to care whether or not the killer would be found, She is the most cold blooded woman I've ever met." Perkins hit the keys on his computer and printed out a second copy of his report.

"Shouldn't probably do this, George, since we're still in the investigative stage, but you need to read this. I've been up since yesterday morning at six, and I'm going home to bed. If Swicker doesn't like you having this preliminary report, you can tell him for me to shove it up his ass." Perkins had that Nevada cowboy smile plastered across his big face again and handed the papers to Andrus, along with the coroner's report, and headed out the door. Andrus didn't move from his chair for another two hours, and then got on the phone and called former sheriff Stan Lyons.

"We have to talk, Stan," was all he said. Lyons was mixing a drink when he got the call and told the DA to come over. Andrus arrived within ten minutes and the two longtime friends settled in over martinis, wheat crackers, anchovies, and a couple of different cheeses, not to mention the reports from Dr. Darling and Deputy Perkins.

Lyons has lived in this house for almost thirty-five years, and it showed his personality in every corner, on every wall, around every piece of furniture. There were pictures from the war, from all the years on the force. He had pictures of every fishing trip he'd ever been on, from every deer hunt, and from every vacation he'd ever taken. If one were to count, one could probably find more than two hundred and fifty pictures of quail hunts alone. One wouldn't have to look very close to discover there wasn't a single picture of a woman anywhere in the home. Hundreds of matted and framed pictures filled every wall in every room, and not a single picture of a woman. But then, why would one look?

The furniture was designed for one person, there were no divans or love seats, and even the bed was a single bed, not double, queen, or king size. There were two chairs at the kitchen table simply because he enjoyed having coffee with friends, and there were two chairs in the living room, facing each other, a coffee table in between, a fireplace, well used, that would warm both occupants. George Andrus had been to Lyon's home many times, and none of this had ever entered his mind. All he had ever seen was a man who knew how to be comfortable. Right now, he could only focus on a dead little girl, and a maniac loose somewhere in the area.

"One bad situation, Stan. Whoever did this is either so angry as to be completely out of control, or just evil. Will it happen again?" Lyons had been thinking the same thoughts all day.

"I had breakfast with Tim Darling this morning, George, and he pretty much filled me in on the crime itself. As horrible as it is, it doesn't give me any thought of a serial type crime, but rather, a crime of passion. What we need to know— and this will test the investigative powers of Perkins and Swicker—is the passion that of a jilted lover, that of jealousy, that of a pedophile turned down, or the passion of one who is mad, not angry, mind you, but mentally out of control?

"There are times I wish I hadn't retired. Swicker isn't up to this and neither is that little puke they elected sheriff. Perkins might be able to pull this off, but he'll need your help. Swicker will dress like a peacock, smell like a whore house, and strut around demanding all sorts of shit. He'll probably end up in bed with Sandi Justus, and Sheriff Fletcher will see an opportunity for a run on the statehouse.

"You've got your work cut out for you, George." Both men understood that Harris Fletcher had run for the office of sheriff only because Stan Lyons was retiring, and both men understood that Fletcher was only a politician, not a member of the law enforcement community.

"Why didn't you run for re-election, Stan? You would have been a shoe-in, and four terms certainly wouldn't be unusual, not for sheriff. Damn, I'll tell you, we're going to miss you. I already do."

"It's very personal, George. Very personal. I gave it long thought, but this is the right time to retire. My life is going to be changing, radically and soon, and I couldn't be the sheriff when that happens.

"I know I'm talking in riddles, old friend, but you will understand soon." Stan Lyons became even more contemplative than was his natural state, and the two men spent the next several minutes just enjoying their drinks and food. Finally, Lyons continued.

"You're an old Southern boy, George; tell me what the feeling is about people who are gay. The feeling from intelligent and educated Southerners. I know what the rednecks say and do in the South, but what about the rest of the population? Here, along the north coast, I feel that some gay people are tolerated while others are shunned. And once in a while, we'll have a hate crime situation involving gays. What is your read?"

The question caught Andrus entirely by surprise. "What the hell brought that up? Does this have something to do with the murder? Do you think some queer shit is responsible?" That last comment actually answered the former sheriff's question, and he let it drop, the same as he had for the last forty years or so.

"I don't know for sure, George. Anyway, we have a few gay people here in the area, we have a few people I might consider potential child molesters, and we have a few people who have enough of their screws not set in place that I would at least look into their activities around the time of the murder."

"In my opinion, we have too damn many queers around here. This whole concept of Sandesta County becoming some kind of art colony doesn't sit well with me, and I wish to hell we could control who comes in here. We'll have more and more trouble like this down the line. I wish to hell you hadn't retired."

Former sheriff Stan Lyons was shaken by this speech and just stammered his response.

"I can't get involved, George. Fletcher would think I'm stepping on his toes or jumping into his domain, but you can. Pass my thoughts on to Perkins and see if he'll run with them. Forget Swicker. Remember, Ken Swicker doesn't understand the relationship between a district attorney and a cop. He considers you an enemy, so just casually mention my thoughts to Perkins."

The two men said good night, and Andrus hopped in his official car for the short ride back to his house, still wondering what the hell Lyons was talking about. "What the hell do queers have to do with this case? I better have a talk with Tim Darling and see what he's thinking. Christ, it's midnight. I'll call the doc in the morning."

Lyons was worrying about the same thing. *I almost went too far. As soon as I broached the subject, I could feel a change in George. I almost... well, at least I was giving it some thought, told him about myself. I can't continue to live this way, terrified that someone will find out, and so desperately wanting to tell the world myself.*

Just a little love, that's all I want, someone to hold, to talk to with complete truth and trust, someone who wouldn't judge or be quick to criticize. I'm a homosexual, not because I want to be, but because I am, and people who have never heard my name more or less know me, hate me for it. There are people in this county who would kill me simply because I'm different.

And now, I have committed the sin of those who hate gay people. I have incorporated the thought in Andrus's mind that a gay person is automatically drawn to children. My God. I'm a homosexual on the one hand, and a homophobic on the other. I just inferred that a gay person should be considered a pervert.

Because of his ability to think through situations such as this, Stan Lyons was an excellent sheriff. People of all stripes were treated fairly and equally. Black people and white, Catholic people and Jews, men and women, gay people and straight, knew they would be treated without bias by Stan Lyons, and now he has done what he has held other people in contempt for doing or saying. *The same can't be said for Ken Swicker, and certainly not for Harris Fletcher. Swicker has no respect whatsoever for women, hates gays, and barely tolerates blacks and Hispanics, and doesn't really try to disguise his feelings. Harris Fletcher on the other hand, feels the same, but as a finely tuned politician, keeps his personal feelings deep under wraps. He has never put anything incriminating on paper, but his mind is filled with hate.*

At that very moment, Sheriff Harris Fletcher was contemplating his future and how best to set things in motion. *When I run for either the legislature or the state house, they're going to be looking at everything in my past. Now would be a good time to hire a black investigator. It would be better to put some black bastard in there than a woman. I can't tolerate the idea of working with a woman. We've had a brutal murder, and a black investigator would be immediately known. I could make him a lieutenant or something.*

The word "hypocrite" fit nicely.

***

Perkins got the call from Andrus early Monday morning and agreed to meet with the DA for lunch. *That's interesting*, he thought, almost out loud. *George Andrus wants to have lunch with me. He must have found something pretty interesting in those files I gave him.* He had to see Swicker first.

"Morning, Ken. I still can't get it out of my mind the way that little girl died. So vicious and brutal. I have to find out why, I think. That may be the only way to solve this case is find out why. The answer to why will pinpoint who." He was turning his thoughts around and through his investigator's mind. "I've got all the preliminary stuff on your desk. Something I found in the river intrigues the hell out of me. It's detailed in the report. Let me know what you think."

Swicker had too much cologne on again, was dressed at eight o'clock in the morning like it was eight o'clock at night, and seemed to be preoccupied with something other than cop shop details. "Just give me a quick idea of where we are on this, Claude. I'm meeting with the press in a couple of minutes, and I want to bring them up to speed on this case. Hell, they might even help."

Perkins snorted at that. Swicker only talked to women reporters, and then only talked to them long enough to get in their pants. The idea of talking with the press without having a full briefing from his officers on the scene, without reading all the reports that have been written, without even knowing what took place during the interrogation of Sandi Justus was unthinkable.

"That may not be a good idea, Ken. You haven't read the reports or seen any of the physical evidence we've gathered. Are you sure you want to talk with a bunch of reporters about this?"

Perkins knew he was on shaky ground, but he also knew he had to say something to this peacock sitting in front of him. Swicker bristled at the comments. His eyes narrowed and Perkins could see him flexing his muscles. Inside, he knew he was right, but he also knew he was about to get an ass chewing.

"You remember your position around here, Deputy Perkins. Don't tell me what to do or when to do it. I'm Sergeant of Detectives, and don't forget it. The press can be very valuable during an investigation like this, can make the town aware that a heinous crime has taken place, that their police agency is on the job, and can even allow citizens to come forward with information we may not otherwise get.

"You're an investigator, Claude—I'm the boss. Let's keep that in mind as this investigation continues. Now, give me a quick overview of what we've discovered up to this point."

Perkins was fuming. In all his years in law enforcement he has never been upbraided like this, and to make matters worse, be lectured about something any first year rookie knows is bullshit. *You're an ass, Swicker*, Perkins thought, *and I'm now your sworn enemy. You'll be buried by this investigation, and if you're not careful, your ass-kissing of the new sheriff will bring him down also.* Perkins had been angry with Ken Swicker before, but not to this degree. *How dare he dress me down like this.*

His thoughts continued as he glared at Swicker. *I'm scheduled to meet with George Andrus in a short time, and I think I'm going to feed this ass Swicker some dumb shit ideas to pass along to the press, and then cajole Andrus into doing a real press conference, one from knowledge, not from egotism.*

He smiled wanly at Swicker. "I guess I'm just a little tired, Ken. As you'll see in the reports, we can't rule anyone out as a suspect at this time. We have some rather vague forensic evidence and very little substantive evidence to work with. At this time, and this is really preliminary, Ken, be careful with the press here, there are indications this might be an act of rage on the part of someone terribly jealous." He was feeling pretty smug with that last comment, knowing that Swicker would jump all over it, and within ten minutes, Swicker did just that.

In the County Court House, there was a conference room on the same floor as the courtrooms, and Swicker met with the reporters there. High vaulted hardwood ceilings, a marble floor, and hard walls made for ugly acoustics, and the TV people were upset. "What the hell are you trying to do, Sergeant, make it impossible for us to cover this story? Are you doing this just for the print press?" The reporter was known for never having a hair out of place, for delivering his reports in a bass voice so well-modulated it was almost comical, and for having an ego unmatched in Sandesta County.

"If this is how you plan to treat the electronic press, then maybe that's our story, not the murder of some drugged-up teenager."

There was a palpable silence, consternation spread across Swicker's face, and the two cute little newspaper reporters just smiled. A couple of cameras fired off, catching Swicker glowering at the TV pretty boy who continued his harangue. "Are you attempting to manage the news, Sergeant Swicker? Are you trying to deny me an opportunity to cover a legitimate news story, or are you just pandering to the print media?

"I'll tell you now, Sergeant, if you don't move this press conference somewhere else, like on the front steps of the courthouse, I plan to file a serious grievance with the sheriff."

Swicker's mind was going fast, trying to find a way out of this mess. "Easy now, Mr. Kelly. I asked my staff to set up this press conference, and I guess they aren't as astute about things like this as the rest of us." He was patently pandering to the man. Everyone except Kelly and

Swicker understood that. "I'm completely in agreement with you about the acoustics in this room, and the fact that nothing would be heard or understood if you taped our talk here.

"I think that's a fine idea to move outside. Let's all adjourn to the front steps of this historic old building, and I'll bring you all up to date on our investigation. I'll also have a few words with my staff afterward about how sound systems work."

There were some knowing smiles among the electronic media, particularly among the veterans who knew that Swicker had screwed up and was blaming his staff. "He really is an ass, isn't he? What the hell is he wearing? God, that stinks." It took about half an hour for the cameras and electronics to set up, and that gave Nancy Carrington of the Sandesta Journal an opportunity to get close to Swicker, and Swicker didn't mind that at all.

"So, Sergeant Swicker, while those guys are setting up their cameras and microphones, can you give me a little background on this case?" Carrington was a fresh faced young reporter who many felt was on her way to the big time, maybe in New York or Washington. Others felt if she got there, it would involve revolving beds and less than ethical tactics. In reality, both sides were right. She had slept with many of those she interviewed, many of those whose stories she wrote, many of those who gave her information withheld from other reporters. There were others, many, who thought if they gave her their story, they would sleep with her also, and found out, after their stories were splashed across the pages of the Journal, they had simply been used by a professional.

Her eyes, big and green, surrounded by a gentle and soft twenty-two year old face, set off by a flowing mane of deep auburn hair, were smiling at Ken Swicker, and the smile seemed to offer opportunity to the big man, opportunity he had missed the last couple of days. As he

71

escorted what he hoped would be his next conquest into his office, he passed Claude Perkins on his way to meet with the district attorney. Neither man nodded, smiled, or acknowledged the other.

As Swicker was slipping his hand under the short skirt of Nancy Carrington, Perkins was getting in the front seat of the DA's official car, looking forward to making the first thrust to the end of Swicker's police career. "Let's go out to the amusement park near the coast, Claude. Your uniform and my car will tell too many people around town what we're doing.

"I hope you don't mind, but I've invited Dr. Darling to join us. I think between the three of us, we might be able to solve this case. For your information, I don't want you to think I'm going over or around you, I met with Stan Lyons after I left your office last night. It was his idea we get together. Tell me about that item you found in the river."

Perkins took in a long breath, listening to what Andrus was saying. His quick mind took hold of the DA's comments, and to himself he was thinking, *Finally, I'm hearing some professionalism. Andrus was an intelligent man with the ability to conceptualize his thinking, and Dr. Darling was brilliant. Yes, George Andrus, I think the three of us will be able to solve this mystery.* He smiled easily as he looked over at Andrus.

"You know, George, since Sheriff Lyons retired, the department has gone downhill quite a bit. I don't want to imply too much here, but Harris Fletcher simply isn't the man Lyons is, and Ken Swicker spends more time kissing Fletcher's ass than he does being a detective.

"I tried to tell him about what I found in the river, and he just shucked me off. You know what that ass is doing right now? He's holding a press conference, and he hasn't read one word of my reports." Andrus almost groaned out loud.

"He'll wreck the case, Claude."

"He'll screw that little reporter Carrington first, then wreck the case." He had a grand smile on his face that Andrus couldn't help but see.

"Do you think Swicker is smart enough to be any help? I mean, he has been a cop for a long time, Claude, and he must have some good points."

"He has some good points, George, he just doesn't remember how to use them. He was a fine cop a few years ago, working hard at some very difficult cases, but because he had such a fine staff, and I'm including myself here, his ego has inflated to a point he can't control it. He believes he has solved every case that's come through the department in the last three years, even though he spends less time investigating than anyone on the staff.

"Truthfully, George, if he spent half the time working as an investigator as he spends trying to screw every woman he sees, he'd be awesome."

"When we get back, I'm going to call in some of the brighter reporters, and just have a chat. Nothing formal. Just a background chat, but I'll make sure they understand that whatever I say is on the record in one respect, just don't quote me by name. That'll slow that shithead down." Andrus was furious at the thought that Swicker would be holding a press conference without knowing the first thing that was in Perkins's files. He was remembering what Stan Lyons had told him last night, and like Perkins, vowing to bring the jerk to his knees.

Tim Darling had a picnic table already staked out at the park, and had buckets of fish and chips along with a pitcher of cold beer waiting when Andrus and Perkins arrived. It was obvious to Claude Perkins that there had been some serious planning for today's lunch, and even more obvious, that they would be there a while. "If there's a next time, please let me know with enough time to ditch this uniform. Damn. Cold beer and I can't have one."

It was District Attorney Andrus who pointed out the

men's room and suggested the deputy simply doff his shirt and badge, remove his pistol belt, and put it all in the car along with his service cap. "After all, Claude, a white T-shirt and trousers a uniform does not make," and Dr. Darling joined in the light humor. Sometimes levity was a wonderful way to break a bit of tension and get a program underway. It worked.

"I really don't want to read the paper tonight, or watch the news. I know that fool Swicker will blow this case and make our jobs that much harder. I read your report, Claude, and like I said, I talked with Stan Lyons about what we know so far. It's his opinion that the three of us should work very close on this case, and be wary of both Swicker and our fine new sheriff." Andrus was solemn as he spoke, and Darling nodded his agreement all along the way. It was Perkins who spoke up next, and the fear was almost palpable.

"I'm a sworn deputy in Sandesta County, gentlemen, you're asking me to sidestep my two immediate supervisors, Sergeant of Detectives Swicker and Sheriff Harris Fletcher." Sweat had beaded on his forehead, and he was almost panicked. He knew it was what he wanted most, but the reality of it happening was frightening. "I don't know if I can do this, Doctor, George, I've never gone around or behind a supervisor, and this is one hell of a case. I just don't know.

"I thought we were going to have lunch, George, and discuss this case, but you're talking mutiny, you're asking me to disregard our chain of command, the one thing that makes law enforcement work. I'm aware, very aware, of Ken Swicker's shortcomings, he's probably screwing that reporter right now, and I'm also aware that the sheriff's office is just a stop along the way for Fletcher, but this is my career. I've spent my life up to this point becoming a damn good cop, a damn good investigator, and a loyal member of the Sandesta County Sheriff

74

Department, and I'm not going to shunt that aside simply because it might make it easier to solve this case if we bypass a stumbling block or two."

Perkins had found himself in a desperate situation, and really didn't know how to get out of it, outside of just leaving. His mind was racing, trying to figure out what to do. *This is preposterous. I've got a sergeant who can't get his mind on anything but pussy, a sheriff who only sees the governor's mansion, and now a coroner and a lawyer who want to run the detective division of the department. My thoughts should be about a little thirteen-year-old girl who never had a chance at life, lying ice cold in a coffin, with a mother who simply doesn't care, and instead, I'm only thinking now how to protect my fucking job. If Fletcher or Swicker hear about this meeting, I'm out, gone, fired, dead meat.*

On the other hand, isn't this why I came out here? I can't continue to work under these pressures. It's hard enough to spend an entire night with the mutilated remains of a teenage girl—now I'm contemplating mutiny. He let his emotions settle, and finally spoke his mind. "Gentlemen, it's important for you to understand how much my career means to me. If I get fired because of something I'm doing with you, behind the backs of my superiors, the problem will follow me for the rest of my life. I'm not a politician, I'm a cop, and my first priority has to be to my department." His mind was whirling, trying to put some kind of sense to what was happening.

It was Dr. Darling who brought things into perspective, both for Perkins and for Andrus. "Claude, I think George might not have expressed himself too clearly a minute ago. We would never ask you to do anything to jeopardize either your career or this case. I'm very aware of your abilities, as is Mr. Andrus, and what we're interested in is what you're interested in. Solving this case as quickly as possible.

"Ken Swicker is a womanizing, selfish, and egotistical person, but he is also trained as a good policeman. He's simply lost the trail, and there is nothing any of us can do about that. You will have to continue to work with him, Claude, because it's your job and your duty. I think what George and I both want is to be kept abreast of what's happening. For Swicker to call a press conference without benefit of knowing how far along the case has gotten, and then to attempt to embarrass the electronic media is a serious display of his lack of leadership.

"I don't think George Andrus wants to simply take over the case, and I know I don't want you off the case. I had a long talk with Stan Lyons yesterday, and George, you had one with him last night. We both are under the impression you are the only one who might have a chance at bringing this thing to a close." He watched as Claude Perkins took it all in, watched as Perkins visibly loosened up, saw a softening in his eyes and the set of his jaw, and understood that there was now a three way partnership.

"You know, at heart, I'm just an old Nevada buckaroo, and sometimes I have to say what's on my mind. I'm very disturbed by what Ken Swicker is doing, I'm equally disturbed by the lack of professionalism shown by our sheriff, and I'm not really sure I can fight the whole damn war.

"I'm a good, well trained investigator, hell, I've put my whole life into a badge and uniform, and I'll do everything in my power to bring this case to a close." Perkins was letting his mind expand on those thoughts, thinking about this possibility of being lead investigator of the department, being in a command position. He was aware that he had been training for this, and it was being offered. Was he up to it, professionally and personally? It was a big question, and he was willing to find that answer. "Gentlemen, just so you know, I'm very proud to be working with the two of you."

The meeting lasted more than two hours, a couple of buckets of fish and chips were devoured, not to mention a pitcher or two of cold beer, and Perkins was relieved to know he would be working with some very professional people. His thoughts on the way back to Sandesta were still just a bit mixed.

I damn near walked away from that table. I sure as hell wanted to, all that talk about just the three of us doing this. When this is over, I'm heading for Nevada and a long ride in the Santa Rosa mountains. Maybe even shoot a chukar or two. If I don't do that, I'll be forced to resign. There would be no way I could continue working with either Swicker or Fletcher. He was as contemplative as it is possible to be while Andrus and Dr. Darling bantered back and forth. For Perkins, he was talking in his mind only.

I don't know right now, who might be responsible for this murder, but I do know that it will be solved. Sandi Justus is out of the picture, as far as I'm concerned; there are just too many people who knew where she was during the time frame of the killing, but I do want to have a long interview with that Jerome Tichner. His name has come up too many times.

For George Andrus, his thoughts were just a little different. *I think I'll call that TV ass first, then little Nancy Carrington. If Swicker got in her pants, she might find it interesting that what he told her about the case might not be the truth. She could end up on our side.*

Chapter Five
Monday, May 11—Tuesday, May 12

Sandesta County ends about five miles from the coastal resort where Perkins, Andrus, and Darling were having lunch. Parkland at the Sea is in Johnson County, and at that moment, members of the Johnson County Sheriff's office were attempting to interview an eleven-year-old boy who was telling them about a man who had offered playland rides, hot dogs, cotton candy and a fun afternoon. The boy had a few bruises on his body; on his upper arms, the bruises were as the shadows of the fingers that had gripped him so tight. There were abrasions as well; a couple on his thighs where the man also held him. What had the detectives incensed were the strong indications of rape. The crying, held in check for a few minutes, started again with little effort. Over and over, terror-filled eyes would fill with tears, and bouts of sobs and screams would follow. Doctors and nurses alike, sobbing along with the boy.

The boy couldn't look any of the officers in the eye, tried to pull back from their hands, screamed in terror when touched. Eleven-year-old Kevin Demetrius was in physical and psychological shock, the trauma seared into his soul, and these men were forcing him to remember how another man had violated his very being. The officers and doctors and nurses were being as kind as possible, fully understanding the boy's trauma, and also harboring hate for the demon who caused it all. The cops silently, each in his own way, vowed to kill the bastard, or at the least beat the shit out of the man. Kevin's description of the sexual molestation was graphic and each of the detectives vowed they might not wait for some judge to let this molester off with a slap on the wrist. Maybe, they said to each other afterwards, they could take him deep into the forest, tear him apart, leave him for dogs and coyotes, bears and cougars.

Detective Jim Roberts was relaying what he had learned during the boy's interview. "I feel sick, Sheriff. This boy wasn't just molested, wasn't just raped and thrown aside; he was tortured, his soul vandalized. I'm going to have more than a difficult time holding myself in check, Sheriff, and I know the rest of the squad feels the same."

The three-county bulletin that went out late on Monday was written by the chief investigator, detective Jim Roberts. It described a van, maybe brown in color, being driven by a white male, about 30-years-old, about medium build and height, with long, unkempt, dirty blonde hair, green eyes, wearing a pair of jeans, and white T-shirt.

Perkins found the bulletin on his desk the next morning. It had been there since late Monday, but of course, Perkins was at the park with Darling and Andrus. His mind picked up on one little detail: "It's interesting that this is given to me and not to Swicker." He walked into his sergeant's office and showed him the bulletin. "That isn't much to go on, but it tells us there is a pedophile in the area, Ken. I'd like to go talk to that boy, and then visit Jerome Tichner. You said he wasn't home Sunday, and it's a mighty short drive down to the coast. I don't have a description of what he drives, but if it's a van, I'd bet it's pretty damned close. Care to come along?"

Swicker was scowling as he read the report. "Why don't I have a copy of this, Perkins? Why the hell would this be given to you and no copy to me? Who the hell runs this department, Deputy Perkins? Do you think you can just take this case on your own, bypass me entirely, run the fucking sheriff's office? What the hell is going on here?"

"You're getting yourself pretty riled up here, Ken.

How the hell would I know why the report was put on my desk, not yours?"

Swicker was riled and even when sitting, made the most of his bulk. "My name is Sergeant Swicker, Deputy Perkins. Don't ever fucking forget that. Get that little communications bitch in here right now." Swicker was more than furious about not being informed of a child molesting incident just a few miles away, even if it was in a different county.

Claude Perkins walked down to the communications desk and told Sara Lane that Swicker wanted to see her. He didn't say anything else. There was a smile on his face as he thought about what might happen. *Sara is just liable to set him back more than a step if he jumps on her case too hard. Communications bitch? I wonder how a federal judge would look on a comment like that? I'm trying to find a murderer, an evil and desperate killer, and he's worried about office protocol.* No wonder Stan Lyons asked the coroner and the DA to keep an eye on this case.

***

Everyone in the court house annex heard the yelling and screaming, heard the distinctive sound of an open-handed slap to bare skin—so loud, heads turned. Those close by heard a thump as if something large and heavy was bounced off a wall; far larger and heavier than say, a basketball. That was followed by the sound of a wooden chair breaking apart from a body falling into or onto it. Muted cries of astonishment, anger, fear came from Sergeant of Detectives Swicker's office. Foul language, recrimination, and anguish were among the sounds echoing in the marble halls of justice.

Sara Lane emerged from Ken Swicker's office, crying as much from anger as from physical pain. Her uniform blouse was all but ripped from her body, with many buttons missing, she was nursing a bloody lip, and was walking with a decided limp. Her eyes, some said her best feature, blazed with hate, and just a little shame. She marched straight into the sheriff's private office, ripped her badge off, loosened her gun belt, and slammed the whole mess on Fletcher's desk.

"You win this round, you sexist bastard, but I'm not through with the war. Note the time and date, sheriff, because in just a short while you'll be getting a call from my attorney. She won't like what I'm going to say." Lane stood straight and tall, didn't even attempt to re-button her shirt front, or even arrange the decidedly open front where it had been ripped, and marched out of the courthouse, head held high, her boot heels ringing from the marble floors and hard walls, echoing up and down the stairways and corridors. In moments, the ancient old courthouse was silent. When Sara Lane got angry, tears began to flow, and by the time she made the two blocks to Barbara Mingus's office, her whole face was wet. She didn't give a damn that people could see her bra through the ripped uniform shirt and missing buttons, didn't give a damn what she looked like. She only cared about one thing: bring down Ken Swicker and Harris Fletcher.

"Sara, in all my years as a civil rights attorney, I've never seen such an excellent case. Let's get a couple more pictures here, then we'll get some testimony. Interesting, isn't it, that the first woman on the force should be run off and come see the only black attorney in the County who is also a woman? There is lots of work to do, my dear, lots of work. The only way this would be a better case would be if you were black, too."

"That fucker reached across his desk and hit me right in the face, Barbara, then that fucker grabbed one of my tits. That's when I slapped him so hard he actually stepped back. He grabbed me by my blouse and flung me against the wall, then tried to rip my blouse right off me. His balls will hurt for a month where I hit him with my fist.

"That filthy pig. That filthy pig. I don't care what it takes, Barbara, I want that bastard out of a job, I want that prick sheriff sent packing, and to make up for all this, I want lots of money." Her hate and anger were focused, and Mingus had her tape recorder going the whole time.

"Just a couple more pictures, dearie." Civil rights was her specialty, and she had the best case of her life standing in front of her. Her smile could have lit a city.

***

Down in the basement, in the cold room where pathologists work over dead human remains, Tim Darling was startled by what he could hear overhead, and putting aside his tools, ventured a look up the stairwell. All he found was empty space and silence. The courthouse was mute. It was George Andrus, completely unaware of what had just happened, who got things started again when he arrived, traditionally tardy, to begin another day.

"G'mornin' Claude, how are you? How's that Florida Justus case coming? The news this morning said there was a young boy who was molested over in Johnson County yesterday. You heard anything about that? Nasty goings on if you ask me. I have to tell you though, those reporters sure didn't much care for what I told them yesterday after what Ken Swicker had told them. They said they were getting two different stories.

"I think I'll drop in on that sergeant of detectives this morning. He really shouldn't be talking to the press if he doesn't know what he's talking about. Maybe I'll talk to that new sheriff of ours, too." He had a nasty little gleam in his eye, knowing he was going to stir a big pot full of shit, but not knowing a nest full of droppings had already been strewn about. Perkins didn't say a word, just smiled good morning and started back to his desk, a cup of coffee in one hand, the morning paper in the other. He wanted to know what Swicker had told the press and what Andrus had told them. This is what mornings are all about, he was thinking, that buckaroo smile cutting across a big open face. "I could ride a horse all day after a morning like this." He didn't get a chance to glance at anything other than headlines.

***

Harris Fletcher had no idea what Sara Lane was talking about, was clueless to the point of just accepting the resignation and letting it go at that. His thoughts, as always, were on bigger stakes. He was mulling over a campaign issue that just might get him near the state house. *If Swicker and these others can put this murder to bed, I can use that to get that job. It's probably just as well that little girl quit. Women don't have any business being cops, for Christ's sake. What was Lyons thinking, hiring a woman in the first place?*

There had been talk, he'd heard it, of a recall attempt on his office, but Fletcher didn't put much credence in that kind of talk. He had other things on his mind at the moment, and called Herb Thompson, the man who ran his campaign for sheriff. "Hello, Thompson, this is Harris Fletcher. How are you today? Listen, I'd like you and your wife to come to dinner at my place Friday, can you make it? I want to discuss the possibility of you handling my campaign for governor. When I find the murderer of this little hot pants item, yeah, that teenager who couldn't keep her pants on, anyway, it will be a good time to kick off the campaign."

"Listen, Harris, I'm not sure about your call on this. That little girl was hideously brutalized, and there's nothing to indicate that sex was involved. While I have you on the line, there's something far more important to your political life than beginning a campaign for the state house. This talk of a recall is gaining all kinds of momentum. That's what we need to talk about."

"Shit, Herb, anytime someone is elected to a controversial office there'll be talk of a recall. Don't think about that at all, just come up with some good ideas for me to use to become governor of this great state.

"And, you're wrong, Herb. Ken Swicker told me this little whore was on the make day and night before she was offed. Get your ducks up and in line before you challenge me, fucker. Now, will you be there Friday?" Harris Fletcher had that conspiratorial chuckle working, the one that usually won someone over to his side.

"I'll see you Friday night, Harris."

Chapter Six
Monday night—Tuesday morning,
May 12 & 13

I t was nearly midnight still Monday by the calendar, when Sandi Justus got home, pissed at the world, drunk as usual, and alone. She paid the cabby, staggered up to her doorway, fumbled for her keys, and stumbled into the living room. For many around her, it was just another night of being a drunk asshole, although there were some who tried to offer condolences. That seemed to generate even more anger. She had cried most of the evening, taking out all her frustrations on the bartender, on his customers, and drinking more than she had in a long time. Even now, she was still cursing and talking to herself.

"That little prick is going to fire me, I know it, and that fat pig he calls mother is responsible. I should have beat her half to death. I should have killed the old bitch, that's what I should have done. Coming in that store, calling me a bad mother when it's her own son who's the fucking queer pedophile.

"Damn it, Florida, how did you get so fucked up? Hanging around with that asshole, probably screwing him anytime he wanted a little young stuff. At least I hope you got some of his money, the cheap bastard."

She bobbed and weaved her way into the kitchen to pour another glassful of whisky, and it took more than a couple of seconds to realize she wasn't alone in there. "What are you doing here? What are you doing in my house? Get out of here, get out!" Her voice was high pitched to start with, and now she was screaming. Anger was turning to fear, drunkenness impeding any chance of getting away.

85

The cast iron frying pan crashed into her skull, and she felt powerful arms drag her into her bedroom. She died with the next blow of the heavy iron weapon. She never felt any of the mutilation that followed—the ripping of her breasts, ravaging and maiming of her most private parts. She never heard the vile things said to her, said about her, shrieked at her. Rage in all its ramifications spilled out of her murderer and across her body: rage, anger, frustration, pent-up hell and fury, and Sandi Justus was dead.

It was over in minutes, and the person responsible felt good. *She should have died at the same time as her evil daughter, that pretty little girl who did so much damage to me.*

Now, both mother and daughter are gone, never to enter my life or my mind again. It is a good thing I've done.

It took a moment to realize there was blood on one of the shoes, but it was too late to do anything about that. *I'll toss the whole pair in some trash can somewhere.* The murderer left by way of the back door, the unlocked back door, the same one used to enter in the first place, found the car, and drove off. If anyone had been watching, the driver would have been seen using a cell phone on the way.

In less than ten minutes, the first patrol unit pulled up to the Justus residence, soon followed by Claude Perkins in his personal car. "Where's Sergeant Swicker?"

"Don't know Claude. I heard the radio trying to reach him, but they haven't had any success."

"Has Dr. Darling been notified?" He didn't mind taking charge of the early phases of an investigation; what he hated was the fact the sergeant who should be doing this wasn't to be found. His mind was going back over the death of Florida Justus and the way Swicker showed up well after the investigation was underway, and didn't seem to care if he got any of the early information. He let fly at the deputy, knowing full well it wasn't his fault.

"Damn that man. I didn't come to this fucking

county to be saddled with a moron. Sheriff Lyons was the only reason I left DEA, and then he retired, I get a fool for a sheriff and a Goddamned rooster, a cock of the walk, for a sergeant. I should have stayed in Nevada, at least people there care about what it means to be a respected member of a community." His thoughts were actually mean, but all the surrounding deputies knew his frustration and agreed with his position.

"Let's have a look."

"She's in the bedroom, Claude, but there's blood in the kitchen as well, and a couple of very good footprints, bloody prints, going out the back door. It looks like the victim may have had her head bashed in with a frying pan, and then she was mutilated almost the same as her daughter."

"How did you find her? Did she call for help? What else do we know?" Perkins was a good cop, well trained by the sheriff in Elko, Nevada and by Nevada Investigations, along with FBI Academy schooling, and his time with the DEA.

"According to my radio call, they got a call at headquarters saying there was some kind of problem here. Screaming of some kind. I think it came from one of the neighbor women, Claude."

"Okay. Get pictures, layout of body and weapons, make damn sure you get as much information as you can from those footprints, dust everything for prints, and Edwards, go outside, around from the front, and see if there are bloody prints leading anywhere out there.

"Be as cautious as possible. We don't want to lose anything here. Get good blood samples, and remember DNA. We're going to have to conduct this investigation as two separate homicides until they can be tied together. Damn, two women with their heads caved in, their bodies destroyed. And within just hours of each other.

"Doc, I'm glad you're here. This is Sandi Justus,

killed almost the same way her daughter was. Let me know everything you find. It looks like that same kind of weapon may have been used. You'd know more than me on that, but she is torn up pretty bad. Jagged rips, not clean as a knife would make them.

"Where the fuck is Swicker, damn it?" He walked out to a patrol unit and called in. "Do you mean to tell me he didn't leave a number where he could be reached, or carry a radio? He's the damn sergeant of detectives, for Christ's sake. Did you get hold of the sheriff?" He knew better than to ask. Sheriff Fletcher had never responded to a crime since being elected.

"I left a message, Claude. He's not answering his phone, and he doesn't even have a radio."

Perkins walked back into the Justus home. "That man runs the most shoddy operation I've ever heard of, Doctor. No sheriff, no sergeant, just you and me one more time. Did they do things like this in the army? I'll guarantee they aren't done this way in any other police agency in this fucking country." Perkins was more angry than he wanted to admit. "You know, Doc, it's not a nice thing to say, but any one of these detective deputies would make a better sergeant that Ken Swicker."

"I hope you include yourself in that, Claude. I assume the sheriff isn't going to make an appearance either. It's called malfeasance if you need to put a name to it sometime, and his actions are corrupting the thinking of others in the department. And I include Swicker in that. Swicker's just ego driven, and the sheriff has an agenda that doesn't include Sandesta County. We pay the price for both." He was shaking his head as he walked back into the bedroom.

"I've heard you say, Claude, that you wished Stan had never retired. I wish Lyons had named you Sergeant of Detectives before he left."

Perkins was looking around the small home, two

bedrooms, one bath, a dining nook, laundry room, and kitchen. The furnishings came from several used or thrift outlets. A single couch, two chairs, two table lamps and a coffee table in the living room, none of it matched. He was talking into his tape recorder as he moved about the house. "There's not a book or magazine in the room, but there is an old television and VCR. No movies though. They must have rented, I guess." The carpet was shabby and worn, covered in places by parts of other old carpet thrown about as rugs.

"This wasn't living. This is just existence." He walked into the bedroom that Florida occupied, and found even more clutter. "No indication this girl might have gone to school somewhere. No books, no desk to work at, not even a lamp next to the bed to read by." Her closet held three or four dresses, a few blouses and sweaters, all very old. There were jeans and shorts in her dresser, limited sets of underwear and socks, nothing one would expect to find in a budding teenager's room.

"Where the hell are the rock star posters, the model's posters? There aren't any souvenirs from school, no pictures of her and her friends, nothing to indicate she had a family. That poor girl died horribly, but she must have lived the same way." He walked back out into the living room just as they were taking Sandi Justus's body out.

"Is there anything in her bedroom that indicates this may have been a family, Dr. Darling? Anything?"

"Not a thing, Claude. No pictures. Nothing."

Perkins stuck his head in and looked around, not wanting to get in the way of the detectives searching for anything that might aim them somewhere. There wasn't even a nightstand at the head of the bed. "You guys take as much time as you need, and then get your reports onto Sergeant Swicker's desk. If you need me, I'll be at home. Use the radio or the telephone." He called Deputy Edmonds aside as he walked toward the door. "Put copies of everything in a file on my desk, too, Edmonds."

He drove slowly home, wondering what in the hell was going on in his police department. *I'm just a beat-up old Nevada cowboy, really, but I'd like to think I'm a good cop. This isn't right; no sheriff, no sergeant. Talk about flying blind. Well, I've got to get some sleep, tomorrow's going to be a bear, big old griz of a bear. I feel it building already.* It may not have been in his mind at the moment, but he had already assumed command of the detective division of the Sandesta County Sheriff.

As he made the drive home, his mind wouldn't slow down. *I'll find Jerome Tichner in the morning. Sandi worked for him. I don't know if she had any other relatives, but we'll get to that in the morning also.* He switched as he neared home, from active mind to active speech. Like most men whose minds were always at work, he talked to himself. "Two murders, mother and daughter, and I have to assume done by the same person. Just too many similarities.

"God damn you, Swicker." He spat the words out. He was thinking that if he could find an extra few minutes during the next day or two, he should call Stan Lyons. He was a damn fine sheriff. *He might just give me a little direction here. It is interesting that he contacted the coroner and the DA to tell them to assist me.* He should have directed that kind of thinking to Swicker. Or even to the new sheriff.

Chapter Seven
Sunday—Monday—Tuesday, May 10,11,12

He was sobbing all the way back to Sandesta, crying like the baby he was, knowing he had to get the van hidden, had to get his clothing disposed of. It was a mad drive home. He didn't see a patrol unit the entire trip, nearly ran off the road twice, passed erratically, and drove well over the posted limit of forty-five miles per hour. He could see himself dead, he could see dead children, he saw his mother standing over his grave, shaking her fist at him, screaming obscenities, and he could see pictures of the pretty little boy. He drove, hard, fast, erratic, to the safety of his own home. His mind was on fire with fear and self-loathing. He was talking to himself in a voice he almost didn't recognize as his own.

"I've got to hide this van. In the garage, and then I'll rake some leaves in front of the doors to make it look like it hasn't been moved for a while." He'd seen that done in a movie once, and it impressed him. "God, I've got to get cleaned up, can't let anyone find me looking like this. God, the blood, and filth. A hot shower."

Jerome Tichner dressed in fresh slacks and a flowered shirt, took his ragmop wig of long stringy dirty blonde hair and soiled clothing into the back yard and tucked them under his compost pile, mating them with clothing from other ventures. Memories of what else was at the bottom of that pile mixed with the memories of other conquests and failures, and again he found himself crying. He was sobbing because his own reality was too close to the surface right now.

Would that trick, hiding things under his compost pile work? Nobody will go through a compost pile of

91

rotting vegetation. Why would someone look under a compost pile for evidence? He hoped the clothing would be rotting right along with the vegetation, and the evidence. And those other problems.

Tomorrow was Monday, and all that Jerome knew was he had to leave, go somewhere out of town. There had been so many Sundays just like this one, he knew the routine. He packed a small bag, called a cab. "Hi, Mr. Tichner. Where to this weekend?"

"I'm glad it's you, Bob. I'm going upstate a little way. There's a new art gallery opening. How's your wife and kids?"

To himself he was saying, "Remember this, Bob. Remember picking me up and bringing me to the bus station. Remember me saying I'm going upstate."

A Blue and Gray bus took him three hours away where he found a motel room, one he'd stayed in so often it "feels almost like home." He stopped at a liquor store and bought two half-gallon jugs of cheap red wine, a deli sandwich, and hopefully, twenty-four hours of solitude. Mr. Jerome's Beauty World was closed on Mondays.

The first glass of wine came right back up. It always did. He nibbled at the crusty sandwich, kept it down, and tried another glass of wine. It stayed down, as did the rest of the bottle, and the next bottle after that. Sleep was what he wanted, but without benefit of being drunk, those horrible dreams would continue, and there wouldn't be any sleep or rest. He told himself so many times, *Drink as much wine as you can, and you'll pass out and sleep away the horror. It'd always worked in the past, and then, late on Monday, raging hangover forcing you to concentrate on it, not what you've done, catch the bus back to Sandesta. When you open the shop on Tuesday, you can tell a grand lie about a wonderful weekend to somewhere, an art gallery opening, fun and frivolity.*

"Lies, frustration, desperation. Is this all I have? Is

this going to be my life forever? All I want is love and peace. Oh, God." He passed out once again, slobbering drunk in a flea-bit bed in a two-bit motel.

***

He did not expect to see a Sandesta County sheriff standing at his door when he went to open Tuesday morning. "Morning, Deputy Perkins. What can I do for you? I rather doubt you're here for a new 'do', eh?" The humor was not accepted, wasn't even given very well.

"I have some bad news for you, Jerome. Let's go inside where we can talk." The two men went into the beauty parlor and Jerome offered Perkins a seat. Both men continued to stand.

"What the hell happened in here? Jesus, Tichner, it smells like a whorehouse in here."

"I'm afraid a couple of the ladies got into it on Saturday. Compared to Saturday, it's pretty clean in here right now. Sandi Justus and my mother had it out, and they broke furniture and bottles of hair stuff, perfume bottles, hair spray. Hell, Perkins, they wrecked my shop."

"We'll want to talk about that. You say your mother was in a fight? That's rather strange, isn't it? And with Sandi Justus? I came to see you yesterday, but I guess you weren't home. Were you out of town?" He was on tender ground here. Interrogating? Or just wondering?

"I'm off on Mondays, so I sometimes get out of town. After the ruckus we had in here, I wanted to get away. I think you can understand that. I went up to Fairview on Sunday, spent the night, and came back last night. What's wrong, Deputy? Has something happened to my mother? What's wrong?"

"On Saturday night, a little girl was murdered, Tichner, a little girl you know. This morning, we found her mother murdered in very much the same manner, a woman who works for you. On Sunday, a little boy in Johnson County was molested. I don't know if all these things are connected, Tichner, but if they are, I feel I have to tell you, I will try to connect you as well." He walked around inside the beauty shop, looking at this and that, not with any particular plan, just looking.

"Tichner, your employee Sandi Justus was murdered, either last night or early this morning. Her daughter, just thirteen-years-old, Tichner, was murdered Saturday night. You tell me your mother and the Justus woman were in a physical confrontation Saturday morning. If there's something else you need to tell me, now is a good time to do it."

***

Perkins had been putting everything together as he drove from the beauty shop, and his answers were jumbled. He turned to the one thing that helped him think—his tape recorder. He started with the date and time, and then just kept talking. "Sunday morning, we find little Florida Justus murdered in Holy Oak Park, and now, Monday night or early Tuesday morning, we find her mother, mutilated in much the same way in her own bed. Jerome Tichner has a direct connection, what is it? Is he a pedophile like Sandi Justus said? She said he was screwing Florida. Or just a homosexual as so many others say? His mother for one. There isn't any connection between gay men and pedophilia, even though it is a consistent theme with homophobes, but in Tichner's case, there just might be. Can a gay man also want sex with a girl child? And his homosexuality. Is there a link to his wanting sex with a boy child? And now, he's become a homicidal maniac?

"This has been the strangest four days of my life, and it's not going to get any better. Somebody better slow down Ken Swicker or he'll go over the top and kill someone, and that dumb ass fucking sheriff, firing Sara and telling Swicker what a fine job he's doing."

At the very moment Perkins was tape recording these things, George Andrus was about to have a second confrontation with Sergeant Ken Swicker. The first resulted in Andrus getting a black eye and broken nose, and the sheriff getting a legal dressing down. That happened Monday morning, and Andrus could remember it minute to minute.

The meeting started off nicely enough, but the district attorney had every intention of stirring the pot. "Mornin' Ken. Glad you're in early, we need to talk about what we release to the press. You were really out of line yesterday, talking about Sandi Justus, talking about Jerome Tichner. We can't bandy names about like that. And, in the future, you need to read the reports from your field people before you go on some tangent that doesn't have anything to do with the case at hand."

He was picking up a chair that was on its side, and was about to sit down when Swicker came around the desk like an animal. "Get out of this office this fucking minute you queer-loving son of a bitch. Get out of here before I throw you out." Swicker was big to start with, and when he got angry, the muscles and veins in his neck bulged menacingly, his eyes narrowed down, and there are those who swore his red beard actually bristled. His fists were doubled up, his shoulders hunched down as if to begin round one. Swicker fought in the collegiate ring, was nominated for the Olympics, knew what getting physical meant. His big hands reached out and grabbed the district attorney by his coat lapel, standing him on his tiptoes.

"Back off, Sergeant. That's the District Attorney you are threatening." Perkins hadn't made two steps toward his own office before the confrontation started and knew he had to say something. Swicker was so big and strong, one smash of those giant hands, and George Andrus could very well end up in the hospital. Swicker paid no attention and slammed Andrus against the wall. When he bounced back toward the detective, he was punched full in the face and crumpled to the floor in a heap of disheveled clothing and blood. Swicker stood over him, waiting for the smaller man to get up.

"Get up, you pansy ass! Get up and talk to me like a man!" Swicker was screaming at the District Attorney like they had been in a barroom brawl, like he was going to pick up that chair that has been battered twice now, and break it over the DA's head. Part of Swicker's anger came from the fact Andrus had said some things to the press about his own comments that belittled him and his position. What's more, Andrus appeared to be defending Jerome Tichner, and that made him a "queer lover" in the sergeant's eyes.

"Sergeant Swicker, my God man, look what you've done." Dr. Darling entered the office, and bent over to attend to Andrus who was groggy and sitting on the floor, holding his nose. "Here, George, let me get that bleeding stopped. Hold this handkerchief over your nose. Not too tight now.

"What the hell is going on? Swicker, have you lost your mind? George Andrus is the highest elected legal authority in the county. What the hell's the matter with you?"

Darling led Andrus out of the office and down to his office to clean him up and see if he needed additional medical treatment, Perkins continued trying to get to his office, and he wanted to smile so bad, but didn't dare. And Swicker stood in the doorway, daring anyone else to say anything to him. Harris Fletcher was that person, but even Swicker knew he wasn't going to punch out the sheriff.

"Your investigation of that murder seems to be going well, Sergeant. Keep up the good work. I see you also got rid of our sniveling little troublemaker, Sara Lane. Women shouldn't be in these jobs. These jobs are for men, big strong, intelligent men like yourself. Keep up the good work." County office workers from various departments had gathered around, and many heard the sheriff.

Now it was Tuesday morning and Andrus was

meeting a second time with the Sergeant of Detectives. "Sergeant Swicker, this is a summons to appear in Justice Court Friday morning to answer charges of battery on an elected official. And, sergeant, these papers are a summons to appear before the board of county commissioners, acting as the police oversight committee, on Thursday morning. I have filed the necessary papers, and it would be in your best interest to engage an attorney."

Andrus turned and walked away, fully expecting to be hit with something. It didn't happen, but Swicker, who had been out all night, also walked out of his office, and never saw the notes on his desk detailing the murder of Sandi Justus. Instead, he simply went down the street for breakfast.

***

Tim Darling worked all the rest of Monday night and well into Tuesday morning before he offered his reports to Swicker and Perkins. Still, no one had heard from Ken Swicker, and the buzz around the office, even as early as it was, centered on the murders and the missing sergeant. "You don't have to be entirely the bad guy, Claude, I gave a copy of this to George Andrus. You can fill him in with what you've found out. Anything I should know?"

Perkins paged through the coroner's preliminary report, and matched the descriptions of the wounds to those suffered by the victim's own daughter. "My first thought is obvious, doc. This is the same perpetrator. Wounds are the same, crushed skull, mutilation with similar weapons." In the report, Dr. Darling pointed out that the wounds were made by the same kind of weapon that Perkins had found in the river the night Florida Justus was killed. "My God, Tim, a knife does horrible damage, but the triangular blade of a beer can opener just gouges and tears at the flesh. Sandi's genitals and breasts were mutilated the same as little Florida's. We have a bad situation."

On the one hand, Perkins didn't like being thrust

into the position he found himself, but still, he had also wanted to be the lead detective, to sit in that office where Ken Swicker held sway. He wanted a command position, and it appears he had one, even if not so appointed, or with any authority other than what he is assuming.

"I really don't like this, Tim. I don't know where Swicker is, and with his temper, I don't know what's going to happen around here. I'm going to find Jerome Tichner and find some answers."

"That's probably not a bad idea. I'm going to go have some breakfast. Let's plan on getting together with George, either this afternoon, or maybe over cocktails this evening."

***

"You say you were out of town Sunday and Monday, Tichner. Can you prove that?" Again, was he interrogating or just asking?

"Sandi is dead? Florida is dead?" Tichner jumped back, his eyes wide, mouthing the words again, silently. Was it shock, or fear?

"When did this happen? Were they in an accident? What happened?" Tichner was shaking, and the questions poured from him, as he wrung his hands, shook his head, as if telling himself, no, this isn't happening. "Sandy and Florida? How, Deputy Perkins? How?"

Perkins could almost feel the sincerity in the questions, but wasn't about to let up on his thinking either. "Little Florida was murdered Saturday night, Mr. Tichner, and her mother was murdered last night. We feel it may have been the same person that committed the crimes.

"Would you make yourself available for some questions? This is not an official interrogation, but there are things we need to know in order to complete the investigation.

"If you'd feel more comfortable, we can do the interview here or in my office down at the courthouse."

98

Perkins didn't give an opportunity for the answer to be "no," and Jerome Tichner was too frightened to say no. He did have his wits about him enough to request an attorney be present.

"I've been out of town, but I will be more than glad to answer your questions. My God, Sandi Justus worked here, that's her station right over there. And her daughter, Florida, came around the shop often. Both dead? Murdered?

"Deputy Perkins, I want to help, but I'd feel much more comfortable if I could have my attorney with me when you interview me. Is that all right? I mean, I've never done anything like this before." There was a big lie, one that Perkins picked up immediately. Tichner has been questioned several times about child molestations in the area even if no charges have ever been filed.

Perkins allowed as how Tichner could have his attorney present, and asked him to meet at the courthouse in an hour. He was about to leave when Ken Swicker came striding in the front door of Mr. Jerome's Beauty World.

***

Tim Darling was exhausted, but wanted to get together with Stan Lyons and bring him up to date on everything that's happened. "Amazing. This is Tuesday morning, and it was just Sunday morning that I had to tell Stan about the first Justus murder. I haven't even had a chance to contemplate what he told me about his personal situation."

Lyons opened the door after the first knock, still in his robe and slippers. "Tim, what the hell brings you out this early? Are you checking on me?" In one way, Lyons was joking, but Darling couldn't help remember the former sheriff had also mentioned suicide on Sunday morning.

He forced a chuckle, and walked into Lyons's living room. "It seems I am again the bearer of bad tidings, Stan. I've just come from the courthouse. Do you have any coffee, I've been up most of the night again."

The two men settled in at the kitchen table. "First, I think we may have a serial killer working. I just finished the autopsy on Sandi Justus, Stan. She was murdered sometime late last night, and the killing was a mirror image of what happened to little Florida. Unfortunately, that's not the worst of the news."

"Slow down, Tim. Sandi was murdered? What could be worse than that?"

"Ken Swicker beat the shit out of George Andrus, right in Swicker's own office, and it gets worse still." He wiped some sweat from his forehead, even took half a second to look at his hand. His fingers were tapping out a beat of some kind on the table as he continued.

"Just moments before, it appears Swicker beat the shit out of Sara Lane, also in his own office." He ran his hand through his hair, wishing he didn't have to continue. "She is in the process of dealing with Barbara Mingus, that civil rights attorney. Sara could end up owning this county, Stan, and George could very well have our Sergeant of Detectives arrested and thrown in his own jail." The sweat poured down his face, the fingers continued their tattoo, and the doctor couldn't sit still.

"I know you're worked up, Tim, so take a big breath and relax a little. That's a tall order, I know, but keep your wits about you."

"I'm trying, Stan. I left Perkins a short time ago. He's going down to interview Tichner. Swicker walked out of the court house before anyone could tell him about Sandi Justus, and I just left him at the omelet shop. He's in a rage, and he's going over to Tichner's shop also."

"My God, Swicker beat up a female cop? Then the DA? Well, one thing, if he swings on Perkins, he'll get a good fight out of it. What an ass. What the hell does Fletcher have to say about this?"

"That's the strangest thing, Stan. I'm the county

coroner, and I've never in my life been on a homicide case, in all the years in the military, and my last few years here, that the head of whatever police agency might be involved, didn't immediately come to me for some answers. Harris Fletcher has not been to either crime scene, Stan, and has not asked for anything from me.

"As always with my cases, I've provided copies of all my reports, autopsies, pathology investigations, to him, but he hasn't asked one single question, hasn't called on the phone, hasn't sent a note." The former sheriff figured the doctor would wear out the tips of his fingers if he kept talking.

"And, here's something very strange—he told Swicker he was doing a fine job, not ten minutes after Sara Lane, still bleeding and unbuttoned, slammed her badge and weapon onto his desk.

"I can't tell you how much we miss you in that office, Stan." He slumped back in his chair and just stared at his coffee.

"Well, at least now I know what that phone call was all about just before you got here. Ray Blocker called and wants to meet with me for lunch. I laughingly told him I had all the property I wanted. You know what a good salesman he is. He said it was political, and hinted at a possible recall of Harris Fletcher. What do you think of that?"

"When word of all this hits the fucking papers, Stan, Fletcher will be at the wrong end of a very hot poker, and we may have to find a new Sergeant of Detectives as well. Fletcher is not sheriff material, and we've known that from day one. To have a recall, there must be someone standing by to fill the void. Would you be there?"

It was just Sunday morning that Stan Lyons had described his own personal sexuality for the first time, out loud, and to another person. He did not run for re-election because of his homosexuality, and now, again the question.

101

"God, Tim. I would be so fearful. I can't face myself sometimes, how could I continue to lie to the citizens of Sandesta County? What would happen if my sexuality was discovered? I would be a liar and cheat, and just as poor a sheriff in most minds as Fletcher is. No, if there is to be a recall, we would want to find another candidate."

If Lyons wouldn't run, who would?

Lyons was having a continuing debate with himself, and as in other times, was losing to his old self. "Others have come out, as the phrase goes, why shouldn't I? It would end this misery I have of knowing I'm not telling the truth, not being honest, with myself or with those who have supported me for so long. It would be impossible, not in the best interest of Sandesta County, and surely not in my best interest." He broke off his thoughts to continue the conversation.

"Let me be as truthful as I can with you, Tim. We've been friends for as many years as I can remember. We served in the same war, even if not the same outfits, we've been involved with many of the same people all our lives.

"What would be the reaction from the public if I came clean about my homosexuality? I'm living a lie right now, but only you and I know that. It's destroying me, Tim. To be as honest as I can be, I'd be happy if someone walked through that door right now and shot me dead. I'm actually terrified of being discovered and having to face the same people who have supported me over the years, knowing they now know me as a liar and cheat."

He put his head down on the table, not to hide his tears, but afraid of the shame he might see in his friend's eyes. Doctor Tim Darling reached across the table and squeezed his friend's arm.

"Do you know anyone who's homosexual, Stan?"

Lyons looked up, his face wet with tears, but he

didn't see shame in his friend's face, but rather, kindness and love. "Yes, I do. In fact, up in the capital, the chief of police there is lesbian. Did you know that? Francine Dermody is lesbian." There was almost a sign of recognition in his eyes.

"I never thought a thing about that until just this moment, Tim. I think a little trip up the coast might be in order, here. Francine Dermody. I owe you more than you'll ever know, my friend. She's a damn good cop, too, and she runs a fine investigative force. Damn me, Tim." Lyons got up, wiped his face with his sleeve, and walked over to the stove for some more coffee. "She might be able to help me find some answers. What does it mean to you, for instance, or to Andrus, or even to deputy Perkins, if I'm gay?

"Will it mean I might have to perform to a higher level, to prove myself? Will those around me have to treat me differently, even deferentially? You know, now that they know I'm gay. Well, I'll be a son of a bitch, Tim. I need to go see Francine." In his mind he was already formulating questions, questions about ethics, about HIV and AIDS, questions about the gay world. To himself he was, probably for the first time, thinking as a gay man might. *Hell*, he thought, *I don't even know what it means to be gay.*

"Let me tell you something, sheriff. Your sexuality doesn't have a damn thing to do with whether or not you're a good person, whether or not you're a qualified leader, whether or not you're a man. Look at you, big, husky, strong as any bull you can name, holder of so many civic awards for good deeds, proud veteran of a nasty war. Hell, Stan, I've read the citations. You were in hand to hand combat on more than one patrol, you've been wounded in combat, you've saved people's lives. You're a fine human being.

"Go up to the capital, talk with Dermody, and let it all hang out. Don't hold back a thing with her. First, it'll cleanse your mind, but more important, you'll get straight answers from her."

"There are so many questions, Tim. Questions I've never given a second thought about. Health, HIV, AIDs. By God, I'm going to find out exactly what it means to be gay."

It was a much happier Stan Lyons who packed an overnight bag and called for reservations at the Capital Hilton. "I'll call you, Tim. No man could ask for a better friend than you. Why don't you call Ray Blocker, tell him I was called out of town, and you'd like to have lunch with him. Scare the hell out of him, Tim. Tell him he'd make a fine sheriff."

***

"All right, Deputy Perkins, come out on the sidewalk, and let's have a talk." Swicker was a mass of nerves, and his eyes were glaring at his lead investigator. He spent a great deal of time working out at the gym, making what he always called a splendid hard-body, and right now, despite a silk shirt and cashmere sport coat, Perkins could see knotted muscles in his arms and neck. He could also see the telltale bulge of a large service weapon. As he drew closer, he could detect the distinct aroma of booze.

"What the hell are you going to do, Ken, punch me out too? That would be a big mistake." Being in barroom brawls from his cowboy days and breaking up barroom brawls from his early days as a cop had Perkins ready and primed if his sergeant decided to really be stupid about the confrontation. It would have been a remake of the Manila Thrilla had the two of them squared off. Even odds at best.

"Why wasn't I informed of the murder of Sandi Justus. I'm the fucking boss, Perkins, and don't forget it."

"Communications has been trying to find you since her body was discovered, Ken." He kept saying "Ken," not "Sergeant Swicker," on purpose, needling, pushing the point. "There's been a file on your desk since seven o'clock this morning. As Sergeant of Detectives, it's your responsibility to inform communications where you'll be and how to get hold of you.

"I'm not sure what your personal problem has been this week, Ken, and truthfully, I don't give a shit, but you wouldn't be acting this way if Stan Lyons was still sheriff. I'm here in my capacity as a detective in the investigation of two murders, and I plan to bring Jerome Tichner down to the office for an interrogation. If you have other plans, now is the time to say so."

Two very strong men, both cops, both armed, both angry, were facing each other in the middle of the sidewalk in front of Jerome's Beauty World. Inside, Jerome Tichner could never remember being more frightened. His mind just went over and over. *Do they know about my trip to the coast? My God, Florida is dead, and her mother? If I can get away from these men, I've got to get away. Where? Where can I go? That would make me look guilty. I'm scared, and I don't have anyone to talk to.*

"The only way you're going to get my job is when I'm dead, Perkins. Understand that? You are not good enough to run me off, so back off now. I want your complete reports on my desk in one hour. I'll interrogate this little queer bastard myself. Now get back to the court house and get those reports for me.

"Believe me when I say this, I'm filing insubordination charges against you with Sheriff Fletcher, Perkins. You've gone too far this time. I got rid of that bitch Sara Lane, and I'll get rid of you too." He turned and walked into the beauty shop, slamming the door behind him.

***

Perkins was smiling as he walked into his office. "Hello, George. How's the nose? I'm glad you're here. We need to talk. Swicker may have just taken me off the case. I

105

don't know where he's been or why no one could find him last night, but he's in one foul mood this morning, and smells like a whiskey barrel. We just had a pretty good set-to in front of Tichner's beauty shop.

"That was a nasty shot you took to the face yesterday, George. How do you feel?" Perkins was genuine in his asking, knew Andrus was not a large man, or very athletic either.

"I'm okay, Claude. Come down to my office with me. We can talk on the way. I wouldn't want Swicker to walk in on us here."

The two men went down the white marble stairs to the main court house offices and into a door marked 'private.' "Sit down, Claude. There's going to be a pretty big shake up around here in the next couple of weeks, and it's important for you to know what is being planned. I've asked the state's attorney general to begin an investigation of the department, since I can't. Swicker, completely unprovoked, smashed me in the face with his fist and broke my nose. I've filed charges, but since I'm the elected District Attorney—under normal circumstances, I would investigate such behavior, but I'm the victim—I can't ask the sheriff to investigate since it is one of his own who is the perp.

"An investigating team from the AG's office will be here either this afternoon or tomorrow morning, and I'm sure they will want to talk with you. No matter what, be as honest and forthright as it is possible. Whether or not Barbara Mingus will let her client Sara Lane be interviewed I don't know, but I sure as hell hope so.

"By the way, she has started the paperwork in federal court, and Deputy Lane could end up taking this county to the cleaners, financially. She has one hell of a good case, even if I have to say it. Again, under normal circumstances, I would be defending the county in the trial, but since I have charges of my own against a department of the county, the county will have to hire an outside attorney for its defense." He took a long breath, trying to let it all settle in. "This is the first time I've actually put all these things into one thought, Perkins." Perkins too was sorting out all the points Andrus had just made, and each one seemed to bring more questions to what was going to happen to him—personally, to his job, to the investigation he was trying to conduct.

It appeared very likely he would either be summarily released from the department, or he would end up where he wanted, as a member of the command structure. Or in the biggest fist fight of his life with Ken Swicker.

"Now, as to you, Claude, there is a group of men gathering at lunch today, to discuss the possibility of forming a recall committee to get Harris Fletcher out of office. You don't know this. Remember that. The most important thing you can do right now is not make too many waves with Swicker, on the one hand, but continue your investigation, even if you have to do it behind his back. We have two people brutally murdered and a sheriff's department in total disarray. Nancy Carrington in the Journal said the department was in chaos. You're the only solid ground we have to solve this crime, and saying it as if it were one crime is said intentionally. Metaphorically, Claude, you're an island of granite surrounded by quicksand."

"My God, George. You're saying that Ken Swicker could be arrested and charged with multiple felonies, and Sheriff Fletcher might face a recall election? This is such a small department, who will lead the investigation? Who will lead the department?"

"I think I'm looking at him, Claude. If Swicker is charged as I think he will be, that will leave you. Fletcher doesn't like you, mainly because of Swicker, but he won't have any choice but to have you lead the investigation.

107

Particularly if he's facing a recall election. He'll have to make the right choices, and you're the obvious one.

"Taking our scenario one step further, Claude, it wouldn't surprise me that if the recall is as successful as I feel it will be, this committee may call on you to be the next Sheriff of Sandesta County. We're not there yet, but keep that in the back of your head. It is a very real possibility."

"Thanks for the vote of confidence, George, but I would think the obvious choice would be Stan Lyons. That's who I would recommend."

"Lyons said the same thing about you."

***

"All right, you queer little bastard, tell me what you know about these two murders. Tell me in plain English, because if you fuck with me, there'll be more trouble than you've ever known."

Swicker was menacing, huge in Tichner's eyes, and the little beauty shop operator was terrified. "I don't know anything, Sergeant. Deputy Perkins just told me about Sandi and her daughter. I've been out of town."

"You better be able to prove that, fucker. You be in my office in ten minutes or I'll come looking."

"Deputy Perkins said I could call my attorney."

"Do you need one, faggot? Ten minutes." And he stormed out of the shop the same way he stormed in, jumped in his bright red Camaro, lit up the tires, and roared back to the courthouse.

Tichner called Barbara Mingus.

Chapter Eight
Tuesday, May 12

"**A**re you sure those are the words he used, Jerome?" Barbara Mingus was walking up the courthouse steps with Tichner, and he was telling her about the meetings, first with Perkins, then with Swicker.

"He called me a 'little queer bastard,' Barbara. It was just him and me in the shop, and he terrified me. My God, he's big.

"When I said I wanted you with me, he asked if I thought I needed you, and he called me a faggot."

"Did you tell him who your attorney is?"

"No, just that Perkins said I could call my attorney to be with me during this interview."

"Good. Don't say a word to anyone connected with this situation, Jerome. I'll do all the talking. Just sit calmly, and listen closely. Not a word now." They walked straight into Swicker's office, not knocking first. "Hello, Sergeant Swicker. It seems you have a penchant for making trouble for my clients. I hear you also beat up our district attorney? Have you considered anger management classes, Sergeant?" Mingus was a small, very thin woman, who could have spent the rest of her life teaching law at Harvard or some other highly respected law school. Instead, she had become one of the East Coast's most sought after civil rights attorneys.

Swicker was scowling, first at Mingus, then at Tichner. "This is your attorney, Mr. Tichner?"

Tichner started to say something, but she stopped him. "That's right, Sergeant, I'm his attorney. Would you like to tell me why you called him a 'little queer bastard,' and then 'faggot,' earlier this morning? I'd really like to know. And, for the rest of this interview, please direct your questions and answers to me.

"I've requested my client to not speak to you or anyone else involved in this investigation. What have you got to say for yourself?"

"Get out of my office now. Get out." Swicker stood up, towering over the seated Mingus and Tichner. Mingus smiled at the huge and angry man, crossed her legs as if to say, *I'm not going anywhere*. Her eyes, big, brown, and alive with the light of anticipated aggression, never left the eyes of Swicker. Swicker was shaking with anger, pointing at the door, demanding they leave his office. Tichner almost wet his pants.

"Or what, Sergeant Swicker? You'll beat us up, too? You really must learn to control your temper. Good day, Sergeant." She rose from the swivel chair, nodded generously to the man, took Jerome Tichner by the hand, and they walked out of the courthouse. Barbara Mingus considered the first round a decisive victory, but was aware just how much danger she had been in. She smiled, squeezed Tichner's hand, and headed for her office.

"Now, that wasn't so bad. was it? Listen to me closely, Jerome. If you have had anything to do with either of these murders, it will be very difficult to present a defense, but if you're clean on this, I'll protect you all the way. Don't lie to me, and we'll get along fine."

"I'm not involved at all, Barbara. I won't lie to you, I'm not involved in this at all." They had had a strange relationship for several years, but she had never represented him before. He had worked on her hairstyles and complexion, talked as beauticians and clients talk, related most of his life to her. She was very good at getting someone to open up.

"I know you have tendencies toward homosexuality, Jerome, and you've told me about some of your fantasies with children, so it's important for you to tell me everything I need to know about why the police are even glancing your way."

Mr. Jerome's Beauty World did not re-open Tuesday. Or Wednesday. Mr. Jerome opened up to his attorney like he had never opened to anyone. Not even in the days when he visited psychiatrists and other counselors. Barbara Mingus learned about Florida and Sandi Justus, learned about Jennifer and Jerome Tichner, learned about fantasies she had a hard time accepting, but did not learn about a trip to Johnson County.

***

Swicker, still angry and mean, called Claude Perkins into his office. "Perkins, I just had a very short visit with that queer bastard Tichner. Do you know who his attorney is? I'll tell you. It's Barbara Mingus. She's the same bitch Sara Lane ran to when she was relieved of duty here."

"It sounds to me like you have a crawful of trouble, Ken. Tell me what the hell is going on with you, anyway? All the years we've worked together, all the cases we've worked on, I've never seen you this hyper. What the hell is wrong?"

"I'll tell you one thing, and you better not forget it again. My name is *Sergeant* Swicker, and I'm the fucking boss here. If you want to keep your position as a detective, you better shape up. We have an opening in communications right now. Think about that, Perkins.

"You listen very close to what I'm about to tell you, because if you screw it up, I'll not only ride you off the force, I'll ride you right out of Sandesta County. That little queer bastard Tichner is our man, I know it. I want you to get him. I've got meetings with lawyers and all kinds of bull shit for the next couple of days. That gay loving ass George Andrus filed charges against me with the County Police Oversight Committee, and the state attorney general.

111

What a fuckhead. A little tap on the nose, and he goes ballistic."

"You broke his nose, Ken. That wasn't a tap, and you damn near ripped the shirt right off a female deputy. Your anger is getting the best of you, and you need to take a good look at why this is happening. A little visit with Dr. Darling or your own doc might be in order. There's a problem, and you need to look at it."

"Get out of here!" The entire courthouse heard the sergeant of detectives, and there were several who anticipated the fight of all time. It didn't happen. Claude Perkins, always calm and intelligent, smiled at Ken Swicker and went back to his own office. He wrote a note to Dr. Darling and DA Andrus.

***

"Hello, Detective Roberts. I'm Deputy Detective Claude Perkins, Sandesta County. Thank you for meeting with me."

"Call me Jim, Claude. Have you got something for me on this child molesting case? I'm sure hoping that's why you're here."

"We have two open murders in Sandesta, just happened, two days apart, but we're almost sure they were committed by the same person. The weapons are identical, and method is the same, and the victims are mother and daughter.

"The daughter was just thirteen-years-old, Jim, and she'd been sexually active. We believe one of those who had sexual relations with her was a man her mother worked for, Jerome Tichner. Tichner has been questioned before on possible child molesting, but we've never been able to pin anything on him. This may be our chance.

"I don't think he committed the murders, but there are others who are trying their damnedest to pin the charge on him. What kind of description do you have of your man, and in particular, the vehicle?"

"Two people dead? We knew about the little girl. When did her mother get killed?"

"Either late Monday night or very early Tuesday morning. Ripped to pieces with a beer can opener, the same as her daughter."

"Jesus. Here's what we have on the guy who molested the little boy. That happened on Sunday. The vehicle description is much more vague. Just a dun colored van. The boy did say there were no door handles on it." Swicker looked at the reports, and shook his head.

"This doesn't look like Tichner. He has short cropped dark hair. But, of course, he does own a beauty shop, so getting a long dirty blonde wig wouldn't be difficult, would it?

"I've got a line into the capital right now to find out what Tichner drives. If it's a van, I'll let you know right away. Anything else I should know?"

"Maybe this. The boy said the man was crying at the end of the attack. He said the man kept saying he was sorry, and told the boy several times that he loved him. The boy swears he's never seen the man before."

"A real asshole. Thanks for your time. If this vehicle thing turns out right, I'll call you immediately. Here's all the info I have on Tichner, his address, where his business is, and a list of the dates we have questioned him on possible child molesting charges.

"It's very obvious Tichner is homosexual—he's got quite a rep around Sandesta—but it's an open question on whether he's a pedophile. It's not illegal to be a homosexual; hell, the chief of police up in the capital's a les, but it is illegal as hell to be a pedophile. We'll get this bastard, one way or another."

Perkins got in his patrol unit and headed back to Sandesta, his mind swirling around with far too many questions; his sergeant acting like a school yard bully, the sheriff not even showing up at two high profile murders, a sexual predator on the loose, and the only sane people he could think of at the moment were George Andrus and Tim Darling. His mind was accelerating into what he saw as his future. He was thinking, trying to see how this might play out. He knew he had to keep control of this investigation, to assume the leadership, even if he didn't get to wear the stripes, at least just yet. He didn't take it to the next step, but several he worked with had already started to pin the top cop position on his resume.

What would Mama think?, he was asking himself. *I know she would have confidence in what I'm doing, where I'm going.* He had a set of stripes ready, he remembered, because she gave them to him. "You'll need these someday," she'd said. He reached for his ever present tape recorder and put his mind back on the case..

"How can someone be so angry as to rip another person to shreds with such a vicious weapon? And do it twice? I can't see a connection between those two dead people and Jerome Tichner, other than the obvious, that Sandi Justus worked for him. Was he screwing Florida?

"Now, I can't even drop in on his attorney because of Swicker. What the hell is wrong with him? Who the hell is under his skin so bad he's taking it out on everyone around him?"

The questions just buzzed around in his head, and when he got back to the station, he dropped in on Andrus. "Here's a description of the man Johnson County is looking for. The guy is small like Tichner, but not much else fits. I'm waiting for a motor vehicle report of what Tichner drives. That might either make him a suspect, or free him up.

"What about you, George? Do you think Tichner is a suspect in the murders here? Swicker does, but I don't."

"I'm not a psychiatrist, Claude, but here's what I think I'm seeing. I don't think Tichner killed either Florida or her mother, but it might very well be his actions that precipitated the crimes. He may have been screwing Florida, and pissed someone off. Why that would bring Florida's death and not his, I just don't know. The same with her mother. In some way, Jerome Tichner is tied to these crimes, but is not the murderer. Does that make sense to you?"

"I haven't looked at it quite that way, but I think we're working on the same link in the chain. I had a nice talk with the guys in Johnson County, and they said that Ken Swicker was stopped by one of their patrol units last night for speeding. Seriously speeding, and he had that little Nancy Carrington, the reporter, with him. They let him go with a warning, but said he came that close to being hauled in for verbal abuse.

"I guess he was his typical ass self with them."

"I guess you haven't seen yesterday's paper yet, Claude. I don't know if Carrington had anything to do with it, but the editorial page of the paper is calling for the ouster of Harris Fletcher, and took Swicker to pieces for attacking Sara Lane, for trying to beat me up, and most of all, for that farce of a news conference he held on Monday. I've got a copy here. You'll enjoy reading this." He handed the paper to Perkins.

It was even worse than Andrus described. He read, "'Harris Fletcher is nothing more than a political hack looking for a boost up, and certainly isn't up to our standards for County Sheriff. After an unbelievably brutal murder just three days ago, and the sheriff didn't even visit the crime scene? Is this the kind of police agency we want for our protection?

"'It's the position of the *Sandesta Leader/Journal* that Fletcher should step down, or be voted out of office. As far as Sergeant Kenneth Swicker is concerned, he held a news conference on Monday of this week, fabricated several portions of the Florida Justus murder case, attempted to control certain facets of the press, and hadn't

115

bothered to read any of the reports he had at his disposal from a fine investigative team led by Detective Deputy Claude Perkins.

"'Reported by sources within the County Courthouse complex, it seems our fine sergeant of detectives also has a penchant for physical abuse. He reportedly hit a female deputy with a doubled-up fist and ripped her uniform shirt right off her body, humiliating her further. The deputy has engaged local civil rights attorney Barbara Mingus. Mingus was unwilling to discuss the circumstances of the confrontation with us. Just a few moments after allegedly physically assaulting a fellow officer, Swicker allegedly attempted to beat up the elected District Attorney for Sandesta County, George Andrus, breaking his nose.

"'These two men, Fletcher and Swicker, are not Sandesta's finest. A recall effort has begun, headed by real estate broker Ray Blocker, a meeting scheduled for noon tomorrow, and if the antics as reported continue, this newspaper supports the effort.'

"My God, George. The whole damn thing is out in the open now. No wonder Swicker is in such a foul mood. His cute little piece of ass turned on him, and he almost went to jail in Johnson County. I would love to have been in that car with Swicker and his honey when she confronted him with her editorial. I bet he really lost it there.

"The man is out of control, George. He's threatened me with my job, he threw Barbara Mingus out of his office. You might not know this, but Mingus has been hired by Tichner to represent him. She's now got Sara Lane and Tichner, and Swicker is up to that thick head of his in legal shit. He called Tichner a 'little queer bastard' and a 'faggot,' and Tichner told Mingus.

"I assume you went to that meeting with Blocker." It was as much a question as a statement, and with the whole department falling apart around him, Perkins needed something positive to think about. "George, I've got two brutal murders here, a child molesting in Johnson County, a sheriff who doesn't give a rat's shit, a sergeant who can't think past his pecker, and now a newspaper throwing my name around as if I'm some kind of hero. How the hell can I think?"

"I went to the meeting, and was surprised to find Tim Darling there as well. I think the best way to describe it is, interesting. I expected to find Stan Lyons there, but Tim said he was called to the capital on some kind of business." Andrus became very contemplative as he continued, almost talking to himself, but directing his thoughts to the deputy.

"I agree this situation is incredible, but not insurmountable. The first order of business has to be solving these murders, and helping Johnson County with their child molestation case if it leads here. All the time we're doing that, Claude, we have to look at what the future might hold for us. Stan Lyons is a natural to return as sheriff, but there's something bothering him that he's unwilling to discuss, and whatever it is, it's also keeping him from becoming a serious contender for the position.

"Our best bet right now, in light of what the paper has said, is to dismiss Swicker from our thoughts. You are being forced to take over this investigation, and if Swicker forces his hand, it will make your job almost intolerable. That's something you must keep in mind every second. Swicker will have to be tolerated, and he could make your life a barrel of shit, Claude, but you must take the lead in this investigation." The two men sat there, one a good cop about to break even more rules within his department, the other, an elected official of the county, about to file a federal law suit against a Sheriff's Sergeant and the department he worked for.

Edwards stuck his head in the door. "Claude, Jennifer Tichner is on the phone for you. Said it concerned her son Jerome."

"Christ, now what? I'll get back with you, George. I really want to know what was said at that meeting."

"Try to be here at three-thirty this afternoon, Claude. The investigator from the attorney general's office will be here. I want you to meet her."

Chapter Nine
Tuesday, May 12

"Hello Francine. Thank you for taking the time to talk with me. I know how busy you must be." Lyons had called the Capital police chief and she agreed to meet with him, but preferred doing it over a late lunch.

"This is quite a hotel. We don't have a single building in Sandesta County that stands more than five stories. Having lunch on a revolving stage of a restaurant, thirty stories above the street is a nice experience. This is a beautiful little city, isn't it, laid out in spoke fashion with the capital as the hub. You must enjoy this very much."

"I do, Stan. But we don't have the Sandesta River flowing through town, or the wonderful rural atmosphere you have. I was raised on a farm, and I do miss the character of a rural setting. You've always been someone I wished I could have become. A county sheriff, respected and re-elected, and a good cop besides. Sometimes I think I have this position just because I'm a woman. Fill a quota or something."

"Nonsense, Francine, don't be silly. You've solved some big problems here, brought order to the race problems you inherited, curbed major and violent crimes, won awards for your leadership. No, no, police chief Francine Dermody is a cop to the bone and someone to fear if one pursues a life of crime."

"But, I'm afraid that's not why I'm here. This is much more personal, and it deals with something that is just as personal with you. What I'm about to discuss with you is very difficult, and I've only told one other person, our county coroner, Tim Darling."

119

For the next fifteen minutes, Stan Lyons, scarred war veteran, mean as a she-bear, retired sheriff, outlined his life. He pulled no punches, let it all out on the table, and Francine Dermody, an avowed lesbian, chief of police of a major metropolitan city, scarred herself, listened attentively.

"To put the whole thing in perspective, Francine, I'm a homosexual, and now you're only the third person in the world to know it. I'm terrified, more frightened than I ever was in Vietnam, more afraid of what my friends will say or think or do, than what I might do.

"I actually gave suicide a thought, but only momentarily, but the thought was there. What do I do? What did you do?"

"My coming out may have been a little bit different than what you're facing Stan, but just as hard, believe me. I lost several so-called friends, faced ridicule and taunts from intellectual dwarves, and became a better person for it. Frightened? My God, Stan, I lived in Iowa when I discovered I liked girls more than boys, and I was forced to leave my first job as a cop. I moved to the west coast, found acceptance, then moved to Boston for a few years, completely accepted for who I was, and then came here.

"There were some serious discussions about my sexual preferences when I was appointed chief here, but my being a good cop, being a good person, being a citizen people could look up to, quieted most of the community's questions. Yeah, you'll have some problems, there's no question, but a weight will come off your shoulders the moment you come out.

"The only advice I could possibly give is to be honest with yourself, and you've already taken that step. You understand who you are, all you have to do is introduce yourself to your community again. Some won't want to know you, but as a cop, you've already faced that. There is one thing though, that of being a public person.

You're not an official any longer, but still, a public person.

"Don't rub anyone's face in your personal life. I learned that immediately back in Iowa. I was seen kissing another girl in a movie theater. There was hell to pay over that. But I've learned, I have my girlfriends, my very close loves, but as good manners would dictate, we don't cavort in public. With men it might be a little different, though. I hold hands with my friends walking down the street, but I don't think you're the type. If you were straight, I don't think you're the type to hold hands."

There was friendly laughter at that, and the two, so alike, so different, looked deeply into each other's eyes, into their own souls. "There's an attempt in Sandesta to recall Sheriff Fletcher. I think I'll come out before it gets rolling, and that will effectively take my name off their select list."

"Don't count on that, Stan. It could put your name on the top of the list. There are a couple of things, though, before we get into that. First, are you set up to get on the Internet?" He nodded, wondering where this might be going. "Good. I'm going to give you a few web addresses that will be a big help. There are a million questions that many homosexuals have had to learn the hard way. STD protection, HIV protection, and of course, civil rights protections.

"Other questions will find their way to you. Such as what does it mean to be a gay. You'll find little paranoid thoughts coming into your mind. Did someone say something just because I'm gay? What did he mean by that? You question whether there really is a place for you in society. Many of us, I myself included, Stan, develop close-knit relationships with others in the gay community. Questions can be discussed, and we all find we really aren't alone, or that much different from our straight friends.

"Now we can get back to official business, and I'm glad we're doing that, because it means I'll get reimbursed for this lunch of ours." Lyons was impressed by this woman and was willing to talk all day and night if she wanted to. "Tell me about this detective sergeant I heard about, Ken Swicker. Did you know he punched out a woman deputy, and then physically attacked the district attorney?"

"My God. It must have happened after I left. He's a hard case, but this is incredible. Fletcher won't be able to deal with this."

"He won't have to. The attorney general is sending Elizabeth Martinez down there to conduct a state investigation, and I understand an attorney down there has called in the FBI to conduct a civil rights investigation.

"Stan, you might very well be at the head of that select list you mentioned." Stan Lyons knew Becky Martinez well and knew Swicker and Fletcher were no match intellectually for her investigative abilities.

***

When Claude Perkins got back to his desk, there was a note from the State Department of Motor Vehicles concerning the ownership of a van by one Jerome Tichner. He was reading the missive as he picked up the receiver. "Hello Mrs. Tichner, this is Deputy Perkins, how can I help you?" The van in question, a 1997 Dodge Caravan, light green in color, registered to Jerome Tichner, doing business as Jerome's Beauty World. Purchased new in Sandesta County, registration renewed two months ago.

"Deputy Perkins, I want that queer bastard son of mine arrested immediately. Do you hear me, deputy? I want that little child molesting prick taken off the streets and put away forever. Chained to a tree and whipped naked."

"Mrs. Tichner, I'm investigating two murders in Sandesta County, and your son's name has come up in the process, but I don't have enough evidence to arrest him for anything." That was not a real lie, just a little untruth, in

Perkins' mind.

"He killed those two women as sure as I'm sitting here, and he fucked that little girl before he killed her. I know it. I'll sign his Goddamned life away, deputy. I want him arrested."

Perkins started to ask why she thought her son was so involved, but she screamed at him, and hung up the phone. What a strange woman. What a strange family life that must have been when Tichner was growing up. Perkins had heard all the stories, but until today, only believed a few of them. *She humiliated him at every opportunity, then I find out she got in a fist fight with Sandi Justus the afternoon before Justus was killed, and now, wants her own son arrested for the murders of Justus and her daughter. And now I'm sitting here with the possibility of being able to arrest the little bastard for child molesting.* He picked up the telephone and called Jim Roberts in Johnson County.

"Hi Jim, this is Perkins. I've got a piece of very good news for you, and a piece of horrible news."

"Well, give me the bad news first. Christ, that's what I need, is more bad news."

"Swicker may have fucked up your case against Tichner at this end. He burst into Tichner's business and called him a dirty little queer bastard, and has since been visited by Barbara Mingus, a civil rights attorney. I've heard rumors of a federal law suit, and a petition to the FBI for a civil rights investigation."

"What's the matter with that fool? Everything I've seen implicates Tichner in this child case. Everything. Is Swicker just a fucking idiot, or what?"

"He may get some jail time, Jim. He punched out a woman deputy and the district attorney. He's over the top as far as I'm concerned, but my own sheriff isn't just a whole lot better. He congratulated Swicker for getting rid of a troublemaker when the deputy walked off the job with a bloody nose and torn blouse.

"I'm working with a nest of fools over here, Jim. One good piece of news for you. Tichner does own a light green van. I'm sending a fax to you right now. I think we need to visit his home. Do you want to get a search warrant from your end, or should I ask our DA to do it?"

"Let's move on this now, Perkins. Get with your DA, give him everything you have, I'll send a fax to you with everything I have, and I'll meet you later this afternoon.

"Holy shit. He punched a deputy? I hope she punched back."

"You obviously haven't seen Swicker. When he punches, you go down. You know how big I am. He's just as big, and he buffs up. Maybe a little prison time will buff him up more." He wanted to laugh, but the situation was too grim, and he grabbed the DMV fax, made a copy of it for Andrus and faxed a copy to Johnson County. He grabbed his Tichner file and walked back down to the DA's office.

"We have a little break here, George. Just a little one, but hopefully, significant. I don't know if this will tie into the murders, but we may be on our way to ending the child molestation case." He showed the DMV information to Andrus, and along with what he already had from Johnson County, suggested Andrus get a search warrant, and that when Roberts arrived from Johnson County, they paid Jerome Tichner a visit.

"We have the goods, Claude. I'll go to the judge right now. What did Jennifer Tichner want?"

"She demanded I arrest her son for the murders of Florida and Sandi Justus. I just might, eh?"

"Florida had not been sexually attacked, Claude. Not the work of a child predator, I'm thinking. As pretty as that little girl was, a pedophile would want some of that."

"I don't know, George. We're looking at Tichner for raping and sodomizing a young boy right now."

124

"The key there, Claude, is boy. We've known that Tichner is gay for some time, but that isn't a crime is it, and now we're investigating the fact he may have raped a young boy. That is a crime, but in both of these outlines, we're talking male on male. Florida was a beautiful little girl.

"I'm not sure there's a connection here. Don't worry, I'm certainly not closing my mind to the possibility, just questioning. Tichner has to be part of it, in some way, even if not the murderer himself. Sandi worked for him, Florida was seen with him more than once."

"That's right , George, but his own mother told me she believed he had sexual relations with little Florida.

"Is it possible we're looking at more than one case? Is the murder of Florida separate from Sandi's death? That's a frightening thought, isn't it?"

"Don't go that way, Claude." Andrus got reflective, sat back in his chair and looked at Perkins. "You know, I've said for some time that we just have too many queers in this county, and it's getting worse. This just reinforces my position. I caught hell in the papers for these thoughts, but I still think I'm right. It may not be illegal to be gay, but it sure as hell isn't right.

"Well." He started out of his chair. "I'll get with you just as soon as I get that search warrant. When we're on our way to Tichner's home, have your communications guy, what's his name, Edwards, Deputy Edwards, contact Tichner's attorney and ask her to meet us there. We won't leave any of the doors unopened here. Swicker has already fucked this up enough—we don't have to add to the problem."

Perkins' mind now was going, but in an opposite direction from Andrus's. He has never had a bigoted thought cross his mind and has never understood those who do. He remembered living close to Native Americans most of his growing years back in Nevada, having great friends to hunt and fish with, having as many dinners at their homes as they had at his. Red, black, white? He knew he couldn't see color, and he sure as hell knew he couldn't see personal sexual persuasion. He was thinking he would have to start looking at Andrus in a different light, and make sure he kept his own counsel.

"This is more than just interesting, this is disconcerting at best. We are dealing with two murders, and a child molesting, and one of our chief suspects is believed to be gay and could possibly be a pedophile, although, many in the health and psychiatric fields don't connect those two." His mind was filled with arguments that he would need when Johnson, Andrus, Mingus, and Tichner all are in the same area, he with a search warrant. "This could be one hell of an afternoon."

Chapter Ten
Tuesday, May 12

"**L**ook Doc, something was said to me the other day that has me worried on the one hand, and confused on the other. I know you're a pathologist, but maybe you can tell me what I need to do."

Ken Swicker has come to Tim Darling's basement compound completely unexpected, and Darling is again understanding why he doesn't like the man. It was early afternoon, but Swicker was dressed as if he were going to the ball, not working as a sergeant of detectives, and he smelled even worse. *This is the most overbearing man I've ever known, and that includes self-important generals in Vietnam. What the hell does he want from me?* He tried to smile, but it wouldn't come, just wouldn't come.

"Well sergeant, I'm certainly available, but your actions lately don't make me feel comfortable. Punching a deputy and the DA aren't exactly what I would consider proper behavior from someone in a leadership position. If you have ideas of being physically violent in my operating theater, I want you to know that my video and audio recorders are on." He hoped that might save him from the same fate as George Andrus.

"I'm not here to punch you out, Doc. But that is why I'm here. When Barbara Mingus came into my office with that little queer bastard Tichner, I was so angry I wanted to shoot them both. And she said I need to control my anger, my emotions. I do need to do that, Doc.

"I've never hit a fellow officer in my life, but I punched that little bitch Sara Lane a good one, and George Andrus, meddling in my investigation of a murder really pissed me off. He had it coming.

127

"Was I really wrong?"

"No one has ever been more wrong, Swicker. You're out of control, and I can see the way your jaw is flexing, the way your fists are balled right now, that you're giving thought to punching me. I can give you the names of a couple of very good doctors, both out of town, who could possibly find out why you're going through this.

"You are destroying your career, Swicker. You have to know this. The state's highest legal authority is investigating your actions, the FBI is being called in, the county is going to be sued for millions of dollars, because of your actions, and you don't know why. You ask me if you're really wrong? You are completely out of control.

"Over the years, you've arrested people and had them jailed for crimes far less violent than what you're being accused of. You know as well as I that simple anger management would probably be enough, but maybe you're just too proud to admit it." He went over to his little metal desk in the corner of the examination room and wrote down two names, addresses, and phone numbers. Here. Call one or both these people. You can say I recommended them or not, your choice, but if you don't call, you'll be talking with a prison psychiatrist before much longer. That's as honest as I can be, Swicker."

"Are you saying I'm crazy? Loony Tunes? Bullshit." His fists were balled, his shoulders set to strike the smallish doctor, and his eyes were narrowed for the attack. For some reason only known to Ken Swicker, he didn't. Instead, he stormed out of the office, and Darling noticed he took the note with him.

***

"All I want to do is talk, Nancy. Please, it's very important." Swicker was standing on the porch of Nancy Carrington's home, nestled in the trees just a few steps from the Sandesta River. Her back yard, lush with spring growth, meandered down to the river, tables and chairs

128

lined the way among great pines, fruit trees, sycamores, and maples, with brilliant flowers everywhere. Nancy Carrington had grown up in this house, and when her parents died, she moved back in.

Her personality dominated this garden spot, and included her flirtatious life style. She offered Sergeant of Detectives Ken Swicker a seat only, no iced tea, no cold beer, no flirting, no friendly smile, nothing.

"You lied to me, Ken. You lied to all the reporters the other day. And now you come begging for my forgiveness? Wrong tree, big dog. You've fucked me for the last time, figuratively and personally. Say what you have to say, and then leave."

"I just left the county coroner's office, Nancy, and he said he thought I have gone over the edge, that I'm bonkers crazy. He didn't use those words, but he gave me the names of two psychiatrists that I should see. He said if I didn't I'd be seeing one in prison.

"Am I crazy? What the fuck is happening to me? I don't know what to do!"

"Listen to me, Ken Swicker. You punched out a woman. A deputy in your own department. You punched out the elected District Attorney for the county. Today I heard through the pipeline you called a suspect a 'queer little bastard.' Does that sound like the actions of a sane and sensible detective? A sane man, regardless of his job?

"Darling is right, Swicker. You've gone over the edge, and you need help. Go see one of those doctors. Do it today. But keep in mind, what you've already done could very well land you in jail. You're fucking dangerous, Ken, and way too good an investigator to destroy everything you've worked for.

"I don't hate you, but right now, I don't trust you either. You hurt me deeply, lying to me, giving me an exclusive that was a lie. Did you do that just to get in my pants, Swicker? You can't get your dick up and you blame me, and then you come back and try again? You called me some pretty ugly names because you couldn't get it up, and now you come to me for help. There's more to life than a hot pussy, sergeant. A lot more. And one that's available, even if you can't get it up for it."

He couldn't remember the last time a woman talked to him that way, and his fury erupted. "You smart ass little bitch. You better run for the house. You better lock that door before I get there," he screamed, chasing her into the house. His rage exploded when the door slammed in his face, and he took his anger out on everything in the garden.

"You worthless bitch!" he howled. He ripped flowers from their bed, threw rocks at the house, and broke more than one window. Swicker was an animal, growling foul comments, finally leaving the property.

Carrigan was curled on the floor of the kitchen, shaking with fright and crying as she made the call to 911, which brought a carload of deputies. Swicker was gone before they got there, but the pictures of his rage were on the front page of the Sandesta Journal the next morning, along with a tearful account of his actions as lived and written by Nancy Carrington.

Chapter Eleven
Tuesday, May 12

C laude Perkins arrived in his patrol unit, with two other units for back-up. Jim Roberts was in a Johnson County cruiser, and had two deputies with him, George Andrus had his official car, and Barbara Mingus arrived at Jerome Tichner's home in a Buick Regal. Tichner was already on the scene, cowering inside, peeking out the window between drapes, shaking and crying. This is what he has feared for so long, and it was happening in his own driveway. Police officers were going to search his property, his home, his garage, his van, his compost pile.

"That's quite a car, Barbara. You're almost lost in it, it's so big." George Andrus and Barbara Mingus went back a long way, and had genuine feelings for each other. He never missed an opportunity to tease her about being so tiny.

"You know George, if you were black, I could fall for you. What have you got here that calls for a search warrant?"

While the two attorneys held a brief meeting on the hood of the Buick, Perkins had three of his deputies begin a look around the grounds. "Don't touch anything yet. Just look around and get a good feel of the layout. We're going to be here a long time, I think. Remember, even though we're in Sandesta County, the crime we're investigating took place in Johnson County, so let's not screw up a good bust." He and Roberts walked up on the porch, knocked on Tichner's door, presented him with the search warrant when he answered, and went into the living room of Tichner's home.

"Please be aware, Mr. Tichner, this is a criminal

131

investigation. Your attorney is present, and she will join us momentarily, along with Sandesta County District Attorney George Andrus. At your attorney's request, we won't be asking you any questions until she is present. Do you understand what I'm saying, Jerome?"

"Yes, Claude. Thank you." The fright of a trapped animal was in his eyes. His lips quivered as he continued to cry; his body, slight to begin with, lost all control, and he sagged into a living room chair. Jerome Tichner was a beaten man, and nothing had been said. "I've talked with Barb and she said we need to talk with the district attorney. I'm really scared."

"Ms. Mingus is talking with George Andrus right now, Jerome. Sit still, and this will be over soon. There's no one here that will hurt you." As Perkins was talking, George Andrus and Barbara Mingus walked into the well-appointed living room. Tichner lived well, with fine art on the walls, good furniture spaced about in an antique, Victorian style, clean and tidy. Tiffany-style lamps decorated end tables and the mantle above what appeared to be a never used fire place. There were lace doilies on the arms of the sofa and large chairs. If one should compare his home to that of his mother, one would never consider the two being related.

"Detective unit two, this is base. Detective unit two, this is base."

"Excuse me just a moment, George, the radio beckons. That sounded like Fletcher, didn't it? I don't think I've ever heard him on the radio now that I think of it.

"This is Perkins, go ahead." Even Mingus looked surprised since it was well known the new sheriff simply didn't take part in department details, hadn't been to a single crime scene since being elected. It was definitely Harris Fletcher.

"Perkins, get your ass down here now."

"Uh, sheriff, I'm in the middle of conducting a

possible crime scene search with the District Attorney and representatives of the Johnson County department."

"I don't give a damn if you're fucking the mayor's wife, get your ass down here now."

"Yes, sir. I'm on my way. Perkins clear." He hooked the radio back on his belt, smiled foolishly at Andrus and Mingus, and started out the door. "Man has a way with words, doesn't he? George, will you tell my deputies, and those from Johnson County where I am? Thanks."

"Keep your temper, Claude. Don't lose your cool, he'll bank on that. Shrewd as they come, so be careful."

"I will. Be back as quick as I can."

It was a short ride downtown, and Perkins couldn't keep his mind on his driving at all. "If I had a million bucks, I'd bet this has something to do with Ken Swicker. What a fool, talking that way on the radio. He probably doesn't even know that every radio, TV station, and the newspaper monitors our frequencies. Then again, he might not even care. He and Swicker are a lot alike, but of the two, Fletcher is the more dangerous. Lots of plottin' and plannin' as we used to say back on the ranch." The ranch. It always seems to come to his mind when things get snarly and dangerous. He was thinking rattlesnakes and badger holes, snakes that bite, and holes horses break legs in. His mind continued working as he made his way to the Sheriff's inner office. "This is a dangerous time for me, just as George said, and this fool Fletcher could be of a mind to set me up, protect his buddy Swicker. I have got to remain calm and be prepared for anything he throws at me."

Perkins walked in on a very angry Sheriff Harris Fletcher. "Where the hell is Sergeant Swicker, Perkins? Where is he?"

"I haven't seen him since early this morning, Sheriff. What's up?" He tried to sound as off-handed as he could. *Be cool*, he told himself.

"Has anybody in this fucking department seen the rooster at all today?" He was bellowing, and used a phrase some of the other deputies had concocted. It surprised Perkins to hear the sheriff call Swicker the rooster. Cock of the walk.

"He came down to my office earlier today, Sheriff. What the hell are you screaming about?" Dr. Tim Darling stuck his head in the boss's office. "He had some personal things to discuss. That was several hours ago."

"What kind of personal things?"

"That's kind of between me and him, now, isn't it, Sheriff?"

"Bullshit. If it had to do with this department, it's up to me to decide what's personal and what isn't."

Darling didn't answer, just stared at Fletcher. Perkins was flushed with anger, but didn't let it show in his voice. "What's this about, Sheriff? I was searching the residence of Jerome Tichner when you called. He may be the child molester Johnson County is looking for, and he has direct ties to our two open murder cases. I have several deputies on the scene now, Sheriff, and I'd like to get back there."

Fletcher snapped, "Read this," and he handed Perkins an official report form, written by a patrol unit just hours ago. Perkins took his time and handed the report to Darling.

"Sheriff, if this is the case, if Sergeant Swicker did indeed destroy this woman's personal property, and did indeed assault her verbally, threatening harm, he needs to be arrested. Sergeant Swicker is out of control, Sheriff."

"I want him brought in, Perkins. Assaulting a reporter in her own home. That's going too far, although she did write some lies about me and him, but one doesn't kill the messenger, now, does one.

"As of now, I'm making you temporary Sergeant of Detectives, Perkins. Wrap this fucking mess up, and bring

Swicker in to me. Get back to that investigation, now." All at once he realized the coroner had the patrol report and was reading it. "Give me that. Get your ass back to your lab."

Dr. Darling had a grand smile on his face as Perkins nodded to him and both of them got the hell out of there "before anything else happens around here." Perkins walked straight up to his desk, fumbled around in the top drawer, took off the little crossed flags on his shirt collar and attached a set of sergeant's chevrons. "Mom was right. She knew I'd get a chance to wear these one day. Very nice, Sergeant Perkins, very nice." Flashes of ranch life continued, but the snakes and squirrel holes were replaced by fields filled with fat cows and rich alfalfa.

He knew he would be in a command position one day, but had no idea it would take a department in complete chaos to get him there. His mind was telling him that the Sandesta Sheriff Department was in more trouble than anyone could believe, and he just might be in a position to do something about that. He also was asking himself if he was up to it. He was in his cruiser in minutes on his way back to Tichner's, and jumped on the radio immediately.

"Edwards, listen very closely now. I've just been made temporary sergeant of detectives and I've taken over the Justus murder cases. I want you to issue a very brief memo to that effect, under the direction of Sheriff Fletcher. If any of the detective or patrol units are able to locate Ken Swicker, he is to be brought to the sheriff's office immediately. Any questions?"

"No sir. I mean, do you mean, arrest Sergeant Swicker?"

"That's exactly what I mean. Get that out now. I'll be at Tichner's home, and the radio will be on."

"Good show, Claude."

"Keep me posted on any situations that might arise." There was a short pause, and Perkins continued.

"While I have you, what have you discovered on your attempt to find out who called in the report on the Sandi Justus murder?"

"Not a single thing, Claude. I've talked with every neighbor in the area, and not one of them says they called. They said they often heard little Florida crying out in pain, but don't remember hearing anything the night Sandi Justus was killed.

"Do you think there's something to this?"

"Something indeed, Edwards. Thank you. Perkins clear." He smiled because he wanted to say, Sergeant Perkins clear. "It'll come," he thought. "It'll come."

He was still smiling when he stepped from his unit in Tichner's driveway.

Two of his deputies walked up to him. "Where the hell you been, Claude?"

"Jesus, asshole, look at his shirt collar."

"Take it easy, guys. Where's Peters? Come over here, guys, we need to talk for a minute." He took the three Sandesta County deputies over by a large tree along the fence line, near what apparently was Tichner's vegetable garden. "Ken Swicker has been relieved of duty and I'm temporary Sergeant of Detectives. If Swicker shows up around here, take him into custody and bring him directly to Sheriff Fletcher. Any questions? Good.

"One thing to remember. Swicker has a Godawful temper, has punched both a woman deputy and the DA. He's armed, gentlemen, so be damn cautious in how you deal with him. This is not the time to get yourselves shot up.

"There'll be hell to pay in the newspaper tomorrow, or maybe even this evening. Our good sergeant threatened that little reporter he's been banging, and busted up some of her personal property."

He paused, sniffing the air. Something wasn't right. "What the hell is that smell? I have to get back to the office. Andrus and I are scheduled to meet with an investigator from the state attorney general's office. Under no circumstances are you to question Jerome Tichner, but I want his home, this yard, and his van sanitized. Regarding that van, I want every hair, every thread, every possible drop of blood, every speck of semen, or saliva, or toe jam removed and sent to the lab. I can't emphasize again the importance of possible DNA evidence. Blood, semen, all that is exactly what I want. God, what stinks so bad?

"Keep excellent forensic records, gentlemen. If Tichner did this, Swicker has already clouded the investigation, and we are not going to make it worse."

"That smell is coming from the compost heap, Sarge."

Perkins' mother had had the best vegetable garden in Paradise Valley, and he knew what a compost heap smelled like. "That's not from vegetable matter, Peters; that smell is from something dead. Blood? A body? Clothing soaked in blood? There's something in that compost pile that shouldn't be there. Get that compost heap torn to shreds first, then the van. Save the house for last, but don't let anything inside get moved out or hidden.

"Keep me posted." And he went inside the house to find Andrus. That little boy smile returned to his long face with its lantern jaw as he joined Andrus, Tichner, and Mingus. Even his walk has changed, from that of a confident detective to that of the boss of detectives, range rider, territorial marshal.

"Sergeant, is it? You can bring me up to date on the ride back to the courthouse. We need to talk." When they got in the car, Perkins held off Andrus for just a moment.

"Coming over just now, Edwards told me none of the neighbors called in the report the night Sandi Justus was killed. The call came from a woman, George. I still think that's significant.

"And, just now, I discovered the smell of rotting

flesh or blood under the compost heap in Tichner's back yard. This is Johnson County's case as far as the molesting goes, but ours as far as two murders go. Can we suggest Johnson County arrest Tichner, or is it too early?"

"It's too early, but not by much. Barbara is sure he's guilty, and I'm sure she's going to be talking to him about copping a plea. I'm going to send everything I have to Farnsworth over in Johnson as soon as we get back.

"A woman? She'd have to be a tough one to take on Sandi Justus. I called my office and told them to alert the AG's rep that we'd be a little late. You know who they sent? Becky Martinez, that's who. You'll go nuts over her, Claude. What a looker. Swicker'll have a hard time keeping his pecker under control when she questions him."

Both men were howling with laughter when they pulled up in front of the courthouse. "Her name is Elizabeth, but she likes to be called Becky. Her parents emigrated to this country from Spain, and she brags she can break a man in five different languages. Rough as a cob, beautiful as a sunrise, and mean as any swamp 'gator, Claude. She'll shape this place up."

"Before we get off the subject, George. Do you think Tichner is a risk for flight? If it's too early to book him on either the murders or the child rape, do we have anything that we can use to guarantee he's still going to be here tomorrow?"

"I brought that up to Barbara, and she just looked at me. She's probably the best criminal defense lawyer in the state, but she's pigeon holed as a civil rights attorney. If we impound that van for forensic testing, at least we'll shut off one avenue of escape. Other than that, all we can do is keep a close eye on the little prick."

Chapter Twelve
Tuesday, May 12

"**W**hen'd you get back, Stan? It's nice to hear your voice, and I have to say, you're sounding a hell of a lot better than when you left."

"I just got in, Tim. Can you get away? Maybe an early cocktail hour at the Blue Lamp?"

"I shouldn't, but I will. See you there in half an hour." He hung up the phone, pleased that his old friend sounded so good. *That trip must have done him some good after all. Stan Lyons is a strong man, and he'll bend a little because of this, but he certainly won't break. I'm proud to know he trusts me. This is a good afternoon for a martini or two."* His mind was trying to understand how two people could hold the same office and be so different.

I wonder what would be happening in the SO right now if Lyons was still sheriff. Fletcher. What an ass.

The Blue Lamp was a little jazz club, tiny really, and it usually didn't come alive until pretty late in the evening. The walls were filled with fine art, some from local artists, some that should probably be in an art museum collection. The art crowd filled the place late, and George Andrus would not have appreciated the number of gay people he would find if he showed up. Lyons knew they would be alone early in the evening, and they were. Attorneys, business types, radio and TV people came in for cocktails in the early evenings; then the crazy action started well after nine o'clock.

"Before we even start to talk about me, what the hell has been going on around here? Ken Swicker punched a deputy?"

"Not only punched out Sara Lane, he damn near ripped her blouse right off her body. Then he punched George Andrus and broke his nose. No, no, wait, there's more, Stan.

"Sheriff Fletcher just issued the order to have him arrested. Swicker went over to that reporter's home, the one he's been having an affair with, tore up her garden, broke most of the outdoor furniture, and threatened to beat her up. We don't know where he is right now."

"What the hell brought all this on, Tim? I know Swicker has a temper, but he's always been able to control it. Hell, I had him go through anger management courses before I'd make him a sergeant, but he always behaved very well."

"Not this week, Stan. Something inside him turned very wrong this week. I don't know enough about psychiatry to have an answer, but something deep inside is bothering the hell out of him. He seems to have lost all reason. He assaulted a deputy, hit a DA, used a personal smear to a suspect. He's over the edge, Stan.

"There's some indication that Jerome Tichner may be involved in a child rape in Johnson County, and Swicker called him a 'little queer bastard' right in his own store. Now, Barbara Mingus is in the picture, twice. Sara Lane went to her, and now Tichner has."

"Chief Dermody halfway brought me up to date on some of this. What a delightful woman she is. Refreshing is the only word I can think of. She said the AG is sending down an investigator after Swicker smacked Lane and Andrus. Do you know who's coming?"

"Your old drinkin' buddy, Becky Martinez. Arrived this afternoon, wearing combat boots and naugahyde pants. Scared the shit out of half the damned courthouse, Stan. She doesn't even try to hide the fact she's packin' that Glock she loves so much. Fletcher ducked back in his office and closed the door, and deputy Edwards followed her around like a puppy dog.

"She's just as gorgeous as ever, Stan. That smile would stop a freight train. It sure as hell stopped Edwards. She's meeting with Sergeant of Detectives Claude Perkins and the DA right now."

"Perkins named sergeant? That's good. You know, Tim, I think he'd make a fine sheriff as well. What do you think? We might need an Old West sheriff around here for a time. Perkins has told me stories about growing up on that ranch in Nevada. He's a good man."

"His name was brought up yesterday, along with yours, of course. This recall move is real, Stan. Fletcher has to go."

"I know. He won't be replaced by me though. You and I have an opportunity here, Tim. Claude Perkins is not only a fine cop, he's a fine person, a man who will stand up to scrutiny, and won't take shit from some namby-pamby politician.

"Let's focus on getting him elected sheriff, work the phones, go to every meeting that might be taking place, do interviews with anybody from the press. We can do this, and Sandesta County will be better for it." He had the smile of a winner on his face.

"Let me tell you about my meeting with Francine Dermody. Have you met her?"

***

While Lyons and Darling were sipping martinis, Becky Martinez was getting a full round of dirt about the Sandesta County Sheriff Department. "You're telling me this sergeant punched a deputy in the face? And then ripped her blouse? I find that hard to believe, gentlemen."

"It may be hard to believe, Becky, but Claude and I were right here. Then the big son of a bitch broke my nose, as you can plainly see." He let his fingers do a tender turn around the bandages still holding all that cartilage in place.

"It's always been such a charming nose, George. I

had to make you gentlemen say that. Actually, I just left Sara Lane's house, and have a meeting scheduled with Barbara Mingus later this evening. Do you find it interesting that Harris Fletcher hasn't stuck his nose in here at all? I mean, the least the little political sleazeball could do is say hello."

"If you think that's interesting, Becky, our fine sheriff never bothered to show up at either of the two murders we're investigating. Hasn't even asked for a report to the best of my knowledge."

Perkins had never met the vivacious state investigator and found himself looking at a tall, thin woman with brilliant green eyes that flashed as she spoke. "I'm Spanish from generations back, Claude," she said when he asked how she should be addressed, "so just call me Becky." She said that with a smile, and Perkins wondered if that smile might not have been an invitation, as well.

She continued to focus on him, eyebrows arched and so flattering to the rest of her face. Andrus saved the sergeant from a serious case of the stammers, and suggested the three of them retire somewhere a little more private than the old courthouse building. Perkins thought of a cold shower, but agreed to a cold beer around the corner at a little deli-pub combination.

"I understand there is a move underway to generate a recall of the sheriff. Is that what kicked Swicker in the ass? He's always been a strange bird, but he's also been a damn good cop. He has a good record, George. Sara Lane hates him with a passion that goes much deeper than a punch in the jaw or a torn blouse. And, according to her, the department has a horrible record as far as women working here. She says Fletcher doesn't want any women on the department, and that Swicker only thinks of a woman as a toy.

"George, as far as I can tell, you're going to have a hard time defending this case, and I'm here to find out if the state is going to join with Lane as a friend of the court. Personally, I'd hate for that to happen, but something has to change or compensation has to be made available to this woman and this community real soon. Barbara Mingus is one hell of a fine attorney, George, I'm not taking away from your own abilities, but in this case, she has a large bag of marbles, and they're all aimed at the county treasury.

"What I'm saying here is simply this; she's going to win." Her fingers were drumming on the long wooden table, her sitting on a bench on one side, Claude Perkins and George Andrus on the other. "Mingus has asked the FBI Civil Rights division to investigate as well. So far, she's willing to let the state proceed first, but if things don't go fast enough or far enough, the feds are walking in the door of that courthouse, and will be running this county's police department."

Andrus started to speak, but Perkins jumped in first. "Becky, I'm a temporary sergeant of detectives with about as much authority as that napkin holder there. There isn't a damn thing I can do in this situation."

"To a point you're right, Claude. George Andrus on the other hand is even more crippled than you. He has to defend the actions of a deputy out of control and a political idiot who's sheriff. On top of that, he has his own case against that former sergeant and the department, and the county. That's why I'm talking to you two. In order for the state to do anything, there must be a plan, and I think the best plan I can think of is the removal of Sheriff Fletcher. To do that properly, it would have to start with Sandesta County losing a major lawsuit because of his ineptitude. Nobody wants to see that. The other option, for him to be removed by a vote of the people. It's very obvious the state can't be involved in something like that.

"What I'd like to see is a plan for the realignment of the department from within, taking into account there are serious problems with civil rights, with deputies out of control, and under staffing because of current policies, particularly as they apply to women and minorities. I have your personnel records right here, Sergeant Perkins, and you're more than qualified to make such a plan. Deal?"

Perkins was quiet for just a moment, looking deep into those green eyes that spoke so many languages. "You sure don't hesitate to use that big hammer do you? Sara Lane and the other women, all gone now, were treated shabbily at best. No respect at all from the top. Lane attended the FBI police academy, is a graduate of police training at university level. She has command potential, Becky, and she was asked to man the radio and make coffee. Sweep the floors from time to time, and dust the furniture. I'm not being as facetious as this sounds. Fletcher and Swicker can only see a woman as something to be found in a bed.

"Can I make a plan for this department? I made one for Sheriff Lyons, at his request, before he retired, and I can have a copy of that for you in the morning. As soon as Fletcher came on board, Lyons's plan was shit-canned. You're damned right I can have a plan for you.

"But even with that, Harris Fletcher would still be sheriff, wouldn't he? And Sara Lane would still be one pissed off hornet looking for retribution. And I still have two murders that need to be solved. And Johnson County still has the rape of a 10-year-old boy to solve.

"You have some fine questions, Becky Martinez, even some good answers, but they can't be implemented without some changes being made that no one at this table has the authority to make."

George Andrus had been sitting quietly, listening and thinking in that Old Southern way of his. "That's a nice little conundrum you've tucked us into, Becky. Get rid of the sheriff or we take over. Make changes or the feds come charging in. I agree though, we have no choice. Twice, you've said that I have a problem with defending this whole pile of pig shit, and I've got to remind you, I have my own charges filed. I won't be defending. The county will have to hire private attorneys for this.

"Claude, you can't be involved in what I'm about to suggest, either. You're a Sergeant of Detectives in the department, and so you can't be involved in trying to oust your boss. Get that plan of yours to Becky first thing in the morning, and then, get back on your investigations of murder, rape and corruption." Perkins knew Andrus was right and didn't try to object.

"I hate everything that's happened to this department, but I'm still a part of it, and now, also, part of the command structure. You'll have a copy of my department plan in the morning, Becky.

"For what it's worth, I'd sure talk with Stan Lyons also before too long. He ran this office for many years, and didn't have any of these problems. These are mostly leadership problems, and corrective action should have been taken months ago. It hasn't been, and we're in a big mess, but not one that can't be changed."

"I like your optimism, Claude. Before I came down here, I tried to find out what the general feelings in the community were concerning Fletcher and the sheriff's office. The community isn't fully aware of some of the problems."

"That's partly true, Becky. Claude, why don't you head back over to Tichner's place and see what's happening. I want to brief Becky on the last few days around here."

"I'll keep both of you posted. It's been a pleasure meeting you Becky." He was still full of questions, but he knew he had to get back to the investigation. Driving back to Tichner's, he had a hard time thinking of anything but sitting across a table from Becky Martinez. "I wonder if George can handle being the middle man with Becky Martinez as top dog. What a woman, Jesus. Then, maybe

145

that's why he wants me back at Tichner's, so he can be alone with her. It sure as hell wouldn't hurt my feelings to be alone with her." But it was two murders and a child rape that were in his immediate future.

***

Dr. Darling and retired Sheriff Stan Lyons had taken a small cocktail table at the Blue Lamp, enjoying cocktails and conversation. It was dark, and the seductive sounds of a jazz saxophone solo supplied ample atmosphere. Lyons had spent a few minutes bringing his old friend up to date on what he had learned while in the capitol.

"If we weren't in the middle of this mess with the sheriff and now with Ken Swicker, it would be so easy to do what Francine suggested, Tim. Simply start living my life the way I want to. I'm certainly not beholden to anyone around here, I'm not answerable to anyone. If I want to have a man friend, have one. She couldn't be more right, and I've been pretty slow in accepting that.

"But Swicker has messed that up, hasn't he? Tell me more about the recall effort and what they're thinking."

"First of all, Stan, I have to agree with Dermody entirely. Simply live your own life. Yes, some people will not like that, but they don't pay your bills, they don't make your decisions. As far as the recall effort, Ray Blocker has put together a committee of about ten or twelve people, some business types, some retired, some working for a living, and they are writing up a list of grievances to be brought before the people, with the intent of recalling the sheriff.

"It's a good plan, and of course your name has come up regularly as Fletcher's replacement. Also, there has been considerable talk about Claude Perkins being the one to replace Fletcher. Fletcher has to be aware of the movement now since the newspaper blasted it all over the editorial page, but so far he's being very quiet. He's a dangerous man, from a political sense, and I'm sure he must be working to fight this recall. He wants to be in that state house awfully bad, and a recall would end that plan immediately."

"When's the next meeting of this committee, Tim? I want to be there. I'll tell them not to look to me, and support Perkins. I'll also tell them they have my complete support. This department has gone downhill a long way since I was sheriff, and I don't like it one bit."

They sat for a long time, sipping martinis, thinking about what might be coming for Sandesta County, for themselves. Darling couldn't keep his mind on the main subject of the sheriff, and kept wondering about his friend's state of mind.

"I have the feeling you're fine with yourself now, Stan." It was a statement, and a question. "I was very worried about you, you know."

"I know, old friend. I was worried about myself. Your prescription to see Francine Dermody was probably the best medical advice you've ever given. I could feel my mind relaxing, my soul breathing fresh air when she talked. The first time I have to admit to someone in public that, yes, I'm homosexual, will be very difficult, but now I understand it's no one else's business but mine.

"If someone doesn't like it because I'm gay, they can go fuck a pig as far as I'm concerned. It's not going to be easy, but I'm comfortable with the thoughts. You got plans for tonight? I could really go for some catfish and hush puppies. You game to be seen out with a gay guy?"

Chapter Thirteen
Wednesday, May 13—Thursday, May 14

Sergeant of Detectives Ken Swicker was sitting in his living room, gun cleaning equipment spread across a coffee table, a revolver in pieces, cleaned and oiled, ready to be put back together. His uniform, which he rarely ever wore, was hanging starched and pressed over the doorway. There was a bottle of Jack Daniels whisky sitting on the coffee table, about half empty, next to a glass that held just a taste of the stuff, and a copy of the latest Sandesta Journal, the one with his picture splashed all over the front page, right next to a picture of Nancy Carrington standing in her back yard surveying the damage, the pictures surrounded by hundreds of words outlining what had happened in the last few days at the offices of Sandesta County Sheriff Harris Fletcher, and in particular, the deeds of one Sergeant Ken Swicker.

"Little bitch. Ungrateful piece of shit, that's what she is. I gave her more attention than I have any woman in a long time. Fuck her. It'll be over for her, and for that bastard Perkins. Who does that sheriff think he is, making Perkins a sergeant? Arrest me? I don't think so. I'm the big man, and they better remember that. I can't get my dick up one time, and they turn on me like the dogs they are. Bitch fucking dogs, every one of them. I can get my dick up any time I want, all it takes is a good woman, not a snivelly cunt like Nancy Carrington. 'Do you need some Viagra, honey?' she says, so sweet and cuddly. I'll show you a big dick, you bitch. It'll be so far up your ass you won't be able to breathe, and then, you ball buster, I'll pull the trigger."

Blustering drunk, talking to the walls, screaming at the large caliber gun he's been working over, Swicker was ranting and very dangerous. Former fellow officers had come to his door several times in the last few hours, but he wouldn't acknowledge that he was home, and they weren't prepared to break down the door. With each tap on the door, Swicker's anger mounted to the point he was ready for a shootout with men who just days before were partners on the same law enforcement team. He only saw impediments, walls put up to stop him from something he couldn't understand, understanding only continuing waves of fury.

"Perkins, you're next after her. You think you're so fucking smart with your little plan to make the department more woman and minority friendly. Why don't you hire a queer, you fucker? Maybe you're a queer? Perkins, you just don't know it, but you're one dead son of a bitch."

The whisky glass was full again, and Swicker was having a hard time keeping his thoughts in line, was still sitting on the couch, stark naked. Even with a good XXX rated video he hadn't been able to get an erection, the same as the other night with Nancy Carrington. It had started, he remembered, about six months ago, and just got worse.

For a man dedicated to making it with every woman he meets, even if only in his own mind, the idea of not being able to get an erection is the end of the world. For someone as dedicated to that proposition as Swicker, it was more than he could handle. Always with a quick temper, always ready to place the blame somewhere else, always ready to accept the honors, warranted or not, the idea of not being able to perform was horrible. He was acting out the perfect victim.

"Go to a fucking headshrink, that's what that asshole coroner said. Go see a shrink and get your dick back. Fuck you, Doc. I've got enough bullets to include you too, if I want. If I want. You hear me, butcher?" He continued to fiddle with his service revolver, he'd already cleaned it several times, drank another full glass of whisky, and tried to get up. He tripped over the coffee table, sending pieces of gun, ammunition, and everything else on the table, including the whisky bottle and glass, crashing to the floor.

Swicker, drunker than he'd ever been, stumbled over the mess, cutting his foot on a piece of gun metal, bounced off a wall, and made it to his bedroom where he collapsed on the bed, out like a light. If he'd thought about it, he would be able to remember that he started drinking pretty heavily right after the first episode of impotence, or as they say in the advertising, erectile dysfunction.

He had been consuming quarts of booze every time he couldn't get it up, and it seemed, regardless of how attractive the woman was, or how available, his personal problem continued to get worse. That coupled with his natural tendency toward anger made him a very dangerous person. Former deputy Sara Lane will testify to that in a matter of weeks, and District Attorney George Andrus discussed it with the state's attorney general office last night.

Swicker wasn't one to contemplate his life, his actions, or those around him—otherwise he might remember that former sheriff Stan Lyons had forced him to attend anger management classes before he would promote him to Sergeant of Detectives. He created problems in the classroom, problems by way of coming to class in his uniform, standing along a wall, his hand on his service weapon. It was an attempt to get him out of the counseling sessions that he was passed. The sheriff was not informed of that.

***

Former Sandesta County Sheriff Stan Lyons was amazed at the number of people that had gathered for the luncheon meeting. "I must have said hello to twenty-five people," he commented, as he waited for the meeting's host, Ray Blocker to begin the introductions.

Conversations centered on Sergeant Swicker, two murdered women, and the complete failure of Sheriff Fletcher to maintain order and peace in the valley. The discussions about Swicker concentrated on the district attorney's broken nose, and Deputy Lane's torn blouse.

Lyons was still nodding hello to many in the room as Blocker stood to get things underway.

"Let's have a nice welcome for our retired sheriff Stan Lyons. Stan, we've been discussing this recall for about two weeks now, and many of us have come to the conclusion that we should never have allowed you to retire. Will you give us some of your views? Harris Fletcher cannot be allowed to remain as sheriff, we know that, but if we kick him out in a recall, who would replace him? I for one, and many people here feel the same way, think it should be you."

There was general applause as thirty or so citizens of Sandesta County welcomed their former top lawman to the podium. The lunch meeting was being held in the banquet facility at the omelet house, and in the crowd was Dr. Tim Darling, District Attorney George Andrus, attorney Barbara Mingus, several reporters including Nancy Carrington, and sitting off by herself, some bruises still showing, an angry former deputy Sara Lane. The room was filled, and expectant, hoping Stan Lyons would say yes.

"Thank you, Mr. Blocker. Ray. Before I begin my remarks, I need to go over a couple of things with you. I have prepared remarks, but they'll have to wait for just a moment. Remember our law here. If Fletcher is recalled, it's a two way street. Another election takes place on the same ballot, an election to replace him. You might find someone you think would be good for the position, but anyone who is qualified will be able to run. Now, into the meat of the matter.

"Harris Fletcher is a good man. Misguided maybe, but not criminal, not evil. He has an agenda, I think we all know. He wants to be governor or senator or some other fool thing, and the sheriff's badge is just a stop along the way. Regardless of how this recall effort is handled, it is important to remember that Fletcher is just a man with faults and imperfections the same as every other human being. The failure of the Sandesta Sheriff's Office right now is most assuredly his fault as he is the man in command, but the problems are correctable. A strong leader, a person who can command and lead, is needed, and most importantly, a person with a solid police background.

"Now, getting to my own remarks, that man is not me. I retired because there are some major changes in my life that I plan to pursue, and feel I cannot bow to two gods— the sheriff's desk and my personal life. In this case, I'm going to be very selfish for one of the few times in my life, and pursue my personal goals.

"Having said that, I would like to remind all of you there is a fine man who might just as well be leading the department right now despite all the disruptions from the sheriff and some of his deputies. Claude Perkins is an old line sheriff's deputy, one who has attended all the special courses and clinics offered around the country, including the FBI Academy, was raised on a big alfalfa and cattle ranch in northern Nevada, so understands the value of independent thinking, and right now, has taken over as sergeant of detectives.

"For what it's worth, our district attorney and our county coroner are both supporting Perkins, and I definitely will throw my support to him. As you can imagine, he can't very well say anything right now, being in the employ of Sheriff Fletcher. I want him to know, he has my support.

"Thank you. Yes, Ray, if you have any questions I'll sure try to answer them."

For the next half hour, Lyons, Blocker, Andrus, and Darling spoke with those gathered for the meeting. As the crowd was leaving, a big, red convertible pulled up to the curb. Drunk and slovenly, Ken Swicker tripped out of the car, waving a .357 Magnum, screaming obscenities at Nancy Carrington.

So many years of training, so many times facing someone with a loaded gun, someone who wanted to kill him, and Stanley Lyons did what he'd always done. A huge right hand, knuckles scarred from war, from training, from working out all the time, slammed into the jaw of Ken Swicker, knocking the big red bearded man across the hood of his car. He still held the pistol, and he was not unconscious, although he should have been, between hits of Jack Daniels and a hit by Lyons.

Lyons jumped on him, grabbed the gun, and the two large men wrestled themselves onto the concrete sidewalk. George Andrus and others tried to get the crowd away and safe, and Carrington collapsed in fright. It was Sara Lane who stepped into the fray and slammed Swicker across the back of the head with her purse, which still carried her service revolver, handcuffs, mace, and a short and wicked night stick. She hit him twice more, drawing blood from his scalp, and Lyons was able to get more solid punches into Swicker's face.

Lane got into her purse, got the short little night stick out and drove it head first into Swicker's ribs, again, again, still more jabs with the stick, then slammed him across the ear with it. Between her beating, and Lyons fighting for control of the service revolver, Swicker was losing.

As Swicker started to go limp from the beating he was taking, he made one last effort to get control of his gun, and it went off. A .357 caliber Magnum is one of the most powerful and dangerous loads available for a handgun, and the bullet can go through several two by fours before expending its energy.

Lyons howled in pain when the heavy chunk of lead plowed through his upper thigh, breaking the femur, but luckily missing the artery. He was on the pavement, bleeding and in pain as Swicker's fight with Lane came to an end.

Lane followed proper procedure, grabbed the gun as Swicker passed out, rolled the former sergeant of detectives over and threw the cuffs on him. Andrus had his cell phone out, calling 911, and Dr. Darling was applying pressure to Lyons' serious bullet wound.

Sergeant Perkins and the ambulance arrived at the same time, and he found former deputy Sara Lane sitting on a groggy and handcuffed Ken Swicker, holding a big pistol to the back of his head. "You continue squirming around motherfucker, and you're dead." She bashed him in the back of the head again with her night stick, just enough to remind him of who was really in charge, and rammed the muzzle of the pistol into the base of his skull so he had no doubt what he was feeling.

"Good work, Sara. We'll take over now." Perkins jerked Swicker to his feet, was amazed to see his nose pushed over to one side from a solid punch, both eyes starting to bruise, and cuts all about his head, some from something other than fists. "What the hell did you hit him with, Sara, a damn pipe?"

"Almost, Claude. I had this little thing made for me. See, it's only about eight inches long, but it's filled with lead. I can wrap it inside my fist and give a hell of a punch, or I can use it like a night stick, either slam it down on a head, or stick it in the ribs. It's a good one."

Perkins nodded and tried not to smile at her. "Stand up straight, Swicker. You're under arrest, anything you say can be used against you. You have the right to an attorney, if you prefer, the state will provide one for you. Do you understand, sleazeball?"

Perkins started to take him over to the police cruiser when Nancy Carrington walked over and slapped the still groggy former sergeant across the face. "You dirty fucker.

You came down here to kill me, didn't you? You'll fry, Swicker. You and that puny little dick of yours will fry."

By this time, half the Sandesta County Sheriff Department was on the scene, but there was no Sheriff Harris Fletcher. Becky Martinez arrived just as the ambulance left rushing Stan Lyons to the hospital.

"Will he be all right, Dr. Darling?"

"I think so, Ms. Martinez. I have to get over there now."

"Take my car, Doctor. It has reds and blues and a big siren."

"Thanks George. I'll try to keep you posted."

"What the fuck happened here, George? Swicker went bonkers or what? Jesus, and I thought I was just coming down to get a little county office straightened up, not get in a murder investigation. Holy shit."

"Becky, let's have dinner tonight. We have lots to talk about." Andrus gave every impression that he had more than official business on his mind, and as the two walked back toward her car, he gave a little thumbs up to Perkins.

"That's very strange," Perkins thought, but put it aside to begin yet another investigation, and this one could also become a murder investigation.

***

"He'll be off his feet for a while, but he'll live." Dr. Darling smiled. "How's Swicker?"

"He'll live with no problem. Sara did lots of damage to his head with that vicious little stick of hers, actually broke one rib and cracked another. Lyons must have done some twisting with the pistol also, because Swicker had two fingers fractured in the fray.

"What the hell makes a man do this kind of thing, Doc? He was a good cop, strange maybe, particularly when it came to the way he treated people. Women in general, I guess."

"That's his main problem, Claude. He never did understand that a woman was not an object, and then when he started having some physical problems, he compounded them with booze. I told him twice what to do about his problem, and he ignored me. He considered himself less than a man because of it, tortured himself with whisky, and lost contact of what we call reality.

"It really is a damn shame too, because it could have been so easily corrected. More than likely a simple imbalance in his system. Now what, Claude?"

"There's a raft of charges against him, Doc. It's all up to the lawyers now. At some point soon, you and I have to get together and talk about these other murders I'm working on. I'm going to call a meeting of my deputies and I'd like you and George to sit in on that. I think I'm coming close to the murderer, I'm still positive it's a woman, and I think she'll make herself known. I need yours and George's thoughts. I'm sure glad this is a quiet little county." That big Nevada buckaroo grin spread across his face, and the two laughed at the irony. Perkins headed out of the hospital. There was a deputy guarding room 407, the room holding Ken Swicker, county prisoner. Sara Lane was in with Stan Lyons.

"You look like hell, boss." She had a big smile plastered across her face, and kissed the former sheriff lightly on the forehead.

"I needed that, Sara. I owe you my life, you know. In some societies, that means I am now your servant, and you have to feed and clothe me, and provide living quarters for the rest of my life." It hurt to laugh, but he managed to get a small one past his wound and sore muscles anyway.

"You'll ruin my rep, you know. I'm supposed to be the big mean bull dyke around here. I can't be living with a man."

"Are you gay, Sara?"

"Christ, you must be the only one who doesn't

156

know it. Why do you think Swicker hated me so much?"

"Jesus shit and damn. Sit down, pretty girl, I have a story to tell you."

Chapter Fourteen
Thursday, May 14—Friday, May 15

"Have I got some good news for you, Kenny baby." Lane had talked her way around the deputy at the hospital door, and stood at the end of Ken Swicker's bed, leering at the big red head. "How's your head, Kenny baby? Aw, does it hurt?

"I beat you, fucker. I whipped your ass, limp dick, and now, I get to put the knife as far into your gut as possible. You had so much fun trying to hurt me with your continual comments about being a queer bitch, and all the time, your own boss was a gay man."

Swicker was half out of it, but could understand every word, almost. "Fletcher's a fucking homo?"

"You stupid pig. Stan Lyons is gay, has been all his life. And you broke bread with him. Spent lots of time at his home. What were you two doing together?" It felt so good to put that needle in, drive that huge wedge into his heart, watch his eyes close in hate. "When you get to prison, you'll get to do some more of that. Well, at least, some of the other butt-fuckers will.

"'Bye now, Kenny."

She patted the other deputy on the butt as she left, and if the music in her head had been just a little louder, she would have danced down the hallway. She got her ass reamed by Barbara Mingus for talking with Swicker, but even that didn't take away the good feelings.

***

"Hey, hotshot. You're getting more front page space now that you're retired than you did all the time you were sheriff."

"Hi, Becky. Have you got all the courthouse people

walking into walls down there?"

"Most of the deputies anyway. That department's a mess. Claude Perkins seems to be the only one running things around there. Is he strong enough to take over the whole thing?"

"Yeah. Perkins is a big old Nevada cowboy with all the right things in his head and his background. They say Swicker is okay. That's good."

"You're a piece, Stan. He tried to kill you."

"He lost his way, Becky. Tim Darling said what's wrong with him is so easily corrected it's stupid he didn't do it. An imbalance in his chemical makeup. Tim said a simple change in diet and maybe some pills, and he'd had his dick up in no time. Instead, he fills his system with booze. Darling told him twice what was needed. Too pig-headed to understand.

"How's your investigation going?"

"Between Sara Lane and George Andrus, Sandesta County could be broke within the year. Perkins has a good plan, and if Barbara Mingus accepts it, Lane will be back in uniform, and there will be some big checks coming her way, but not as big as if the county decided to fight it in court and lose.

"As far as George goes, he's going to own everything that Swicker has now, will have in the future, anything he even thinks he might own. George says he's going to keep it a civil thing and not sue the county unless someone in county government tries to do something stupid. Then, he and Lane will own the county together. Joint tenancy.

"While we're on the subject of Lane, I talked with her and she said you had something to tell me. What's up, hunk?" Her green eyes were trying to get a reaction from Lyons, but they weren't working. Neither was her smile.

"It's kind of a long story, Becky, and at least for the short term, I'd like what I'm about to tell you to be between us. There are a few people around, Tim Darling and Sara Lane among them, who know this.

Chapter Fifteen
Friday, May 15

Perkins was sitting at his desk, three deputies in chairs, George Andrus pacing about, and Dr. Darling was holding up a wall near the doorway. "Here's where we are. Florida Justus was mutilated with a beer can opener, the type referred to as a church key, after her head was caved in with a big rock. Sandi Justus was mutilated with a beer can opener after her head was bashed in with a cast iron frying pan.

"We have footprints from the sand near the murder scene at the river that seem to match bloody footprints from the Justus home. We have the rock that caved in Florida's skull and the probable mutilation weapon, and we have the cast iron frying pan that killed Sandi.

"The footprints are indeterminate. They could be from a small to medium-sized man, or a medium to large-sized woman. The soles indicate the shoes were made by a manufacturer that supplies just about every el cheapo department store in the country. Millions of them, and the sizes are small, medium, and large. This shoe is a medium. This narrows our suspect list to about 75 million people." His smile slid across his big face, but his eyes were still narrowed, still angry as they searched the room for answers.

"There is a bright side to this. When Florida was killed, it was a couple of teenagers who discovered the body and called us. When Sandi was killed, we got a phone call from a woman who said she was a neighbor, and she heard screaming at the Justus home. None of the neighbors in the area admit to making that call.

"That's significant to me. That tells me this woman

wanted that body found that night, not discovered at some point down the line. I'm going to move into a very delicate position now.

"As you know, Sergeant Swicker has been relieved of duty, and is in custody recuperating from wounds incurred during a scuffle with former sheriff Stan Lyons, and former deputy Sara Lane. Sara was our communications officer for a long time, has been through some good training as far as radio communications are concerned, and, Edwards, I'm not taking anything away from what you've done on that job since we lost Sara, but George, would we be jeopardizing anything if we let Sara listen to that tape?

"If it is a woman, she'd know. If it's someone trying to sound like a woman, she'd know. I've listened, as have all of you, and I think it's a woman. Edwards, so do you, but George, you seem to have a doubt. Do we dare ask Sara?"

"I talked with Becky Martinez about that, Claude. Mighty soft ground. Sara wants to continue her career in police work, and she understands very well that she has this county over that big old barrel. Becky is going to talk with Barbara Mingus today, and we'll just have to wait."

"Okay. Going under the assumption the call was from a woman what does it mean?"

Tim Darling straightened up, paying attention for what appeared to be the first time. "It means one tough broad killed Sandi Justus, and we already know that Jerome Tichner's mother got in a physical altercation with Justus the morning before she was killed. We also know Jennifer Tichner followed young Florida out of the beauty shop that morning and had a long talk with her."

"That's true, Doctor, and we know that Jerome Tichner speaks with a naturally high voice and is currently under investigation by Johnson County for child molestation." Claude Perkins was in a quandary, and he wanted one of his deputies to jump in with something.

"Along with the murders of Sandi and Florida Justus, we have the possibility of at least one and maybe two more murders. Pieces of a body or bodies were found in the compost pile at Tichner's, gentlemen, and that little prick now is a possible suspect in murders in Sandesta County, and child molesting in Johnson County. An arm, a skull, and various other human parts had been in that compost pile for a long time, and we're going over every report of missing children within an area comprising five counties.

"Blood samples and dental records are being looked at, and DNA evidence is being examined as well. This is a huge investigation, people, and we're being hampered by the internal problems within the department. I want input from you. I'm not Sergeant Swicker, and I want us—you and I—to come to conclusions that can be brought to court.

"When you took apart that compost heap at Tichner's, you found a large pile of bloody clothes. Some appeared to be old, and one group was fairly fresh. Have we got anything back on them? Is the blood from the freshest all from the same person? We know what type that little boy over in Johnson County has, and we know what type Florida and Sandi are. Have we made a match? Do we need to involve ourselves with even more DNA testing here?

"Doc, do we have a record of Tichner's blood type? Has Johnson County done a blood test on the bastard? Let's follow up on the various blood types from those body parts, rags and clothing at Tichner's, and see if we have a match of any kind. Also, while I'm on it, do we have anything at all on Jennifer Tichner? I mean as far as blood goes. George, how hard would it be to get a court order on that?"

"Probable cause, Claude. It would be very difficult."

"We have an opportunity to wrap up two murders,

some possible missing children cases, and one child molesting. Gentlemen, let's do it. Give me your thoughts." He continued to contemplate the differences between his command, the opposite of Ken Swicker's. This was his command now, and he needed to let his deputies know things were different.

"Swicker always demanded reports from you, backed up by enough evidence for him to take credit for solving whatever was being investigated. This is a new era in the department, and we're working as a team now. Let's discuss what's on our minds and solve this."

His mind was alive again. He was back in his law enforcement student days at the FBI academy, at San Jose State University in California, on the Humboldt County Sheriff Department, and his long and dear time with Elko County. "I loved men and women sitting, discussing a case, putting little pieces together, finding answers. Lyons did that with us, but Swicker then spoiled the effort by taking all the credit. No more rooster."

In the room, they saw a contemplative sergeant look all about him. He had decided the only way to break these people out was by direct questioning, letting them understand, it was his way now. "Peters, tell me what's on your mind."

"It seems to me that Jerome Tichner would be our prime suspect. We've known for some time he's probably a pedophile, he's under suspicion for that in Johnson County right now, and he had a relationship with Florida Justus. It was that relationship that caused the blow-up Saturday morning in his shop.

"He would be at the top of my list, Sarge." Perkins liked that. *Sarge*. It came easy to him, and sounded good. Swicker hated to be called Sarge. It was always Sergeant Swicker. Claude Perkins could live a long time being called Sarge.

"I'm not so sure." Edwards was getting involved.

164

Perkins always had to prod the young man, force him to do whatever a young investigator should automatically do. He wasn't really sure if Edwards would be a good detective. A good cop yes, but he had his doubts about him being an investigator.

"Why not, Edwards?"

"I think he's too obvious. According to your own report, Jennifer Tichner came to your office and demanded he be arrested for Florida's murder. The minute Florida's mother was aware of her daughter's death, she fingered the little queer."

"Whoa, Edwards. We don't talk that way in this department as long as I'm Sergeant of Detectives. Every person is a human being first and will be treated with the dignity that demands. Tichner is a self-proclaimed homosexual, and that's not a crime. He is a probable pedophile, and that is a crime. The two are not one and the same. A gay man is not naturally lured by children, and most pedophiles are not homosexual. Jerome Tichner is not a good citizen as we look on them but he's still a human being, and a citizen of our county. He's not been convicted of any crime.

"He will be treated with that respect and dignity until he proves he's not worthy. A part of one of the potential lawsuits aimed at this department and this county derives from the way Ken Swicker spoke to Jerome Tichner. I don't want to hear that around here again. If anyone has an argument with what I just said, speak now."

"That's quite a speech, Claude."

"I know, George. This isn't the way Swicker did things, it isn't the way Fletcher feels, but it is the right way. It's my way."

Tim Darling was amazed. *No wonder Stan Lyons likes this man. He's honest and brave. Two of the things Lyons appreciates more than anything in a person. I've got to remember to talk to him about this.*

"Now, Edwards, let's get back to what you were talking about. You're going in the right direction I think. Keep going, and let's see what develops." He chewed the guy's ass out moments ago, and now he credited him with good ideas. Darling was taking it all in, as was Andrus.

Perkins was trying to run a double murder investigation, and Darling and Andrus were working to find a new sheriff. All focus was on Perkins.

"If you had a thing for young children, and were having more than just a one-time fling with a young girl, and you killed her viciously for some reason, and then killed her mother in the same way, would you go to Johnson County the next day and attack a little boy?

"It doesn't add up for me. Both his mother and the little girl's mother fingered him immediately. And the mother of the little girl is then killed. If Jennifer Tichner believed what she told you, she should be hiding under her bed right now, terrified that she would be next."

"And the phone call reporting Sandi's death came from a woman." Peters spoke up. "Edwards might be right."

"You've been awfully quiet, George. We have fingers pointing at Jerome and his mother. There is always the possibility it's someone else, but these two seem to be prime right now. Talk to me, George."

"I'm being quiet because I'm hearing something I haven't heard in this division for a long time, Sergeant Perkins—a sound and reasonable assessment of a case under investigation. I know you tend to swing to the idea of the murders being committed by a woman, but they are so brutal, so vicious. Maybe it's my Southern upbringing, but I find it hard to picture a woman doing to another woman what was done to those Justus women. Physical brutality of that nature is usually perpetrated by a man, and we know from what Johnson County has told us that Jerome Tichner is not a kind man.

"If he's their man, he brutalized that little boy. And Peters, from your report from the Tichner home, there were body parts and lots of bloody clothing and material in that compost pile, bloody from other encounters with children, no doubt.

"My mind isn't closed on this, Claude. Not closed at all, but I'm inclined to believe we're looking for a man, and I'm also inclined to believe that man is Jerome Tichner."

"Dr. Darling, do you have anything to add to this before we wrap it up here?"

"Only to add to what you said a little earlier. A homosexual person is not the same as a criminal pedophile. A gay person is not a criminal. A pedophile is. It is a distinction that must be burned into your brain. Jerome Tichner had a lousy youth, and it wouldn't surprise me his wishing to be with children stems from that. He probably looks on them as being safe.

"He probably also feels because they are children, he is in charge, something he's never been around adults. Even his help at the beauty parlor told him what to do, and his mother was totally dominating, not just in his youth, but even today. I wouldn't rule him out just yet, but I'd certainly want more information about some of the women Sandi and Florida Justus knew.

"I'm inclined to believe the murders were done by a woman, and probably by one inflamed with jealousy. Or fear. Afraid her position of control is being threatened. In my opinion, Jennifer Tichner is not only domineering, but is mentally unbalanced."

"Thank you, Doctor. Here's what I'd like now. George, see if Barbara or Becky can get us a chance for Sara Lane to hear that telephone tape. Peters, I want you to have a nice little talk with Jennifer Tichner. Just a conversation, Peters. Don't let her believe she's under any kind of suspicion, or that she's being investigated. Get names of Jerome's friends, if he has any, find out what she talked about with Florida that morning, get some understanding of where her mind is right now.

"Edwards, I'm going to get one of the patrol people to take over the radio shack. I need you out in the field. Go over all these reports again, feel comfortable with what we know so far, and find out everything you can about Sandi Justus and her circle of friends, Florida Justus and hers, and Jerome's.

"Big orders, my friends, but we have big problems here. A double open murder, a former sheriff recuperating from bullet wounds inflicted by a former sergeant of detectives, state attorney general investigators looking into every trash can, and the threat of the FBI coming in as well.

"As far as the detective division of this department is concerned, our only job right now is to solve these murders. Let's try not to be side tracked by all the other bull shit. I'm not Ken Swicker. My office door is not closed or locked. Come talk with me and keep me advised of what you're doing.

"Saddle up."

***

"What do you think of our new detective sergeant, George?"

"I think he'll make a fine sheriff, Tim. My only concern is about the way the two of you feel about queers. I think you're dead wrong. I've never been able to get along with queers, ever. I think it's a cop-out for a man, and I don't think you're right about queers not being pedophiles. I've seen 'em."

"Well, I've seen many straight men and women who love to fondle little children George, and that certainly doesn't mean all straight people do. I can't accept that a gay person is automatically a criminal. I've known many myself, and many I'm proud to know."

This certainly wasn't the right time to bring up the

name of Stan Lyons, Darling knew, but he was worried about what George Andrus's reaction would be when he found out about Lyons. "I've got to get over to Stan's, George. We're going to fight it out for Sandesta County champion in scrabble. See you this evening."

"By the way, did you and Becky get your dinner?"

"Tonight, Tim. Tonight." The smile answered any other question the doctor might have thought of.

***

Perkins found himself alone in his new office, still surrounded by some physical reminders of Ken Swicker, but slowly taking on his own personality. There was a painting of a young cowboy roping a calf, done in oil, but showing a strong resemblance to a younger Claude Perkins, a set of silver spurs hanging from the hat rack, and many official documents indicating all the schools and conferences he has attended over the years.

The broken wooden chair has been replaced with one from the squad room, and he spent hours cleaning the windows and light fixtures. "Swicker was a real pig in here. Leftover food in the desk, shit behind everything, and I don't think he ever dusted anything. Probably figured it was Deputy Lane's job." He was smiling over that thought, trying to bring his mind back to the investigation, when he found himself looking deep into a pair of bright green eyes set directly above a delicious smile.

"Hi. Hope I'm not interrupting anything." Becky Martinez dropped into the high back swivel chair, crossed her long legs, and continued her devastatingly sensuous attack on Claude Perkins. Her legs were wrapped in a pair of tight jeans, and her sport coat was open enough for anyone to see a large semi-automatic pistol slung in a shoulder holster. Her baby blue blouse wasn't open at the neck, and she wore a necklace as a man would wear a bolo tie. She had boots on, tall and black, with her jeans tucked inside. A fashion piece carrying a big piece. *Formidable,* was the first thought in Perkins's mind.

"I'm glad you're here, Becky. Can we set aside the boy-girl, man-woman bullshit and talk cops and robbers?" He was really bothered by this Attorney General investigator, and he didn't like it. "To be very honest, Becky, you are a disruption to my thinking process." He could see her on a horse, Western-style boots and extra long legs reaching from stirrup to saddle, sitting straight and tall. He could also see her bare-ass naked, sprawled across his bed, and that enthralled the hell out of him. He had visions of Becky Martinez with George Andrus, and that simply pissed him off.

"I know. I do that on purpose most of the time, Claude. It gives me an edge, and that's half the battle in my line of work. Big tough Nevada cowboys get their edge by physical intimidation, I get mine by sensual intimidation.

"If you'll quit intimidating me, I'll quit intimidating you." Perkins had never met a woman like this, honest to a fault, yet able to distract with such a simple phrase.

"I intimidate you? My God, Becky, I can't even breathe when you're in the same room. OK, here's the plan. I won't rope and tie you, I won't wear spurs when I attack you, you can ride sidesaddle anytime you want, but please quit looking at me that way. I'm a male black widow spider in your company. If you have to have me for lunch, just don't make it hurt too much." Honesty from both sides now, and in the open for both to understand.

Several minutes went by with the two just looking at each other, each sizing the other, debating pros and cons over the coming match, knowing they should never be allowed to be alone with each other, ever, under any circumstances. Martinez broke the silence but not the spell.

"Is there anything I can do to help you with your murder investigation? You've used our resources at the capital before, Claude. Do you need anything from us?" Saying "us," not "me," kept Perkins on track, because he was ready to discuss anything this vixen had in mind.

"I'm not sure where we're going with the investigation at this time. It looks like we have a woman perp, Becky, but then sometimes, I'd swear it was a man. One thing bothers me a lot, and Swicker may have fucked us out of a chance to get a defining answer.

"On the night Sandi Justus was killed, we got a call from an alleged neighbor telling us about loud screaming at the Justus residence. Edwards, our communications officer believes the caller was a woman. I've listened to the tapes over and over, and I think it's a woman also. Edwards replaced Sara Lane who has sat at that radio and phone bank for a couple of years now, and I can't use her expertise. She would know, I feel sure.

"Do you have anyone or anything that would nail this down? You've heard Jerome Tichner speak, could his voice be lifted enough to sound like a woman's? I'm sure the two murders were committed by the same person, and right now, I believe that person is a woman. Have you read through any of the reports?"

"That's why I'm here, Claude. I believe as you do, and I think, for the same reason. I think we should be looking for a woman, deeply troubled and insanely jealous of something. But you're right, Jerome Tichner could almost be considered part woman, and yes, sometimes he even sounds like one.

"He's homosexual, but talking with you, Barbara Mingus, and him, he wouldn't have any difficulty passing himself off as a woman. Has he got any kind of record of being transsexual? Has he ever been seen dressed as a woman, or found to be acting as a woman? If not, I would almost cross him off the list.

"On the other hand, we know he's a pedophile. Well, he hasn't been convicted of being one, but Jesus, Claude, there's enough evidence right now to bring him in. Why is Johnson County holding back on arresting him?"

"I don't know, Becky. I asked George if there was enough for us to hold him, and he said no also. My God, the van, the body parts, the bloody and filthy clothing, the wig, and an amount of time he can't—or won't—tell us about? That's pretty convincing to me, but I guess not to lawyers. They are a unique breed, aren't they?"

The two investigators smiled over that thought, and sat another couple of minutes just looking at each other. "Interesting, isn't it. You're investigating the department I'm now running, working to bring this office to its knees, wanting to send my predecessor to prison, hoping to represent a former employee in her attempt to get justice, and at the same time, you're offering professional help to me to solve a double murder.

"Is there an irony here? When this is over, when murderers are sent to prison, when pedophiles are done in, when out of control former cops are sent off somewhere, how would you like to spend a weekend with a beat up old Nevada cowboy somewhere down on the coast?" It was so easy to ask the question, but only because he didn't give himself time to think about it, otherwise, he would have chickened out as he has so many times over the years.

"We'd kill each other, Claude." She sat so straight in the chair, eyeing him, smiling softly, toying with her necklace. "But, one has to die sometime, doesn't one?"

Chapter Sixteen
Friday, May 15

"Our new sergeant of detectives has a set of balls, Stan. He's a good man, and will make a fine sheriff, I think. It looks like you're feeling better. That bullet did some damage, but you'll be up and around in no time. The therapist will be in shortly with some crutches. Don't give her a hard time, and learn to use them properly," he said, chuckling to himself, seeing a picture of Lyons fighting the crutches.

"I'm sending you home tomorrow, so learn how to use those walking sticks. Or, hire a housekeeper." Tim Darling spent an hour outlining what had taken place in Perkins office, paying special attention to the fact that Perkins held no intolerance, no bigotry, toward homosexuals, but that George Andrus was seriously homophobic.

"I picked that up one evening when he was over at the house, and it bothered me at the time. I've come quite some way, eh? I'm glad though that Claude is holding up under some incredible pressure. From deputy to sergeant with no warning, in the middle of a double murder, and with the state investigating the department, is more than most cops go through. I never have, and I know I'd be taxed.

"How's Swicker doing? I'm told he's just down the hall from me. I hope he gets himself straightened out."

"He tried to kill you, Stan, Jesus. He'll be fit to go to jail in a day or two. Sara beat the shit out of that boy. She's one tough little lady."

"I'm glad she's on our side. Did you know she was gay?"

"You didn't?"

***

"Hello, Jerome. How are you holding up? It's been a tough time for you, I know."

"I'm okay, Claude. Thank you for asking. Barbara said it wasn't good for me to talk with you unless she was here."

"I know. I'm not here to discuss this Johnson County business, Jerome. I want to talk to you about the deaths of Florida and Sandi Justus. Sandi worked for you, and there may be some things you can tell me that will help me catch whoever killed her. Can I come in for a few minutes?"

"I suppose so, Claude. Is it true Sheriff Fletcher is going to be recalled and that you're going to be the new sheriff?" he asked as the two walked into Tichner's living room, just as neat and clean as the last time Perkins had been there. Tichner had been drinking a glass of white wine, the glass sitting on a table next to an easy chair, and a copy of *The Guide* was open as well. The magazine was a gay travel magazine, and Perkins noted that immediately.

"Can I get you anything, Claude? Coffee, tea, a glass of wine?"

"No, thank you. I'm concerned about the night Sandi was killed, Tichner. You told me you were out of town, and I know you did have a bus ticket to back that up, but can you give me any idea who might have a reason to kill her?"

Tichner didn't hesitate a second. "My God, Claude. That woman was the nastiest person I've ever known; mean, cruel. She hated everyone, had nothing good to say about anybody or anything. I would think there might be many who would want her out of their lives.

"Hell, she even got in a fist fight with my mother." As soon as he said it, he knew he shouldn't have.

"I know. I saw the results. Your mother has quite a

174

temper too, as I recall, Jerome. She came by my office a few days ago and suggested you might be responsible for Sandi's death. In my mind, and to make you feel better, I don't think of you as a possible suspect, but I would like to know more about both Sandi and Florida. Anything you can think of would be a help." He watched as Tichner became more and more uneasy with the current situation. Perkins's thoughts were always concise, something that kept him on an even keel. He saw that Tichner became agitated when he added Florida to the conversation. *He'll talk about Sandi, but he's worried about having to talk about Florida. He's a strange man.* Perkins was thinking that he better not bring up that compost pile either. *Body parts and bloody clothing. More murders? Were those body parts children, or maybe men lovers?*

"I don't know what I could tell you, Claude. Sandi would come to work angry, would be angry all day, and go home angry. She took her anger out on me, on our customers, on her co-worker Carrie.

"She was an excellent cosmetologist, Claude. Probably the best I've ever had in the shop, but she was horrid with our customers. I lost business when I hired her, and I should have gained. She treated pretty little Florida the same way."

Perkins knew he had to be very careful here, because every indication was that Tichner had been having sexual relations with Florida, but he didn't want to frighten the little hairdresser off now. He brought up the name Florida, and it would be natural for the deputy to follow through.

"According to the coroner, Jerome, little Florida had been physically abused by someone over a long period of time. Are you saying you believe Sandi was responsible for those injuries?"

Tichner again tightened up, picked up his wine glass, even though it was empty now, and just stared at his equally empty fireplace for a long moment. He was being put in a corner, and he didn't see a way out. *I'm really afraid of this man. That other big sergeant scared me physically, but this man is so smart. He's trying to make me say something I don't want to say.*

The agitation was obvious to Perkins, and he knew he couldn't go too far or he'd scare Tichner off.

"There are things Florida told me, Claude, and I promised I wouldn't tell anyone. I'm really afraid right now. I think I should call Barbara." Perkins saw fright written across Tichner's face, saw his hands tremble, watched as his eyes darted about the room, almost as an animal looking for an escape.

"It's all right, Mr. Tichner. I'm aware that you and Florida Justus had a relationship, aware that it may even have been sexual, aware that she had been sexually active for some time, and probably you weren't the only adult she had been to bed with. I'm not interested in that right now.

"I'm trying to find out who killed the two women. It's obvious to me you had sincere feelings for Florida, and I don't want to violate any pact you may have had with her, but if there's anything you can tell me that will bring me closer to her killer, that too will make you feel better."

Tender eggshells still filled with eggs, Perkins was saying to himself, and watched as the small man tensed and relaxed, felt tightness and release. Tichner was having trouble, and Perkins was going to go as far as he dared with these questions.

"Jerome, it will be points in your favor if you know anything and tell me about it. Florida was brutalized while she was alive, Jerome, and her killer did horrible things to her at the end of her life. She was your friend, Jerome, and you might be able to help me bring her killer in.

"Was it Sandi who terrorized her daughter for so long?"

"Yes," Tichner whispered. "Florida told me her

mother beat her. We had a very special relationship, Claude. My mother never beat me, but she emotionally destroyed me, and Florida and I could relate to each other. I probably shouldn't be telling you these things. Barbara wouldn't want me to, but I have to tell someone.

"My mother humiliated me at every opportunity, Claude. Every day when I was growing up, and Sandi beat the hell out of her daughter every day. We needed each other." Tears were flowing across his sunken cheeks, he was averting his eyes from everything in the room, grasping the arms of the big chair he was in, pulling his knees up, almost to his chin. Jerome Tichner was a beaten man; physically he was helpless, and emotionally, he was a little boy, spanked and stood in the corner, had been all his life, and now everything he had ever done was coming together as an evil presence.

"I don't know what to do, Claude. I don't know what to do." He was bawling like a ten-year-old boy who fell off his bike in front of all his friends, blubbering great cries of emotion. "There's no one in my life, Claude. Does that mean anything to you? No one. No one to even feel a speck of warmth toward me. My mother hates me, the police want to kill me, Florida is dead.

"What am I going to do, Claude?" It was a plaintive cry of one in total despair, and Claude Perkins didn't have an answer. It was impossible for Perkins to relate, and thoughts of his own mother, his life as a boy on a ranch, the love that spread through so many members of his family. He simply could not relate despite understanding to a degree what Tichner was saying.

"Talk to Barbara Mingus, Jerome. Tell her everything. She's a good woman, she obviously has your best interests at heart. Talk to Barbara, and maybe she can get you some personal relief." To himself, he was saying that Jerome Tichner needed to spend the rest of his life in confinement, with or without mental counseling.

Tichner watched the big squad car pull out of his driveway, poured himself another glass of wine, cried for an hour, great sobs of crying and moaning, and called his mother. He would have been better off to have called Mingus.

"You told the police to arrest me? You told them I killed Florida and Sandi Justus? You told them I was a pedophile? I hate you. I hate you!" It didn't make him feel any better, and it was even worse when she just laughed at him.

"I've hated you since the day you were born, Jerome. I hope the police put you away forever. You've embarrassed me for the last time, having sex with men and boys, having sex with little girls, hurting people, and everyone in town blames me, Jerome. Do you understand that? They think I'm responsible for your sick behavior, that I'm a bad mother. I am not a bad mother, Jerome, but you are an evil person.

"I hope the cops put you away forever. I hope they kill you. You hate me? You don't know what hate is." He heard the line go dead and slumped back into his chair. He'd been all but living in that chair since the day all the police arrived to search his home, search his life. It took a few minutes, but he finally called Barbara Mingus and unloaded his life on her.

"I have nothing left. There's nothing, no warmth, no love, no friends, and soon, no home. They're going to put me in prison, and then even more people will be able to hurt me, and it's all my mother's fault. She did this to me, she made me who I am, she's responsible, not me. Barbara, I beg you, make sure the cops know that, she's responsible.

"I am not responsible for any of this. Poor little Florida, so pretty, so young, and now, just dead. Her mother, so mean and terrible, so frightening, and now she's dead too. I am not responsible. That poor little boy over in Johnson County, all I wanted, all he needed was some kindness and love, some tender love, but he fought me. It's all my mother's fault. I'm not responsible." The sobs continued, even after Mingus told him she would see to it that he got the kind of help he needed. She couldn't tell him he wouldn't go to jail, she couldn't tell him he wouldn't be subjected to years of pain, even ridicule, but she promised to get him as much help as possible.

It was several hours later, well past sunset, that Jerome Tichner got up from his overstuffed easy chair and dressed to go out.

***

"George, I think Jerome Tichner is getting ready to run, to get out of Sandesta County. Listen, George, he's either going to run or do himself in. He's emotionally unstable, could kill himself or run. I've already alerted Johnson County about my thoughts, and I know you and Barbara Mingus are close enough you can talk to her. I think she needs to be alerted to this."

"What did Johnson County say? Are they going to put out a warrant?"

"Roberts was a little vague, George, but if we don't do something, he'll be gone. I've got a deputy keeping an eye on the house, but we don't have complete surveillance. At least we impounded his van, but he's very much aware of bus schedules in and out of here."

"I'll call Barbara right away. Peters was in looking for you a few minutes ago. He just came back from talking with Jennifer Tichner. Boy, she and her son are a pair, aren't they?"

"How's that?"

"Peters said Ms. Tichner flew off the handle when he knocked on her door. Called him some pretty bad names. I think you need to talk with him, and then her also.

"Are you going to get any help from Becky Martinez? I heard you talked with her about Sara Lane."

Perkins wondered how he knew about that. Did

Andrus have designs on her? "Why is it bothering me? Get your head on, cowboy, she's way out of your class. I won't let this little attorney get in my head this way." To Andrus, he simply said, "I don't know yet. The state has some audio experts who want to listen to that tape as well. I still don't think Jerome Tichner is responsible for those murders, but I'm keeping an open mind.

"Let me know what Barbara Mingus says."

He was sitting back at his desk wondering why Becky would tell him about their conversation. *I wonder how much she told him. I hope this isn't going to develop into some kind of political thing. I could really fall for her. We'll just have to wait and let the dust settle some, I guess.*

I don't think I'm ready for this sheriff stuff. I like sergeant, that's okay, but I'm not a political person. I have that sense of a cop, take what someone says with a grain of salt, believe them to a point, but don't always look for an ulterior motive. It seems most of the politicians I know, never quite tell the whole truth, always feel they have to hold something back. He got up and walked down to the radio room.

"Call Peters for me, and have him meet me at the hospital. I'm going to see how Stan Lyons and Ken Swicker are doing. I'm taking my own car, but I'll have my radio with me."

His mind continued to work, more on the case than on Becky Martinez, but it was hard to get her out of his mind. He needed to talk, get his thoughts out where they can be heard, and as he'd done for his entire career, he reached for his tape recorder. "If Tichner does decide to run, I hope we can get him first. I wouldn't want to lose him. Roberts surprises me, though, He should be on his way over here with a warrant, but he didn't seem to feel any urgency. Strange. This isn't the way I would do it, but Roberts didn't see the travel book or the look on that man's face. I have this feeling that Roberts has another agenda and I don't know what it is. Those around him say he's a good cop, but I sure wouldn't give Tichner this much leeway. He's going to run, I know it." He shut off the recorder and made a note to call Roberts as soon as he got back to the office. The tape recorder was switched back on.

"Peters is a queer duck. I hope he didn't do any fancy strutting when he went to Jennifer Tichner's. I told him not to, but he's pretty full of himself sometimes. Takes after Swicker.

"Tichner had a bad childhood, emotionally, and Florida Justus had one physically. Is that what tied them together, or was it just raw sex? She was a pretty little girl, and Tichner does like children. He could have been bullshitting me, but those tears were damn legitimate. Did the sex start the process and then they discovered their similarities, or the other way around?

"I can't see him as the killer, but the deeper I think about it, he is the one. I can't get those body parts in his compost pile out of my head. Those lab reports better come in pretty quick. And then, that damn phone call. Was it Tichner calling as a woman, was it Tichner calling and his voice was just high from the excitement of the moment, or is there someone else who was with him? Or is our killer a woman? Damn it, too many questions." He was still working out answers as he pulled into the parking lot at the hospital. Peters slid his squad car right next to Perkins's.

"I tried to find you earlier, Sarge. That Tichner woman is one serious case."

"Did you do as I asked, Peters? I hope so, because she is emotionally unstable in my mind. She was in a fist fight with Sandi Justus the day before that woman died, and she has made serious allegations about her son being a killer. Tell me you handled this as I asked."

"I did. I went up to her door and introduced myself, and that's as far as I got. She came out through the screen door in some kind of terrycloth robe that didn't cover anything, screaming obscenities at me. She had a can of beer in one hand and a damn pointed can opener in the other. I'd bet she was drunk as shit.

"I never got another word in, Sarge. She splashed that beer all over me, was swinging her arms around like a windmill, and that church key came mighty close more than once. I remembered everything you said, and felt the best bet was retreat. She is one weird woman, and in any other circumstance, I think I would have arrested her for her actions."

Perkins straightened up at the mention of a beer can opener. "Was she using that can opener as someone who may have used something like it as a weapon, maybe recently?"

"There's no question, Claude. She was going to rip me up."

"Okay, buddy. Do me a big favor and write your report as you just told me. Don't leave anything out. Also, while I'm thinking about it, help out with the surveillance on Jerome Tichner. I have a suspicion that he is planning to run. I wish I knew his part in these murders. He's involved, Peters, I just don't know how yet.

"Keep your eye on him. and don't let him get out of town. If he takes a cab anywhere near that bus station, you arrest him immediately on suspicion of child endangerment, and child molesting. These would be Sandesta County charges, separate from Johnson County, stemming from his relationship with Florida Justus. I don't want that man to get away."

"I'll get that report on your desk right away, and coordinate my actions with the others watching Tichner. Where will I get hold of you if I need to?"

"I'll have my radio with me at all times. As I said earlier, I'm not like Ken Swicker." The lanky cowboy turned and walked toward the hospital, wanting to have a long talk with Stan Lyons. He's been off the range for years, many years, yet he still walked as if he just stepped down from a comfortable leather saddle. "Hey, Peters. You said Ms. Tichner was drinking a beer? What kind was it?"

"One of those cheap kinds. You know the ones, don't have pop tops, and sometimes the cans get rusty."

Perkins's eyes lit up. "Thanks, Peters. Put that in your report. That's damn important." He headed into the hospital with a whole new outlook on life.

Peters might make it yet. Developing a good attitude. I really like Edwards, but he's so damn lazy. I have to tell him everything I want. Maybe that's what I'll do is have a little meeting with those guys and pep 'em up a little. Mom used to say she was going to put 'pepper in your pants,' when she wanted me to think for myself. Never did, bless her soul, but it made me think. And act. He had that crooked grin on his face as he strode through the hospital corridors.

"Hi Sheriff. How 'ya feeling?"

Lyons was nursing a bowl of bread pudding with lots of raisins, even a dollop of whipped cream, and was scowling. "Hurts like a son of a bitch, Claude. Tim says I can go home tomorrow, and the nurses here say they won't let me out unless I start eating. Bread pudding? There's a lot of irony here, my friend.

"I've got scars everywhere from a war we all hated, and now a broken leg from a cop I hired. Big tough Stan Lyons, and eating bread pudding. I want a steak."

Perkins was chuckling, watching his former boss carry on. "My mama used to tell me if I cried one more time she'd have to fix me a sugar titty, sheriff."

"Don't you start, too, now." The two professional police officers smiled warmly at each other, understanding the humor and little jab Perkins took.

"I'm glad to see you still have your humor, though. That was a nasty shot you took. I just popped in to see how you're doing. Things in the department are almost completely out of hand with Fletcher hiding out somewhere, Swicker in custody, the AG's office investigating, and threats of FBI agents coming in as well.

"I sure do miss you."

"I recruited you out of that office in Texas, Claude, because I have lots of respect for the way you do things. Congratulations on being sergeant, and I want you to give serious consideration for making yourself available for the office of sheriff if this recall election takes place.

"You're fully qualified, and I'll give you my complete backing. Have you given this any thought yet?"

"The idea has crossed my mind, sheriff, but I'm so involved in this double murder, and a child molesting case from Johnson County involving Jerome Tichner, I haven't really thought hard about the prospect."

"My God, there's a lot going on. Makes me wish I was back, but that can't be. It's not easy to work murder cases and try to think about an election at the same time, Claude, but it would please me no end if you would try. While I'm thinking of it, try to call me Stan, will you?"

"That might be hard. I respect you so much as a man and a sheriff, I don't know if I could call you by your first name, but I'll try. The idea of being sheriff of this county is high on my list, I have to admit, but even if I made that decision right now, today, I would still have to give most of my interest to the investigation. That's primary right now."

"That's why you'll make a good sheriff. Have you heard how Swicker is doing? What a shame for a good man to get himself so turned around, and all because of something so simple a couple of little pills once in a while would correct the problem. Tim Darling said he has a chemical imbalance, and it is easily corrected. And look at what's happened. An entire career destroyed because he was too damn proud to admit there might be a problem."

"After visiting you, I was going to stick my head in

his room and say hello. It's the least I can do. He's arrogant, proud, egotistical, but he's still a guy I worked with for some time. I never liked him, never considered him a friend, but I did work with him.

"He's about three doors down the corridor. Want to pop in with me? Maybe that's not a good idea. I'm sorry I brought it up, I mean, shit. After all, he's the bastard shot you. I'm sorry."

"Don't even think that way, Claude. I need a little walk, let's go down there. My robe is in the closet there. I refuse to walk around in these hospital gowns with my bare ass showing."

As he helped the former sheriff into his robe, Perkins could see the pain Lyons was still feeling. "Have you ever been shot? Between being a cop and a soldier, I've got way too many holes in this old body."

"I have four holes across my shoulders in my back, Stan, but it's from a pitchfork, not bullets. Damn fool I was working with got angry at something and threw his pitchfork, and I was in the way. Sheriff back there wanted to arrest the idiot, but I wouldn't file charges. Just one of those stupid things that happen to people."

"Could have been pretty serious, Claude."

"Yeah. It did some damage, but nothing that wouldn't heal, and the fool just lost his temper, is all. He wasn't aiming at me." They walked out of the room, Lyons and Perkins, the former sheriff, the possible new sheriff, to visit the man who shot Lyons and would gladly shoot Perkins.

Perkins always admired Stan Lyons, but his level of confidence in the man increased as they walked down the hallway. *He's one tough bird, this Sheriff Lyons. Damn near killed by a former employee and now he wants to visit him and see how he's doing. I wonder if I'd be that generous?*

One thing I do know, I want Lyons and Sara Lane

on my side in any kind of fight. She's damn near as tough as he is. I wonder if I can get her back in the department. Listen to me. I'm talking like I'm the sheriff. Be careful, Claude, old boy. That's one big step you're looking at. He was smiling at these thoughts, weathered lines around his eyes crinkled, his deeply chiseled face taking on a kinder expression.

It was just the night before, sitting in his rocking chair, going over notes from Andrus and Darling, that he thought about this job, this idea of being sheriff, this concept of being in that command chair. He said to himself so many times, "I've spent my life learning to be the best cop, a damn fine investigator, a student of people, and now, I might have the opportunity to put it all together. Am I strong enough? Am I as good as I think I am?" It was a long night of introspection, and there were far more pluses than negatives. He slept well last night.

Now, walking with his friend down the hall, he asked, "Is there something I should know as far as why you don't want your old job back, Stan? Something going on in the county or in the department, other than the chaos that's part of it right now?"

"There is something you should know about, Claude, but it doesn't have anything to do with the department. Maybe after our visit with Ken, we can take a few minutes and talk, eh?"

The deputy at Swicker's door gave a big hello to his new sergeant and former sheriff, but wasn't sure if this visit was the best thing that could happen. "Sarge, he's in one pissy mood. I had to tell him if he threw one more coffee cup, one more bed pan, or cussed one more nurse, I was going to put him in restraints. He's really being an ass, Claude."

"We just want to say hello and see how he's doing. Won't be a minute." Perkins opened the door and held it for Lyons. Swicker erupted in a volley of profanity as they entered.

"Get out of here you butt fucking queer son of a bitch! I hate you, Lyons, you queer bastard, I hate you! Get out of my room, out of my sight! I hate you!" He was screaming at the top of his lungs, thrashing around in his bed, and Perkins hustled the sheriff out.

"What the hell brought that on? What the hell was he screaming about queers? I'm thinking that old boy has gone way over the top."

"No, Claude, actually, he hasn't. Let's go have that talk now, shall we?"

Chapter Seventeen
Friday, May 15—Saturday, May 16

C laude Perkins, brand new Sergeant of Detectives, possible candidate for Sheriff of Sandesta County is sitting across the dinner table with the most beautiful woman he's ever been with. And his mind is on everything except Becky Martinez.

"Stan Lyons believes himself to be gay? That's the most incredible thing I can imagine. Sara Lane is a lesbian? My own department is falling apart, with a sheriff who simply doesn't give a damn, a former sergeant in custody for attempted murder among other charges, another former deputy suing the department and the county, a district attorney with a broken nose, and the state's attorney general investigating the whole fucking mess." He looked into those electrifying green eyes and tried his damnedest to smile. His mind was spinning, and he couldn't slow it down. "I'm about to spend a few hours with a goddess, and I can't get away from the office."

"You have every right to be in another galaxy, Claude. More problems? Please don't tell me another deputy has gone out of control."

"I'm sorry, Becky. I'll try to put it aside. My God, I would much rather just sit here and stare into those eyes of yours than think about cop shop shit. Does your job ever overwhelm you?"

"Sometimes it tries. I know what's happening to you, though, and I sure as hell don't envy you. I spent several hours with Stan Lyons today, and even broke a dinner date with George Andrus just to be with you. Intimidate me, Claude, because I'm tired of bullshit. Any good news?" Her smile was so sincere, her eyes said all the things a man wants to hear, and she reached across the table to take Perkins's hand in hers. Warmth spread up his outstretched arm, and his mouth and throat dried up like the Nevada desert in the middle of August. Many murder investigations just went out the window, and he relished the idea of her breaking a date with Andrus so she could be with him.

"Tell me something to make my heart skip a little. I pack a big gun, I investigate other cops, I even destroy lives and careers, Claude, but I'm not the tough little AG's investigator people think. I'm soft and warm, maybe not your fuzzy little Raggedy Anne, but I am cuddly, and right now, I'd like to just be with you. Not the Sandesta County Sheriff's Office."

This big Western lawman personified what Becky always wanted in her life. Raw and mean when necessary, warm and loving when needed, and tough and strong as a bull. Claude Perkins stood tall and wide in her eyes and she wanted him to know it.

"I'll try not to stammer and sound like a fool, Becky, but around you I'm just another little adolescent boy. I could sit and hold hands like this all night and be as happy as it is possible. I'm probably going to sound silly, or even foolish, but I want you to know, you intimidate the hell out of me on the one hand, and excite the hell out of me on the other.

"I own a small part of our family ranch back in Nevada, and I'd sure like to take about three or four weeks and show it to you when this mess is over with. Together, we have a couple of sections around Paradise Valley, but each of us kids has set up our own little places around the perimeter. I've got mountains and streams, antelope and deer, a broad valley and cabin where we could just sit and look at each other. God, you're beautiful."

She took her hand back, clasped her two provocatively under her chin, and looked deep into the eyes of this rangy hunk in front of her. "Just how big is this 'little place' of yours?"

"Each of us kids took 160 acres. That's a quarter of a section, a quarter of a square mile, Becky. It's big, open, the highest and bluest sky you've ever seen, with water so cold and pure it makes your teeth hurt to drink it." She saw thousands of square miles sparkling in big brown eyes when he talked about Nevada, and could almost feel herself drawn in.

"We can't have a relationship for real, Claude, until after my investigation. You already know that, but I want you to know, if you say the wrong thing, make just one wrong move, look at me one more time that way, I'll not only be in your bed, and your heart, I'll be Doña Primera at the Nevada homestead." His heart turned somersaults, and he blushed like a high school boy with his first taste of a woman. His thoughts were tempered by thoughts that she would have been sharing this table with George Andrus if certain things at the hospital hadn't taken place. Or was her decision based on him, not what happened earlier in the day? He couldn't be sure, just yet.

Their dinner lasted hours, and they had a hard time saying good night when he brought her back to her hotel room. "You can't come in, hot shot. If I let you in, I'll never let you leave, and that wouldn't work ethically with what's going on."

"I know. Can you come into the office in the morning? There's some shit happening that you need to know about. We'll try to keep us separate from investigations, if we can. Offices are off limits, okay?"

"That's a good way to put it." Their goodnight kiss lasted a while, and they rocked back and forth wrapped in long and strong arms. "You're in serious trouble, Sergeant of Detectives Claude Perkins, I want you to understand that. Very serious trouble. If I don't say good night right now, we'll create quite a scene right here in the hall." She laughed, punched him gently, "You didn't say the hall was off limits now, did you?

"See you in the morning, Sarge."

***

The timing was perfect. As he approached his car, his radio came alive with a call from headquarters. "Yeah, this is Perkins. Go ahead."

"Edwards has been following Jerome Tichner for the last few hours, Sarge. He's gone to dinner, by himself, and to a movie, also alone. Edwards says he's at a bar, some kind of jazz club, right now. Should he stay with him?"

"Absolutely. No question. Why am I just now hearing about this?"

"I guess because I just heard, myself, Claude."

"All right. Perkins clear." He drove to the Blue Lamp and found Edwards parked around the corner, eating a hoagie from a convenience store.

"Edwards, why did you wait so long to report what Tichner is doing? My God, man didn't you hear me this morning when I said he has to be considered a prime suspect in these murders?

"Didn't you understand when I said later today that I feared he was a flight risk? Edwards, you've been to the training sessions, you have an opportunity to be a good cop and a good investigator, but you've got to start thinking. When did you get that sandwich?"

"Just a couple of minutes ago, why?"

"Because it would take Tichner about two minutes to walk out that door, turn down the block, flag a cab, and be gone without you knowing it. Jesus." Perkins picked up the radio microphone and called in.

"Send a car to the bus station. Look for Jerome Tichner. Call me as soon as you know he's there or not there. I want to know either way.

"Now, Edwards, I'm going in that bar and have a

191

cocktail. If Tichner is not there, I'm walking straight out of there, and you're on suspension. You don't move until I come back."

His anger at Edwards boiled, but he knew he couldn't let it cloud his judgment. He had to walk in that little club and find Jerome Tichner. He didn't care if he was seen or not, he had to know the hairdresser was there.

Clouds of blue cigarette smoke filled the air, and the sounds of some serious jazz wafted through as well. The club was crowded with people, some dancing, some at cocktail tables, and some at the bar. Perkins sidled up to the bar and ordered a Scotch on the rocks. He didn't always appreciate jazz, country music being more to his liking, but he didn't hate it either. His eyes slowly took in the crowd, and it was several nervous minutes before he found Tichner, sitting in a booth with two other men, one of whom appeared to have his hand inappropriately in Tichner's pants.

"Jesus. How can they do that in public?" He finished his drink, keeping an eye on the table, and then walked out.

"Edwards, I want to see you in my office at 10:00 o'clock tomorrow morning, no questions asked. Understood?"

"Yes sir." Edwards still didn't seem to grasp the gravity of the situation.

"Tichner is in that club, lucky for you, with two other men. I don't care what time it is, or where they go, I want that information relayed to headquarters immediately. Again, understood?"

"Yes sir."

It was a sad Sergeant Perkins who drove home, wondering if he would be able to salvage the career of Deputy Edwards. " So far, fear doesn't seem to work, and I have never bought in to the theory of management by intimidation anyway, but there has to be a way to get into that man's head.

"There are so many things I don't know, about Edwards, about this case, about my new life as sergeant, and mostly about one Elizabeth Martinez. I sure as hell enjoyed the first part of tonight, though." He let his mind drift, thought about sitting on a big quarter horse, shoulders squared to a Nevada wind, trailing a mule deer high into the Santa Rosa Mountains, thought about having Becky on a horse right next to him, and then his mind returned to the present.

He needed to spend lots of time with Dr. Darling, with George Andrus, and with Stan Lyons in order to bring this case to a close. "I've almost got it, and just need a piece or two. Body parts in that compost pile have me in a quandary, though. I want to believe that Tichner is not responsible for the murders of Florida and Sandi Justus, but if those human remains are telling me he has killed before, I might need to change my thinking.

"Darling can tell me about some of these things, like age and sex of the remains, if they are from one or more individuals, and maybe how they were killed. An ID would be even better. And then how do we tie him to the Justus killings? Damn." He called one last time to his communications deputy, was satisfied that Edwards was still on Tichner, and headed for bed. There were visions of purple sage, high blue skies, and Becky Martinez floating through drooping eyelids, and all at once, the alarm went off. For the first time since young Florida's body had been found, Claude Perkins had had a good night's sleep.

***

It was just after 7:00 A.M., and Tim Darling seated himself across the desk from Perkins. "I guess that was a bit of a shock when Stan told you why he wasn't going to offer himself as sheriff again? Are you okay with everything?"

"As close as you two are, it shouldn't have

193

surprised me that he let you know, but no, I don't have any problem with what I've learned. Someone's personal life is their own, I've always felt, and I certainly couldn't judge anyone. A person suspected of a crime, I can arrest, Doc, but I sure as hell can't judge another person because of what their sexuality might be. Personal philosophies are just that in my mind. Personal.

"I've never given the least amount of thought to having a sexual relationship with a man, I can't imagine it, but I certainly can't condemn someone if that's what they want or need. I found Tichner in a bar last night with two men, one fondling him, and it turned my stomach, but that's his life. It sure isn't mine, and wouldn't be.

"What surprised me as much as what Stan said to me about himself, was what he said about Sara Lane. She told him she was gay. It was quite a day yesterday, I'll say that."

Reflectively, he thought back on his visits with Jerome Tichner and Deputy Peters, with Stan Lyons and Ken Swicker, and finally, his dinner with Becky Martinez. In the back of his mind was his upcoming meeting with Edwards. "It was quite a day, Doc.

"Tell me about jealousy and hate. Is it possible for someone to feel so threatened and so afraid, they will kill? I can't get it out of my mind that our killer is a woman who is insanely jealous on one hand, or filled with hate, or even frightened on the other. Does jealousy have to be about another person, or can it be about a situation? In other words, can someone be terrified of losing a position? My suspect right now is terrified of something, so afraid she has killed two people. Am I going in the right direction? Would killing be the result of a threat at that level?"

"I think so, Claude. To kill might be perceived as self-protection, or protection of a serious belief. Even protection of a love. How did the interview with Jennifer Tichner go? She's on your short list, isn't she?"

"I have to think about her, her very strange son, and maybe someone we don't even know of yet. Peters got himself thrown off her place. I guess she went off the deep end with him. I just hope she did it because that's the way she is, and not because of something he did.

"One thing, though. She intimidated that deputy with a beer can opener, Doc. The kind we think was used on both Justus females. That's important to me right now, but I'm also concerned just a bit about Peters. He spent way too much time learning to emulate our former sergeant, I'm afraid. Jennifer Tichner has to be a head case, Doc, but she's never been accused of anything. She started or at least took part in a fist fight with Sandi Justus on that Saturday morning before Florida was killed, but no charges came from it. She doesn't even have a bad driving record, and as far as I know, she hasn't been treated for any kind of mental problem. At least, nothing I can find.

"We know Jerome Tichner was having a relationship with Florida, and we also know Florida was not chaste. I mean, she had sexual relations with many men, as near as we can tell. This doesn't mean Jerome is off the hook for diddling, but it does mean they may not have been as close as he might have wanted. Did he kill her in a fit of rage because of other men, and then have to do in her mother as well? Is it possible Sandi found out some way, and threatened to call us? You remember, the first thing she said when we told her about her daughter was to arrest Tichner. Even his mother said the same thing. And Tichner told me he could just barely tolerate Sandi Justus at his shop.

"Taking this another step, since Johnson County has enough evidence to pull the asshole in, and hasn't done so, is there something about that bastard we don't know? I can't get the fact there are body parts in his compost pile out of my mind. Has Jerome Tichner killed in the past? Is it possible we have a jerk who also diddles his mother? And she got jealous and killed Florida and Sandi?"

"Well, that one might be off the chart, Claude, but I see where you're going. We know Jerome had a miserable youth, but was it miserable enough for him to need the closeness of children? And does it mean that Sandi, if she found out, was a big enough threat that he killed her?"

"My God, Doc. That means Jennifer might be in dire trouble. I need to get a car over there, if only for surveillance. That asshole could kill his mother. She's been telling anyone who'll listen that he killed Florida; she could be next." He punched his phone line into the radio room and gave the deputy on duty directions to protect Jennifer Tichner.

"I'm going to call Andrus, Doc. We may need to pick up Tichner, if only for his mother's protection. George will have to coordinate this with Barbara Mingus, but our job is as much to protect good guys as it is to arrest bad guys. Maybe I've been wrong about the killer being a woman. The more I think about this, the more I see Jerome Tichner as our number one suspect. Give me your thoughts." He said this as he was dialing George Andrus.

"I think you're onto something, Claude, but I wouldn't rule out the idea of the jealous woman, just yet."

He asked that Andrus call back when he came in. "Listen, Doc. Have you got anything back on those blood samples, from either murder scene? And what about the DNA samples? Are they going to be any help? Questions, questions, I know, but right now, that's all I have.

"What about those human remains from the compost pile? Do we know anything about them yet?" The doctor wasn't given the time to answer.

"Hi. Am I interrupting? I can wait, if you need me to." Bright as the sun, the smile enveloped Doctor Darling and Sergeant Perkins.

"Come in Becky, we're just going over all the revelations of the last couple of days. Between finding out about sexual preferences of former bosses, former co-workers, and murder suspects, it's just a normal every day in the life of the Sandesta County, S.O." Perkins smiled and pulled a chair to the desk for her. "You're mighty perky this morning."

"I spent a great deal of time with a cowboy dream of mine last night, Sergeant. What do we know about all this mess?"

Tim Darling picked up on the looks between the two, and started to excuse himself from the group. "No, no, Doctor. I, that is, we need you here. What about all those blood samples?"

The county coroner sat back down, glancing nervously at the two others, and opened his brief case. "The blood at Florida's homicide is all hers, and the traces on that beer can opener are hers as well. The blood from Sandi's homicide scene are also all hers. If either of the victims fought back, they didn't do any real damage." Perkins jumped in right away.

"That surprises the hell out of me. Maybe not about Florida Justus, but certainly about her mother. Everything we know about that woman indicates violence. You're telling me she was savagely murdered and didn't fight back?"

"Maybe didn't have the opportunity, Claude. There is some big news from the Tichner compost pile, however. The remains found there are from two juveniles, boys, and I think I'll have ID's on them before the end of the day. The blood on all the clothing, rags, and debris in the pile indicates that whoever is responsible for that compost pile has been involved with more than half a dozen people who have shed blood. Because of previous problems with the Sandesta Sheriff, we have samples of Tichner's blood. Some of the blood in that pile is his. You'll be glad to know that in more than one case, his blood is on the same item as the blood of someone else. That could be significant in court."

"Jesus. I wish Andrus wasn't always late. Can you put all that in reports for both me and George? This is more than I expected, and I think we are going to want to take Tichner into custody. I mean real soon." Dr. Darling got up to leave, said goodbye to Becky Martinez, who answered in a riddle as far as he was concerned.

"Yes, Doctor. Thank you, and we must remember, the office is off limits."

Chapter Eighteen
Saturday, May 16

D r. Darling left a copy of his blood sample and human tissue report on the desk. "I already have a copy for George, Claude, so I'll drop it off on his desk. Are you in a position to simply arrest Tichner?"

"No. George has made it clear that we have to have damn good evidence. We're close, Doc, but remember, the little shit's attorney is Barbara Mingus. That idiot Swicker has already put a big cloud across the face of this investigation, so George wants to be absolutely sure of himself before we arrest the fool.

"Swicker. What a stupid way to destroy a career. Can't get Big Buster to perform, so you shoot the former sheriff, destroy property and threaten to harm a reporter, besides clobbering the DA and beating up a female deputy. What a fool. Anyway, doc, thanks for all this. We'll be coming close now."

"Before I leave, there's something, I don't know how to put it, but something that might change some of our thinking. I went to a little hamburger stand for dinner last night and found George and Barbara together, sitting in a booth, and holding hands. I don't know what it means, but I thought you should know."

Darling left, but not before giving another close eye on the two left in the room. "Those two have something going also or I'm not as good an investigator as I think I am. Well, good for them. And George and Barbara? In the middle of this investigation?" He closed the door, and true to their word, Perkins and Martinez only did business in the office. Cop shop business.

"There's one thing I can't understand, Becky. Both

the Justus women were slaughtered, mutilated, with what we believe is the old style beer can opener, the one us red neck cowboys used to call a church key, and that doesn't strike me as a Jerome Tichner way of doing something. Strangled with lace panties, I could understand, maybe, but not the gruesome way those two were killed.

"I think we have several sets of homicides here. I still think it was a woman that killed Florida and Sandi Justus, and probably Tichner that killed whoever those human remains belong to, and I'm afraid for Jennifer Tichner as well. If it was Tichner, then his mother might be in danger."

"What if it was Jennifer?" The question Perkins had been evading, he knew, but a legitimate question.

"There's some serious possibility there, Becky. She's mentally unstable, has proved that many times, but has never been arrested for anything, or seen a shrink as far as I know. But she is volatile, got in a fistfight with Sandi Justus the morning that Florida Justus was killed.

"My God. Becky. When I sent that deputy to talk to Jennifer Tichner, he told me she was swilling beer from a can. An old style can, he said, and that she was threatening him with a church key type opener. Holy shit, where is Andrus?"

"You're on to something here, Claude." Becky's eyes were saying something else entirely, and Perkins wanted to follow up on those thoughts, not this investigation. She unfolded her long body and legs from the chair, giving what she now considered her Nevada buckaroo a large and inviting smile. "I have to go see the sheriff about my own investigation, but keep me posted on what's happening. You've got some real kooks in the county, eh?" She was laughing as she kissed him very lightly on the cheek and headed out the door. The smile she threw back at him was glorious. All he could do was pick up the phone again and try once more for George Andrus.

"George. You're actually in. We've got a couple of possible breaks here. I'll be right up." He hung up the phone before Andrus could say anything, picked up all his file folders, and headed for the DA's office. "I should have invited him down here, but then again, this office holds some bad memories for the old bastard." He was too busy to even think about George Andrus and Barbara Mingus having their own affair.

The DA was going over the coroner's report when Perkins walked in. The office reflected Andrus in every detail, with pictures of Southern elegance, mansions, big trees dripping with moss, standing in swamp water. There was a mounted big mouth bass, and a couple of mounted quail and ducks. On his desk, Andrus had pictures from hunting trips spread across the continent, with so many local and state officials both he and Perkins knew.

"You've made a real home in here, George."

"I stuck my head in your office yesterday, Claude, and saw your changes down there. Very nice, indeed. I'm just finishing Tim's reports here. Wow. We've got a hell of a bee's nest. That bastard Tichner appears to be more than just a pedophile, Claude, but a murderer as well. This part about his blood and blood from one of the human remains could very well land him on death row.

"I assume you're here to ask for an arrest warrant. Everything tells me we should act on this right now. He knows we took that pile apart. He must know what we found. That coupled with what Johnson County has on him, his days of hair styling are over. The only thing really missing is identification of the body parts. If those are children, and we know who they are, Tichner is a death row candidate."

"There's more, George. I don't think Tichner is responsible for the Justus murders at all. When I asked one of my deputies to have a quiet little talk with Jennifer Tichner, Jerome's mother, she ran him off. He said she was swilling a beer and threatened him with a beer can opener."

"Well, hell, Claude, I've been known to have a beer before lunch once in a while. That doesn't make me a murderer."

"Of course it doesn't, but if you were mentally unstable, known for getting in a fistfight with one of the victims, and you were swilling a beer from and old style beer can, and threatened a deputy, and both of our homicide victims were maliciously chewed to pieces from an old style beer can opener, I might want to arrest you." He sat back and watched the facial expressions change from delighted little grin to something akin to anger.

"So Jennifer Tichner drinks from an old style steel beer can. Well, I'll be damned. I suppose you would like me to get you a search warrant? And an arrest warrant for her son?

"By the way. I heard from Ray Blocker at the recall committee. They are going to announce later today their recall drive. They want me to get a go ahead from you to put your name up to replace that fool Harris Fletcher. The law says to start a petition of recall, they have to offer a replacement. It also says that anyone else can then join in and offer themselves for the office.

"Generally, the person recommended by the recall committee is the one that gets the nod if the recall is successful. You know damn well that Fletcher will have a cat fit when he hears that his new sergeant of detectives is trying to oust him."

"Jesus, George. This is horrible timing. I've almost got a multiple murder investigation completed, and now you tell me this. Fletcher will fire my ass immediately, and then what the fuck do we do? No. Let me at least wrap this case up to the point where it can progress on its own. I very much would like to be sheriff of Sandesta County, but saying that, I have to say my first priority is to be a detective. A good cop first, George, then sheriff.

"Please don't do this yet." Perkins couldn't understand where this kind of thinking was coming from, and wanted Andrus to back off. "Look, Blocker is a fine real estate salesman, a good one, but he doesn't know from diddly about cop shop work. That sheriff will fire my ass today, and we don't have anyone to finish this investigation.

"Tell Blocker to go ahead and talk to the press about how the committee is working to create a recall petition, that they are searching for the right person to replace Fletcher, what the hell, even bring Stan Lyon's name in to the story, but leave mine out. I'm not asking, here. George, I'm begging." The two men sat on each side of George Andrus's big desk, just looking at each other.

"I understand your concern, Claude, I really do. I think you have a good plan, and I'll pass it on with my blessing. Have you heard the rumors going around the court house that Lyons is a fucking queer? And Sara Lane, too? Holy shit, I've been working with a couple of damn ass-fuckers and didn't even know it." He had hate written large across his small face, and Perkins thought he looked like he would puke if he kept thinking about it.

"Whoa, George. Stan Lyons may be gay, but he's still one of the finest men I've ever known. I have nothing but respect for the man, and I won't listen to that kind of talk. He's a wartime veteran, a retired sheriff elected twice to that position, and an honorable man. You may not have much tolerance for a gay person, but don't let it cloud your thinking when it comes to Stan Lyons." Animosity has taken over from generous praise as these two leaders of Sandesta County glared at each other across Andrus's desk. "Talk to Dr. Darling before you get too carried away, George."

"I just don't like anything about queers. I won't work with them."

"Apparently you have, George. Let's get back to

this investigation, okay? Can you get a search warrant for Jennifer Tichner's home and properties, and can you get an arrest warrant for Jerome Tichner?" The two eased back in their chairs and let the steam of the moment pass away.

"I'll get on it right away, Claude, and I'll call Blocker too. Let's not let any of this spoil our relationship. I'm just an old Southern conservative kind of guy, and I also tend to say what's on my mind."

"I understand, but don't let it get in the way of what we're doing here. I'm going to put together a couple of teams of deputies, so let me know when you have those warrants." He got up and offered his big calloused hand to the little Southern gentleman, and the two shook to their slightly strained friendship.

***

Edwards was waiting in his office when he returned. "I'm glad you're here," Perkins said. "I have some serious doubts about your career as a detective and I want you to clear them up for me. If what you want from a career in law enforcement is just a job, then you need to change your career. This is a business that takes dedication and perseverance, and a high level of intelligence. It's a fine picture to see a snappy uniform, black leather and shiny badge, a big gun on the hip and dark glasses to intimidate, but I'm afraid that's a stereotype that only exists in a few minds.

"To make it today, you better understand customer relations, compassion, and above all, you better have the ability to think on your feet. I want you to give what I've just said some serious thought because after last night, I'm not sure you fit that mold. The man you were sent to keep an eye on may be arrested later today for multiple murders and pedophilia. He may also be looking to kill again.

"You could have been responsible for letting him get away. We got lucky, Edwards—he wasn't trying to get away. He sure as hell could have made it. I'm not going to spend a lot of time chewing on your ass because I hope you're smart enough to see where I'm coming from. Go to Tichner's neighborhood right now and relieve deputy Chance. Take a handheld radio with you, drive an unmarked car, stay out of sight as much as possible, and if that man so much as lowers a blind, you call it in. And while you're there, take as much time as you need to think about what you want to do with the rest of your life. One thing we don't want to happen is for him to have visitors we don't know. You call in everything, even if it's a fucking robin taking a shit on the porch. Do you understand?"

"Yes sir, I do. I'll be a good cop, Claude, I promise you I will." He never sat down during his dressing down, and now left the office, consternation written all over his face. Perkins followed him out the door and headed downstairs to see the coroner.

"Hi doc. I just spent half an hour or more with George Andrus and he's going to get an arrest warrant drawn up for Tichner. I can't thank you enough for getting those blood samples tested as fast as you did. Good work, doc." Darling couldn't help but think back to the days when Swicker wore those stripes. He had never in his time there thanked the coroner for anything. All he had ever done was gripe and bitch. He smiled as he thought he could really get used to this new approach to working closely with detectives.

"Before I get to the meat of why I'm here, I just spent quite a bit of time listening to George Andrus get himself in a pretty good knot over the fact that Stan Lyons is gay. That man simply hates anyone who is not straight, to the point of suggesting that Lyons and Sara Lane are, in his delightful words, 'butt fuckers.' I hope you don't feel that way too. That would ruin everything I've hoped for these last few days."

"I know how George feels. He said about the same

things to me, but that is not the way I feel. I think in the thick of things, I'm Stan Lyons's best friend and have been for a long time. I'm the one suggested he come out about his homosexuality, and support him fully."

"That makes me feel a lot better, doc, thanks." He thought about the differences in people, just in this small little county complex and wondered how someone in a really big command position was able to handle all the personalities. "I hope I'm ready for all this, doc. Sheriff? I like the idea, but it sure as hell scares me to death. About this investigation, there's something else. When I asked that deputy to have a chat with Jennifer Tichner, she chased him off, apparently half in the bag. He said she had a can of beer in her hand and a church key type opener. He just casually mentioned it was the old fashioned kind, a steel can opener.

"That's what was used to mutilate the Justus women. Andrus is going to try to get a search warrant for Jennifer's home and other property. If he does, want to come along? You've been at the scene of both murders, want to be there when we try to put a cap on them?"

"In less time than it takes to get an oil change and lube job, the whole concept of the Sandesta County detective division has changed. Swicker would never have told me what you just did, and if I had found out, he would have denied me the opportunity to participate. You are damned right I want to be there. That woman probably should have been put away years ago, but until someone actually commits a crime, that can't be done. Shame.

"If she's not guilty and Jerome Tichner is, at least I think we both know she is at least partially responsible. There is no excuse for doing what that man has done, or at least what I feel he's done, but his actions had to have been brought on by the way he was raised by that woman. Barbara Mingus will bring that up in court—you can bet that farm you talk about all the time. It's not a defense in

206

my mind, but at jury trial, that little puke sitting up there bawling like a baby, describing the way his mother treated him, will bring some on a jury to feel sorry for him."

"You are able to see into people's reactions pretty good, doc. Tell me about Jennifer and Jerome. Will he try to kill her? Will he try to run away? Will he try to kill himself? And let's put those same questions about her."

"I've thought more about him than I have her, Claude. I have doubts that he might think of suicide, but since finding his blood mixed with that of at least one murdered person, I have to believe that he is also a killer, and it wouldn't surprise me if he got some balls and went after his mother. He has to hold her responsible, and he has to know his world is collapsing around him.

"What a family, eh?" That broke the tension a little, and Perkins was trying to picture what it must have been like living with Jennifer as a child.

"She ridiculed him at every opportunity, doc. She whipped him in public, chased off every friend he ever had, made him the laughingstock of every school he ever attended. Yeah, I agree, if he doesn't hold a serious hate for that woman, he sure as hell should. I've got people watching him around the clock, but what about her? She's said more than once that people hate her and ridicule her because of what he is, that is gay. And probably pedophilic. Is she a physical threat to him? And could that be the jealousy factor we're looking for?"

"That's a tough call, Claude. She has been a mental threat to him his whole life, but is there anything in their past to indicate that she was ever physically abusive? In school, more than once, she pulled his pants down and blistered his ass, but that's obviously not the same as the kind of treatment little Florida got from her mother. At this time, I have to believe that she wouldn't kill him. Kill others because of him? That's a tough call too.

"But that's not the same as saying she wouldn't beat

the shit out of him, either. It is possible that when she was at his shop on that Saturday morning, she was physically angry, even to the point of getting into a fist fight with Sandi Justus. She has blistered his butt in public, and it wouldn't surprise me she could be just far enough off plumb to get into a physical confrontation with him."

"But not attempt to kill him, right?"

"Right. I think."

"I'll call you as soon as George gets that paperwork for me. I'm going to try to put together a couple of squads of deputies right now, and we'll coordinate serving the papers so one won't be able to alert the other. Thanks for everything, Doc. We wouldn't be this far without you."

Chapter Nineteen
Saturday, May 16

"**Y**ou keep that bitch out of here." As soon as he said it, he knew it was too late. Elizabeth Martinez had already opened the door to his inner office and was coming in.

"That's no way to talk, sheriff."

"You get out of my office. Who do you think you are, just waltzing in? Gladys, I told you to keep this woman out of here. Now, leave." Harris Fletcher was red in the face with anger, his voice ringing down the marble halls at foghorn level, blustering as politicians who don't get their way often do. Becky on the other hand was cool as they come, that threatening semi-automatic very much in view.

"Is that any way to treat a fellow investigator, sheriff? By way of introduction, my name is Martinez, and I'm here at the request of the state attorney general to do a full investigation of your department. Here are my papers authorizing me to complete the job." Her face appeared to be smiling, but it wasn't the beguiling smile she heaped on the deputies or the one that sent shivers up and down Claude Perkins' private areas. Becky was smiling with her mouth only; her eyes were as a snake's might be at the moment of a strike.

"Give me any shit, Sheriff, and I bring in the troops. I can have five or more state investigators here in less than an hour. Is that what you want? More newspaper headlines? More shit brought out in public? Or would you rather cooperate with me and get this over with nice and easy? Your choice." She continued glaring at the deflated sheriff and told Gladys to get her pad and come back in.

"I'm going to record everything we say here,

Fletcher. Every word, and at the same time, I'm going to have Gladys here keep notes on everything we talk about. When we're through, Gladys, I want you to type up those notes and see to it the sheriff, the district attorney, Barbara Mingus, and I get copies. Any deviation from our recorded conversation, and you'll be charged with aiding and abetting. That's right, Gladys, you." She put a little tape recorder on the top of the desk and pointed out that it had been on for the duration.

Gladys Sample, fifty-three years old, matronly and professional as they come, has worked for Sandesta County her entire working life, first for the county commission, then for Sheriff Stan Lyons. It was pretty well known around the court house that she and Fletcher Harris did not get along, but with her time in service he hadn't been able to do much about it. "Don't worry, Ms. Martinez, I'll take exact notes." She looked over at the sheriff and smiled an almost nasty smile. Becky had to hold one in.

The preliminaries went quickly, the sheriff giving name, rank, and what not and then Gladys doing the same thing. Becky then added the time and date, and the interrogation was underway. It did not go smoothly. Harris said he had never called Sandesta County Deputy Sheriff Sara Lane a bitch, and Becky asked if Gladys had ever heard the sheriff call someone a bitch.

"He called you a bitch, Ms. Martinez."

"Yes, I know. I heard. What I meant was, have you ever heard him call any of his own employees a bitch?"

"Oh, yes. Many times. He and Sergeant Swicker often laughed with each other after one or the other had reprimanded a female employee, and both called women bitches all the time."

"Thank you. Well now, Sheriff, what about this other thing, the one about telling then-Sergeant Swicker what a fine job he was doing after he hit one of his deputies and almost ripped her uniform shirt off? Did you do that?"

"Fuck you, Martinez." Fletcher picked up the tape recorder from the top of the desk and threw it to the floor, then stomped it into pieces. "Take your skinny bitch ass out of my office. This interview is over." Becky and Gladys walked into the outer office, leaving Fletcher to fume and cuss.

"Let's go to George Andrus's office, Gladys, and you can type up your notes while I call my boss in the capital. By the way, don't worry, I know Harris Fletcher well, and I have another tape recorder here in my pocket, so he isn't getting away with anything. Get your purse."

Gladys picked up a steno pad, some papers and pens, and followed Becky toward Andrus's office. "I'm frightened," she said.

"The important thing right now is to keep you safe." They went to the DA's office and told Andrus's secretary what had happened. "Claude, I need you in the DA's office right now. No questions. Just get up here right now." She hung up the phone and slumped into a chair in Andrus's private office while Gladys and George's secretary commiserated over the morning's goings-on.

"I've never seen anything like it, Theresa. The man is a fool. Ms. Martinez is an investigative attorney for the state attorney general. What the hell is the matter with Sheriff Fletcher?'

"Hello, Sergeant Perkins," Theresa smiled. "Ms. Martinez is in George's private office. Please, go right in." Claude was wondering what Gladys and Theresa were doing huddling over some notes and Becky was in Andrus's office, but he didn't have time to give it any thought.

"I want you to hear this before either one of us says a word, Claude. Just sit down and listen," and she started the tape. He was dumbfounded, speechless, when it ended, and just sat back with his mouth open, his eyes staring at the ceiling.

"My God, Becky. My God."

"I just got off the phone with the attorney general. Five or six investigators are on their way, and I'll get a fax momentarily naming me as acting sheriff of Sandesta County. The AG doesn't have the authority to fire Fletcher as such, mainly because he is an elected official, but does have the authority to remove him from active participation in the sheriff's office.

"Claude, I need an undersheriff, one who knows what the hell is going on in this department, that is from a police point of view, and one who will take over as sheriff per sé. I can't maintain an investigation of the department and run the department at the same time.

"I don't feel I have to ask, Claude, but just to make this as official as possible, will you assume the position of Undersheriff, Sandesta County until further notice?"

"My God, Becky. My God. Yes, of course, but are you sure this is what you want? My God."

"It's almost what I want. Next will be when I call you Sheriff, and then when I call you lover, maybe even husband." That smile spread across the whole room and Perkins knew he had to sit down, and right now. His knees were weak, his pulse was racing, and his eyes were blurred.

"If you were a pretty little kitty cat, you caught your mouse. I'm trapped and you can do with me as you wish. We said we would maintain an office dignity, but we're not in my office or yours, little lady." They hugged and kissed, and did those things some more, finally breaking off when Gladys and Theresa knocked on the door. He was trying to understand what just happened, but he knew in his heart that it was the best thing that had ever come about.

"Undersheriff. Just a few days ago I was a simple deputy in the detective division, and now I'm Undersheriff. I've wanted a command position for a long time, but I really thought I would have time to adjust. My previous positions and training will sure as hell be put to the test now."

He wanted to pat her on the butt, would have if the two secretaries weren't already in the room, and instead just stood there like a ten-year-old boy with half a cookie in his hand.

The changes came furiously fast, faster than most could keep up with, and all within an hour of the capital city contingent's arrival. The sheriff was forcibly ejected from his office; newspaper and TV reporters were all jumbled up with state AG investigators, state police, and Sandesta Country deputies. In the meantime, George Andrus had his warrants, both of them, and Claude Perkins, now Undersheriff, decided the best bet was for him and a couple of deputies to converge on Jennifer Tichner's home and Andrus and a couple of deputies to meet with Barbara Mingus at Jerome Tichner's at about the same time. Becky Martinez was planning to spend hours poring over records and files.

**

"I'm glad you're riding with me, Doc. Can you believe any of this? All of this has come down in less than a week, and my head is swimming. Two known murders, possibly two others, a sheriff told he's not welcome in his own office, a sergeant of detectives under arrest for attempted murder, and to top the whole damn thing off, I've had time to fall in love. Holy shit."

Tim Darling was literally holding on to himself, his arms wrapped tightly, he was laughing so hard. "When you make a power play, you go for the jugular, eh? I'm just so glad you are on board. What a disaster this would be if you weren't here.

"You've asked about our DNA investigations, and I have to tell you honestly, DNA won't help us in the investigation of the Justus murders. All the blood and samples we have are from the victims and we know who they are. But, DNA might help us establish the identity of the human remains found in the Tichner compost pile. There is so much blood, actual body parts with flesh, bone, and some fluids, we might be able to find out who this is. Or who they are."

"I'll make you a friendly little wager, Doc. How much can you afford to lose? I think we'll find there are two sets of human remains in that pile."

"No bet, Boss Hogg. I've had that in my mind from the time we found them. I have the pieces in the cooler if you want to come down and take a look. From what I've gathered so far, I've got pieces of a leg, maybe two legs, and pieces of skull. The skull is fractured, but that could have happened in the compost pile. Teeth are going to be as big a help in identifying these remains as much as DNA, I'm hoping."

Claude picked up on that. "You don't think that Tichner was planning the same fate for Florida, do you? And then got scared about something and just reacted?"

"Not in what we might think of as his normal behavior, but possible." Claude looked over at Tim Darling, his mind working as fast as it ever had.

"Right now, I've two suspects with equal weight. Jennifer Tichner, absolutely capable of the murders, and Jerome Tichner, possibly capable. If we hadn't found those remains, he would not be so high on my list. Have you any way to establish age without some kind of ID?"

"No. Other than I can tell you the pieces I have are from young people. But exact age, no. If I was asked on the witness stand, all I could say is it is my opinion that the victims were young people. That could be refuted." Perkins had moved from the astonishment of being appointed number two in the department back to detective, a position he thrived in.

"Here we are. I don't think we'll have any reaction from Jennifer that might lead to serious danger, Doc, so just stick close to me. She's nutso, and will probably fly off the handle, but I think my boys can handle her."

Perkins, with Dr. Darling at his side and flanked by a pair of deputies, walked up the concrete driveway toward the front door. "Where's Peters? He's supposed to be with us."

"Got a call just as we were leaving. Said he'd catch up."

"It was that important a call? Damn it, if Swicker had trained like he was supposed to, Peters and Edwards would both be better cops. Okay, Fred, go around back and make sure nobody gets out that way. Least force possible here, even though this is a capital situation. Stick close, Doc. Jack, stay off to the side so whoever opens the door only sees me. Doc, you stay on the other side. Here we go." While one deputy hightailed it around to the back of the house to join a deputy already there, Perkins and his two shadows walked up to the front door of the Tichner home. After several hard knocks on the door, there was no answer and they could not discern any movement inside.

"This door is kindling now." Perkins put his two hundred-plus pound frame into a lunge that shattered wood and opened the door. Perkins was on his radio almost instantly. "Fred, we've entered the house forcibly. Stay where you are in the back, but draw your weapon and be prepared for anything." He had his service revolver in hand and moved catlike through the living room, kitchen, bedroom, and bathroom. They found nothing, and walked toward the inside garage entrance. "Careful now." He threw open the door, and looked at an empty garage.

"Sandesta Control, Sandesta Two."

"Go ahead, sheriff."

"The Jennifer Tichner home is empty. We're beginning our search." He looked around the room and then remembered he was missing a deputy. "Where the hell is Peters?" His radio came alive with a call from Peters. "Where are you, Peters?"

"I'm turning onto the street at this moment. I just got a call from Ken Swicker, and Claude, I think he's about to jackrabbit on us. Said he's not going to prison for any butt-fucking queer. He's really a head case, Claude."

Perkins kept his cool and went outside to meet with his deputy.

"Mrs. Tichner's home is empty, and we're just now beginning our search, Peters. I want you to stay here and be the command officer. Do you have any problem with that?"

"No sir. I'll do the best possible."

"Sandesta control, this is Perkins. Double the number of deputies watching Ken Swicker at the hospital. He may be thinking of escaping. I'm going to Tichner's now to meet with George Andrus and his team. Keep me informed of everything that's happening. Perkins clear."

Chapter Twenty
Saturday, May 16—Monday, May 18

Perkins answered his cell phone as he finished his call to headquarters, and both Peters and Dr. Darling could almost see his face turn rigid and red. "That stupid son of a bitch. All right, Becky, thanks." He didn't attempt to say anything to those near him, but immediately made another call.

"George, don't say one word of what I'm about to tell you to either of the deputies with you or to Barbara Mingus. Leave immediately and meet me back at the courthouse. Do not use your police radio under any circumstances. No questions till we meet, now move as quickly as you can.

"Damn, George, no. Okay, make sure those deputies with you take that house apart. You know what we're looking for. Now, get to the courthouse immediately.

"Fred, Jack, I want you to take this place apart, inch by inch. What we're looking for is anything that might tie Jennifer Tichner to the Justus murders. Bloody items of clothing or footwear, beer can openers, or something that might tear a body to shreds. Remember those canvas type shoes that appear to have been worn by the killer at both homicides. Doc, you need to come with me."

His mouth was more grim than anyone had ever seen, his eyes were on fire, and his massive, work-strong hands were about to break the steering wheel in pieces. That strength was about to rip his shoulder right out of his shirt, or destroy his police car. "Doc, we're in trouble. That phone call was from Becky, not from my communications deputy. Swicker just broke out of the hospital, and the deputy guarding him is in critical condition with a gunshot wound to his chest. The man must be considered mad and as dangerous as they come. Becky has put out a statewide alert for the fool. Since Jennifer isn't here, and Andrus just told me that Jerome isn't at home either, I'm running out of deputies. I have four at Jennifer's and four at Tichner's.

"Damn it." He picked up the radio and made another call to his communications officer. "Get at least two people, pull them off traffic patrol if you have to, but get them over to Tichner's salon right now. If Tichner's there, arrest him. If not, just keep a watch until we arrive. Perkins clear." He looked over at Dr. Darling. There was no smile on the big face.

"I'm seriously worried about Stan Lyons," Perkins said. "Swicker could either be looking to finish him off, or is simply running. Jerome Tichner isn't home, and no one saw him leave. There's at least one deputy going on the carpet for that one, and I don't know what to think about Jennifer at this time. Becky has called Lyons and he's headed for the courthouse to meet with us. At least we can protect him there. Of all the stupid things. I can't believe just how ignorant that fool Swicker can be."

The group went straight to the sheriff's inner office. Becky, Perkins, Darling, and Andrus were waiting when Lyons arrived. "I heard before I'd taken three steps inside the court house. Keeping radio silence, Claude?"

"Yes completely. We're doing everything by cell phone. I've alerted the agencies in the surrounding counties, issued warrants detailing his escape and attempted murder, and right now, I fear for the lives of my suspects." His cell rang and he talked for just a couple of brief minutes.

"I'm beginning to think everyone of the people I consider a suspect is guilty. We now have beer can openers at Jennifer Tichner's and at Jerome's. Stan, you know Swicker better than anyone here. Would he try something as stupid as kidnapping? I remember how he blew up at

218

you in the hospital room, and what he had to say about gay people, and about pedophiles. They're the same in his mind, and Jerome is gay and a suspected pedophile."

"Swicker right now is a loose cannon, Claude. I think we would be better off to search for the two suspects in these murders. George, you know Barbara Mingus pretty damn well, see if she might know where Tichner would go if he was scared and just wanted to hide."

"I wish I wasn't here right now. I'm not in agreement with many of the things that Ken Swicker has done in the past, but his thinking about gay people may not be wrong, at least in my mind. I'll call Barbara, but only if Claude wants me to."

"Call her, George, and I mean right now. Stan, stand up please, and raise your right hand. As Undersheriff of Sandesta County, with that authority, I hereby appoint you, Stan Lyons, deputy, and chief of detectives. Anymore nonsense about authority around here had best end right at this moment. I won't tolerate bigotry in my department." He was glaring at Andrus, angry to the point of shaking, but kept his professionalism under control. "We are a team. I want that understood. I am lead detective on this case, George, you are elected District Attorney, and Stan, you are chief of detectives. Our job right now is to solve two murders and possibly a pedophilic attack that took place in another jurisdiction. Those are the only things that should be on our minds right now. Becky, I'm going to have to depend on your people to sort out the Swicker shit, at least for right now." A long speech for an old cowboy, but one that carried the authority of his position, and everyone had been put in place, so to speak. He looked around the room to find every eye, first on him, then on Andrus. George Andrus still had bandages on his nose from Swicker, and Perkins wanted to break the man's nose as well. Perkins, however, was far more professional than that, and had his mind on solving murders.

"I think if I were Jerome Tichner, and I didn't feel safe in my home, I just might head to my little beauty parlor. And if Tichner's mother follows her previous patterns, we'll find her there also." He started out the door when his cell rang again.

"All right. Yes, I understand. We'll be there right away." He turned back to the group, consternation written bold across his big face. "They just found Deputy Edwards's body in the garage at Jerome Tichner's. He was slashed in a similar fashion to the Justus women. Let's take two cars, and get there right now." Becky rode with Claude as did Stan Lyons. Dr. Darling and George Andrus rode in the other car.

"The call came from Barbara Mingus, Becky. She didn't offer any details other than what I mentioned. Three people now, ripped into pieces, and if that's not bad enough, a former detective sergeant on the loose after trying to kill another deputy. Ideas, beautiful?"

"I'm going to keep my council until I get to the scene. Shoeprints from the same type found at Florida's and Sandi's death scenes will be pertinent. Same type of gouging wounds will be important. Those shoes still rattle around in my cage, Claude, and I don't know why."

"I think I do."

"Okay Stan, your turn. Do you think those shoes are important, and why?"

"I bet those shoes, if we actually had them, will fit both Jerome and Jennifer. He's smallish for a man and she's large. You said the shoes are usually found at major discount stores. We don't have any discount stores in Sandesta County, but we know that Jerome takes trips out of town, supposedly to art and music openings in large cities that surround our county."

"Jerome's your man, Claude."

"That's a strong argument, cowboy. What do you think?"

"Here, use my cell, Becky, and get the deputy at Jennifer's and have him bring any tennie runner type shoes he finds at her place, in evidence bags, to Jerome's. We'll see what we find at his place also. I'll bet Stan is right about this, but I won't give up my thought these killings have been committed by a woman." Two deputies and Barbara Mingus met Perkins and company in the driveway, and Tim Darling was right behind.

"He's back here, sheriff." The deputies had already assumed that Claude Perkins would be their boss. "Naked as the day he was born, and slashed to ribbons. Just like Florida that night. His head is mush, Claude, smashed with a rock from the garden." Dr. Darling was already making his way to the garage.

"Thank you. George, you said Jerome wasn't here when you and Ms. Mingus arrived. Barbara, have you heard from your client at all? I know I'm pressing, but if he's not responsible for these murders, his life is in big jeopardy right now."

"I haven't heard a word, Claude, and I would tell you."

"He's in the biggest trouble he's ever known, Barbara, with body parts, probably children's, found in his compost pile and evidence of an attack on a child in Johnson County found here and in his van. Do you think he's running?"

"He's terrified, Claude. I don't know what might be going through his mind." Perkins looked Mingus up and down, smiled weakly in recognition of what she said and turned his attention to Becky Martinez.

"No Jerome, no Jennifer, no Swicker. Is it possible that Jennifer and Jerome are in cahoots on this?" He answered his own question before Becky could. "Bullshit. Jennifer is our key, though."

"I'm going to put my money on Jerome, Claude. He was diddling Florida, hated her mother Sandi, and killed

Edwards in order to get away. I'll bet he's running as fast as one of your Nevada jackrabbits right now." It was Andrus's time to intercede.

"You two go look to Edwards. I'm going to see what's in Tichner's closet. I'll bet I find tennie runners, as you call them Claude, and I've already seen beer can openers like you've described.

"Coming, Barb?"

"Would you look at that?" Becky pointed to the pair, heading into the house holding hands. "That son of a bitch is as bigoted as they come when it comes to gay people, and he's making time with a black lady. Maybe he's not quite the ass I have him pictured." Perkins, Martinez, and Lyons headed for the grisly job in the garage.

***

"Well, we're not in the office, and we're not in my hotel room, Sheriff Perkins, so there are no out of bounds."

"Two days without a clue. Let's go up to my place, Becky. Jerome and Jennifer have dropped off the face of the earth right along with Swicker. I have some steaks and a nice bottle of wine. Is it all one tangle? Whose blood was that at Tichner's salon, and why was Jennifer's car parked across the street, filled gas tank, and with spots of blood all over the seats? Is rare okay for your steaks? That's the way I like them.

"We'll get blood results from Darling tomorrow, from Tichner's garage, from his salon, from Jennifer's car, and we'll have a ballistics result on the bullet Swicker fired at that deputy. How about a green salad with dinner, and some good old fashioned country music? The real stuff. Hank Williams stuff."

"Let's just drink some wine and let me look into your eyes. You have some very pretty eyes, Sheriff. And when I've looked as deep into your soul as I can, let's go to bed and save crime-solving for tomorrow. You have all your people out on the job and I have all my people out there as well. The Tichner Gang will get caught, and Swicker will be found. Right now, cowboy, you're mine. Everything you say and do will count toward our lives together, and don't ever forget that." He wanted to carry her across the threshold but knew that was just too corny, so he grabbed the bottle of wine, two glasses, a candle, and led the way upstairs.

It was hours later that sleep overcame the lovemaking, and with knees and elbows twisted, twined, and tangled, the two dropped off, Perkins saying something about being guilty and begging for mercy.

Chapter Twenty-One
Tuesday, May 19

"You make a nice breakfast, cowboy, particularly after a long ride in the saddle."

"We shouldn't have slept in like this, but what the hell, I'm the boss, right?"

"Boss of the range, Claude. Your desk will be filled with reports and so will mine. I'm just about wrapped up here, and I'm trying to think of ways to prolong my having to leave and go back to the capital."

"I could smack George Andrus, if you like." Gentle snickers filled the kitchen, but Becky wondered if he might just do that at some point if Andrus kept up his homophobia. "They found Fletcher last night. I cheated and called in, saying I would be late.

"Harris Fletcher didn't run away with Swicker like I thought, but holed up in his home. The county commissioner and other community leaders had talked him into resigning, and he was trying to figure out how to save his political ass, what there was of it.

"My people think that Fletcher was just a weak politician, and the state isn't even going to follow through with any kind of action, but George Andrus sure as hell should. That guy should get one hell of a dressing down in the courts. Both Andrus and Lane could end up getting regular paychecks from that fool for many years.

"I think that Barbara Mingus might have a lot to say about that, don't you? That was kind of cute, the two holding hands, but he might still be facing her in court. How the hell do you face someone you have feelings for in court?"

"I'm going to talk with Mingus this morning and try

to get Sara back, if she'll come back. Maybe the department as such won't be sued by her. Swicker will, but the county won't. As far as Fletcher goes, Mingus plans a civil action against him on behalf of Lane."

"That's good news, but I just can't figure Swicker out." She was wiping up egg yolk with some well-buttered toast. "He must have snapped something in that thick head of his. I don't know where he would go." Perkins had been worrying the problem since the news that Swicker had escaped, and couldn't put any kind of answer to it.

"Neither do I, Becky. Where would a well-trained cop, egotistical beyond belief maybe, but still well-trained, where would he go? You can bet he's getting as far away from Sandesta County as possible. He has to be paranoid, and not just in the psychological meaning. He'll see cops where there won't be any, and he's going to have to lighten his baggage. He proved his mental condition by challenging Stan Lyons and Nancy Carrington in the middle of the day, and then shooting his former boss. He's dangerous, and the FBI will surely have him on their list of top ten criminals. He'll stand out in any crowd with that flame red hair of his. I bet his beard is already gone. He's one of those guys who grows hair everywhere, and even if he dyes the hair on his head, his body hair will give him away.

"He'll get caught, it's just a matter of time. I want those blood samples just as fast as I can get them. If Swicker did what I think, kidnapped both Jerome and Jennifer Tichner, I want to know whose blood is all over that beauty salon, Jennifer's car, and that garage. I'll bet those two are dead, and it'll take me another year to solve these fucking murders." His frustration level was right on the surface and even with last night's wonderful respite, he was wound tight.

***

Dr. Darling was first in Perkins's office. "We have

blood from Edwards in the garage, Claude, but like the Justus deaths, no other blood. It appears there is blood from several people around Tichner's salon. I'll have those results within the hour. At least we know what blood types the three are.

"Take a look at this." He handed a sheaf of papers to his new sheriff.

"Well, this clears up nothing. More damn mud. You're saying the little tennis shoes that we found at Jennifer Tichner's match the shoes we found at Jerome's? And the tread pattern matches those that were used at both Justus murder sites? Were there any prints left at either Tichner's garage or his salon?"

"Page two, Sheriff. They're the same. One difference at the salon though. There was another print, bloody as well, but from a boot, a large boot."

"Damn me. A boot the size that Swicker would wear?" He was getting his hopes up.

"According to the records, Swicker would wear a larger size. Those in the salon would be about a ten and a half, probably E width. Swicker wears a 12 double E, so he wouldn't even be able to get his foot in a boot like that. In men's sizes, the tennis shoes are both eight medium, the same size that Jerome and his mother wear."

"Oh, how sweet you've made it, doc." He wanted to put his head down and cry. "Just one more suspect to bring into our soup pot, eh? How could this happen?" he was thinking. "One more person now in this mess, one more unknown, and why was that bootprint there? Was it from a jilted lover that followed Tichner, or was it from a parent or relative of some child Tichner had approached? Was it a boyfriend of Jennifer's? Any thoughts?"

"None that make any sense. Tichner runs away to the salon, his mother kills Deputy Edwards and follows Jerome, and then some guy unknown to any of us comes in and slashes the hell out both of them, and abducts them?

No kind of sense at all, Claude."

"I remember back in Nevada once, I was working for the Elko County sheriff, and we had a rustling ring that was taking hundreds of thousands of dollars' worth of cattle off the range. And one of the rustlers was killed, and it took forever to find the bastard that did it. Turned out the killer had nothing at all to do with any of the rustling or other gang activity. Killed because of something completely outside the case, a perceived threat from years before.

"Would Jerome have some lovers that might be jealous? Did Jennifer catch him in the act of something, lash out, and Jerome's lover defended him? Where the hell are we going with this case?

"And while I'm thinking about it, how the hell did Jennifer get into the garage, or whoever, and kill Edwards? Where the hell was George Andrus and Barbara Mingus? The last thing I said to George was to keep a tight eye on the place, and I can't help thinking I should never have posted Edwards there. His mind hasn't been on the job at all. He's dead while his killer just sauntered into the garage and bashed his head in? Doc, this is getting out of hand."

"With your permission, Sheriff, I'm going to make another forensic sweep of all three locations. The salon, and both homes, and of course, Tichner's garage. Just to make sure we haven't overlooked something."

"Do it Doc. You need any people? Any help I can offer is yours, I hope you know that."

"I have one person and that's all I'll need, but thank you for that. What a change from Harris Fletcher." He headed out of the office shaking his head, but with a large smile on his thin face. He passed reporter Nancy Carrington in the hallway, and the look on her face told him Sheriff Perkins's day was about to get worse.

"Sheriff, I'm not here as a reporter, but as a concerned citizen. I think Ken Swicker may be stalking me."

"Have you seen him, Nancy?"

"I think I saw someone about his size early this morning across the river from my home. Swicker vowed to kill me, Sheriff, and I think he's after me now."

Perkins picked up his phone. "Becky, can you come up to the office right away? It's very important." He put the phone down. "When was the last time you were in the state capitol, Ms. Carrington?" The arrangements were made and Nancy Carrington was on her way to the capital under the protection of the Attorney General. Perkins then sent two teams of deputies to the area of Carrington's home, one team on each side of the river.

"Don't get caught up short, guys. This fool is as dangerous as can be, and remember he's already shot one deputy. Don't fall into a trap, and protect the hell out of each other. Swicker is to be treated as armed and dangerous, a wanted felon. He's not your former sergeant. He's a criminal."

He sat at his desk looking at Becky Martinez, trying to understand what was going on. "You said you thought you had most of your investigation of this department wrapped up. I sure need your continued help with this case. Between Swicker, the Tichners, Johnson County, and dead bodies all over hell and gone, I'm just about at wit's end. It's going to take me quite a bit of time to get this department back on track, Becky. More time than I want to think about, but I hope soon we'll have a trip to Nevada in our future." They had talked about it last night, but no kind of date was brought up. Too many obligations to think about running off somewhere.

They flirted dangerously with each other, eyes darting about, little smiles working, teasing, knowing they were in the office, and they had decreed this place to be 'hands off.' Perkins toyed with the idea of locking that door and accosting her, and he would not have been surprised to learn she had the same thoughts.

"You know, Claude, you awoke things in me I forgot even existed. I want to spend one hell of a lot more time in your bed, and if it means sneaking away on weekends for both of us, it's okay with me. Nevada I'm looking forward to, but sack time is on my mind." Her eyes were blazing, and he read lust in them as she read lust in his. They had decided that out of the office, they were just man and woman, while in the office, she was an AG's investigator, he was acting Undersheriff. She finally broke the spell.

"How's the case coming?"

"It's really complicated, and I don't think we have it figured out at all. Tim Darling is helping all he can with forensics, but it's going to be awhile before we put a wrap on the case. We just discovered another person, one we don't have the slightest idea of who, might be involved.

"I've got as many questions right now as I did two days ago. Jennifer Tichner is a nutcase, hates her kid, tried to beat up Florida's mother, took the young girl for a long walk on the day she was killed, but is she crazy enough to have killed her?"

They sat on either side of Perkins's desk, staring at each other. "She often gave the impression of mental instability, but this is way past that, isn't it? I remember you telling me the stories that have circulated around town about Jerome's youth. It must have been horrible. If she is guilty of killing Florida to save her from Jerome, and that's what you're alluding to here, why would she have killed Sandi Justus? Conversely, my friend, Jerome has ample reason to kill Florida if she was about to divulge their relationship, to his mother or anyone else, and that would force his hand, and he would probably kill Sandi for the same reason.

"How do you plan to separate these two? Or is it possible that Jennifer killed Florida and Jerome killed

Sandi? I may not be on your side, though, Claude. My money would be on Jerome being the guilty one. I assume that you're working on Jennifer first, right?"

"Did she kill Florida because the girl told her about her relationship with Jerome, and that she didn't plan on ending that relationship? Did that trigger hate, jealousy, anger? She was a horrible mother, hated her kid, but could it be she hated even more the idea that someone else could love him, even if that someone was a thirteen-year old girl, prompting a jealous rage?

"Did she kill Sandi because she blamed Sandi for being responsible for the girl even being here? Did she kill Sandi because Florida told her about her miserable life? Did she kill Sandi because of the fight they got into at the salon? There aren't any answers right now." He got up, walked around the desk, had a crooked smile plastered across his big face, pulled her to her feet, and gave her a long, passionate kiss. If someone had walked in, they would have found his hands on her delightful little butt, and hers damn near ripping his uniform shirt off his back.

"I thought we had an agreement about the office and stuff.."

"It's lunch time."

"Okay with me." They went back to her hotel room and had a special lunch, without room service. During lulls, breaks in the action, they just looked into each other's eyes and smiled. It was those little smiles that kicked off the next round of fun and games.

"I can't postpone getting back to the capital as soon as possible. My boss has been screaming for my reports, but I'm going to leave a couple of people here, Claude. And, I'll be back every weekend, I promise. I have the authority to give you full responsibility of the department, hot shot, and that doesn't give you the right to smack any deputies or districts attorney."

It was agony to think about her having to leave, and

it was going to be another long session of self-examination, knowing he would be in complete command, and knowing he wouldn't have her there to help.

***

"What's the scene on those human remains, Doc?"

"The remains are from two people, ages are basically unknown, although I feel they are from young people. What we do have is very good DNA samples from both, and we're running them through all the databanks we know about that deal with missing children. We're doing the same with dental records. Often with children, dental records seem to provide the best results. There are literally thousands of missing children, Claude. We can't break this down by sex yet, either.

"We know Tichner had relations with Florida Justus, and we are certain he's the man responsible for the attack on that boy in Johnson County. He is one of the few gay pedophiles I'm familiar with, one who preyed on boys and girls. It's not common for a gay person to also be a pedophile, and then for a gay man to also have sexual relations with a young girl is very abnormal. Tichner's psychological profile will probably end up in some textbook down the line. He professes love for all these children, the ones we know about and the ones we don't, but did Jerome Tichner kill the children, or whomever those parts belong to? That's your job, I'm afraid, Sheriff."

"Well, circumstantial it might be, but it's pretty damn strong circumstantial. Keep me posted on identification. While we're on the subject, what might have happened to the rest of the bodies? We aren't looking at very much of a person in those remains."

"I'm doing tests now. Did they turn to dust? Bodies do that. Or were the bodies butchered and buried all around the place?"

"I'm going to get Andrus to get us another warrant, doc. I'll turn every inch of that property if I have to."

"You know, in ancient times, native Americans buried a dead fish when they planted their corn. Human remains would act the same way. Excellent fertilizer, Sheriff, excellent. Look around the yard and find where the flora is thriving, you might find more."

***

The Sandesta County Commission meeting got underway at ten o'clock that morning with just one item on the agenda, that of naming an interim sheriff. The old courthouse was filled with deputies, businessmen and women, and reporters, primed to welcome Claude Perkins.

There was very little discussion, a nomination was made and seconded, the vote was unanimous, and Perkins, almost Will Roger-ish, managed to get to the podium to accept the position.

"The only thing missing from this little gathering today is Sheriff Stan Lyons. It's because of him that I'm even in Sandesta County, more or less acting as your new sheriff, and it's with tremendous sadness that I accept the honor knowing I'll never be able to thank the man enough." It was a somber gathering, naming Claude Perkins acting sheriff of Sandesta County, acting that is, until the next election. The County Commission didn't hesitate a moment before asking him to serve.

"I've given a lot of thought to what I'm about to do, and I think I'm right in my thinking. It takes a special breed of person to be a cop, and there are many levels of police work. Some is brain intensive, as in investigations, some is physically challenging, and once in a while, we are fortunate in finding an individual who has the capacity to think and to act. Sheriff Lyons's life was saved just a couple of weeks ago by a cop like that.

"Sara Lane, humiliated by former members of this department did not let that deter her from knowing she was a good cop, a trustworthy comrade, and was willing to put her life on the line to save another good cop. Deputy Lane jumped into a fray involving a man twice her size who was brandishing a powerful weapon. She never gave it a second thought.

"Her former boss, her mentor, was in physical jeopardy, and she had the means and training to do something about it. Sara, step up here, please." There was sincere applause as she came to the podium, dressed in civilian clothes. A prim blouse covered by a summery suit coat, and matching skirt. You could tell she was still nursing some tender bruises. The black eye was almost invisible, the nick on her cheek was healed, and her pride was in place.

She wanted to smile, but since she had no idea what was about to happen; she tried to simply look professional. She had told Barbara Mingus that she wanted to continue her career in law enforcement, and if Mingus said she felt it was okay, she would enjoy working for Perkins. He was among the few who understood her desire to be a good cop.

"You're out of uniform, Deputy Lane." Everyone laughed, and the worry lines that had been creasing Lane's face disappeared.

"A sheriff is only as good as the people who work for him, and this department has lost several bad apples recently, making plenty of room for some very good people. Sara, I haven't said a word about this until now, but I need a lieutenant to run the detective division, and I just can't think of anyone more qualified than you." There was a hush in the audience as what Perkins was saying became obvious. Sara Lane was speechless for one of the few times in her life, and Dr. Darling was looking on with sincere pride. "Will you take the job?"

The only person in the group, standing in the main rotunda of the Sandesta County Courthouse who was not pleased with the nomination was George Andrus, and that was very plain by the look on his face. Darling walked over to him, and stared long and hard at the man. "You're far too intelligent and educated to have these kinds of feelings, George. Between Stan Lyons, Francine Dermody in the capital, and Sara Lane, we know three very upstanding citizens, very fine people. It's time for some serious introspection, George, and you'll know what I'm saying is the truth."

"I doubt it, Doctor. I seriously doubt it." He was a bitter man as he turned toward his office, and was planning his letter of resignation, thinking how much he would be missing, working with Perkins, working with Darling, living in Sandesta County. "I can't abide queers, and I certainly won't work with any."

"You've been working with gay people for years, George. How can you justify what you just said?"

"I didn't know."

Chapter Twenty-Two
Wednesday, May 20

"**G**eorge, are you sure of this?" Barbara Mingus was seated in the DA's office looking over Tim Darling's forensic reports, Sheriff Perkins investigation reports, and those from the District Attorney himself. "Are you open to any kind of negotiation? Jerome Tichner is a sick person, very sick, George, and what you're showing me here makes that plain."

"The only thing I can promise you, Barbara, is that I will be seeking the death penalty. At least two children dead, the bodies butchered and placed about his yard as fertilizer, a young boy kidnapped and brutalized, sodomized, and his own confession to having sex with a young girl whose body was mutilated. Yes, Barbara, I am seeking the death penalty.

"The only questions not answered so far, concern who killed the Justus family. Help me with that Barbara, and I'll help you if I can. The way I'm looking at this, your only hope for saving your client is proving he is mentally incapable of knowing what he's done."

"That's the only answer I have, George. I have to plead him innocent by way of insanity, and plead with the court to put him in a mental institution for the rest of his life. I can't save his life any other way.

"As far as the Justus murders, I don't think Jerome is responsible. What I'm about to say is client privilege, on the one hand, but he's said this to many. He knows he's responsible for the death of those two children whose remains have been found on his property, but he has been adamant about not being responsible for the Justus murders, Florida's in particular."

"Then, Barbara, will you let Sheriff Perkins and myself interrogate the bastard?"

"I will sit in on the interrogation, and I will say if something is out of line. I will let Jerome know that the only way he is going to live through this is to tell the truth, and if I'm sitting with him, I think he will.

"Before I leave, George, do you know where Claude Perkins is?"

"I think he went over to Johnson County to talk with Jim Roberts, the detective over there. Tim Darling has identified one of the children whose remains were found at Tichner's, and it appears the child is from Johnson County."

"It just gets worse, doesn't it George? If this ever ends, can we get together again some night? I'd love to look in your eyes and think about something other than murder."

George Andrus smiled his answer and escorted the attorney to the door. "Cocktails, dinner, and dancing, lovely lady. That's a promise." He walked back to his desk wondering just what he had accomplished. He had permission to interrogate Tichner, but he didn't have Tichner. "Where would that queer prick go? Dr. Darling thinks that's his blood in the salon, along with blood from his mother, and maybe indications there was a third person on the scene. Where would he go?" He put some notes on his calendar, one in particular, to work on a new county ordinance controlling the arts population. "Just too damn many queers."

***

"I want you to ride with me, Sara. Dr. Darling has identified one set of remains from Tichner's compost pile. They are from an eight-year-old boy who lived in Johnson County. I'm going over there to talk with detective Jim Roberts."

"I can't help but be amazed at the differences between you, Harris, and Swicker. First you get my job back, then you bump me to lieutenant, and now you want me to actively take part in an investigation. You couldn't stop me from going with you." Perkins nodded and they walked to the car.

"You have college level training in police work, Sara. You've attended the FBI academy, and while Lyons was sheriff, you were an active deputy. Stay focused and you'll go a long way in police work. I can see that, Stan Lyons could see it, and those who trained you knew it. I'm proud to have you on the team."

The trip to the Johnson County courthouse was quick on this late spring morning, and Perkins was thinking he wished Sara Lane was Becky Martinez and they were heading for a weekend on the beach, not bringing even more bad news to some family that has been mourning the disappearance of a child. "I have always hated this part of the job, telling someone that a relative or loved one is dead. This kid has been missing for two years, Sara, and the family is just now going to be told he's dead. The sick feeling in the stomach never goes away."

"I'm glad I'm with you. There's a lot of love and caring in your soul, isn't there, Sheriff? I've known you as being tough as a board, actually mean as cat shit is the way you've been described, but you have soft spots all over. I'm glad to be working for a man like you. You know I'm gay. Is that going to bother you or create any kind of problem down the line?"

"'Mean as cat shit?'" He was laughing like hell, glancing over at his new Detective Lieutenant. "When Stan was still in the hospital, he sat me down and told me the whole story, Sara. There have always been rumors around the department about you, and I think it's a good thing to have everything out in the open. You and I have a lot in common, Sara. We both like girls." Genuine laughter from both broke any tension, and Perkins continued. "There have been many things said about homosexualism over the years, many stereotypes painted large, and most are bullshit. Being gay is part of your personal life, shouldn't have a bearing on your professional life.

"Gay people have existed from the emerging of the human race, and I think we all would be amazed if we knew just who some of them might be. I have a lot of confidence in you as a person, as a cop, and hopefully, as we work more and more together, as a friend. The only thing you need to be aware of is this. George Andrus is not open to working with gay people.

"He is homophobic, and I've already told him I don't want his personal feelings to interfere with our jobs. He indicated to Dr. Darling that he might resign, but I doubt that. He's very intelligent, just not willing to accept this part of life. It's a shame. I have to tell you the same thing I told him. Don't let your feelings or his feelings interfere with our responsibilities to the citizens of Sandesta County.

"End of speech."

"Are you and Becky Martinez going to get married?"

"We're in a company car, Sara." But that big old cowboy grin had returned and Sara Lane took that for at least a maybe. Perkins hadn't thought about marriage, just the idea of having a wonderful time with a wonderful person. Now other thoughts will be dancing in his head. "You've just made it difficult for me to concentrate on multiple murders, Lieutenant. I had Becky escort Nancy Carrington to the capitol. The reporter thinks that Swicker might be after her.

"His mind is gone, Sara. Gone. He was a fine cop and let such a simple thing as a chemical imbalance destroy his life. His entire life, everything that counted in his mind, hung between his legs. Nothing else mattered, and now, he'll spend the rest of his life in jail."

**

George Andrus did not offer a letter of resignation. "Tim, there is nothing you can say or do that's going to change my attitude. It's the way it is." He was in his office, facing the coroner. Dr. Darling tried to open a discussion on homosexualism, but Andrus wouldn't listen. "Thank you for these files on Tichner. I'm going to press for the death penalty. Two children sexually tormented, killed, and then buried in a back yard only to be dug up by dogs. This is the most disgusting case I've ever had to work on. He is what I've always been against, Tim, a queer pedophile." Dr. Darling just shook his head.

"George, what you can't get through that thick head of yours is this. Gay and pedophile are not the same word. Are not synonyms. For God's sake man, you can't believe Stan Lyons would have had feelings of pedophilia? You've worked with Sara Lane. You know she doesn't even like kids. And, my God, George, Francine Dermody is the staunchest supporter of children's rights in this state. Find a good psychologist, one you can trust, and ask that doctor to describe for you the differences. Don't let these feelings destroy everything you've worked so hard for."

Andrus sat at his desk, chin in hand, staring blankly at the coroner. "I just can't help my feelings, Tim." The thought of hating queers, as he had always put it, and having that interfere with his career was, in his thoughts, absurd. "You know I'm not racist, I'm not a hateful man, but I can't stand the thought of a man having a sexual relationship with another man. That to me, is hateful."

"You're not racist, George. Hell, watching you around Barbara Mingus proves that point, but you are a bigot, and deep in your soul, you know that. Is there anything else you hate? For instance, green Chevrolets? You might not be able to see yourself in a relationship with another man, but why would you deny those two you hate so much an opportunity for love?"

"Let's concentrate on the case, Tim. I hate it when you start to make sense. Does anyone have any idea where Jennifer and Jerome Tichner might be?"

***

"Detective Roberts is on leave, Sheriff. Is there someone else that can help you?"

"I hope there isn't a problem. I have some vital information about pedophile cases here in Johnson County, cases that Roberts has been working on."

"I think that's why he's on leave, Sheriff. It seems that a nephew of his, a child, disappeared a few years ago, and Detective Roberts was informed yesterday that the boy's body had been identified in Sandesta County.

"Didn't he come to you? He said that's where he was going."

"You're going to think this a very strange question, Deputy, but do you know what size shoe Roberts wears?" Lights flashed in Sara Lane's eyes as she realized where Claude Perkins was going. Perkins looked over and saw the recognition in her face. "Just exactly when did Roberts leave?"

They hustled back to the patrol car and Perkins got on the radio to his office immediately. "This is Sandesta One. Ask the District Attorney to contact me on my cell right away. This is of the highest priority."

"Right away, Sheriff."

"As soon as we get back, Sara, I want you to mobilize your deputies and find Johnson County Detective Jim Roberts. I'm going to bet every dime I have that I finally understand this whole thing.

"Sara, while you were on your special leave—that's a joke, girl—I couldn't understand why Roberts was holding off in arresting Jerome Tichner for the attack on that little Johnson County boy. I'll bet he had just a hint of information that Tichner was involved in his nephew's disappearance years ago. Wanted us to make the case for him. Now, I'll bet he is holding both Jerome and Jennifer hostage, if they're alive at all, and we have to find him.

"None of which clears up our own two murders of the Justus women. Jerome? Or Jennifer? Or, Jerome and Jennifer?

"You find Roberts, Sara, and we'll end this damn case one way or the other."

"I'm on it, boss. You can bet on that."

Chapter Twenty-Three
Friday, May 22—Saturday, May 23

P erkins had asked that everyone be in his office at eight-thirty sharp on this Friday morning of what was starting out to be a warm spring day. Flowers blooming everywhere in the valley, trees in full bloom, the river surging at spring level—none of it stood a chance at making things warm and fuzzy in the sheriff's office.

"Thank you for coming. As you know, we have a sticky situation on our hands here. There have been multiple murders in the county, at least two dating back several years. On top of that, we have a former member of our own department now wanted on a charge of open murder. We lost our jailer to his wounds, shot by Ken Swicker, and another deputy murdered. And, we have a Johnson County detective wanted for possible kidnapping of our own prime murder suspects.

"Six people that we know of are dead, three of them little children, one the mother of one of the children, and now, two of our own. I said sticky because of the multi-jurisdictional situation. At least one of the dead children is from Johnson County, and the possible kidnapping suspect is a Johnson County Detective.

"Becky Martinez will be back in town later today to join in this investigation, at my request. I'd rather no one except me or District Attorney George Andrus speak with the press, and I insist that every item deemed important come across my desk. In this case, deemed important covers just about anything you see, hear, or stumble upon during this investigation.

"Stan, what have you found so far?"

Lyons liked the way Perkins had taken complete

control of what had been his department, and has had people fanned out working every angle. "The bloody shoe prints, or boot prints, at Tichner's salon match the shoe size of Jim Roberts perfectly, but we haven't made a match from his closet or from his police locker. If the prints are his, it might mean he's still wearing the shoes, or he has junked them somewhere.

"As far as the little canvas shoes we've found at both Tichner residences, all five pair match the prints at the murder scenes, but none have discernible blood stains. Sizes and sole patterns all match perfectly. It is possible the shoes worn during the commission of these crimes have been disposed of."

"Thank you, Sheriff." Claude couldn't bring himself to calling him anything other than "sheriff." "Lieutenant Lane. You've been called on to find the Tichners and Johnson County Detective Roberts. Where is your investigation leading?"

Sara outlined her work over the past couple of days, saying there simply wasn't any trace of the Tichners or of Roberts. She had asked for help from all the surrounding counties, and had contacted Martinez in the capitol as well. Perkins told everyone to keep at it, and keep him informed of anything that came up, and sent them on their way. Dr. Darling held back when everyone left.

"You always like to bet that last dime of yours, Claude, what would it be on today?"

Perkins smiled, thinking how he did tend to say things like that. "Oh, I don't know, Doc. This Roberts thing has come out of nowhere, and it's really screwing up my thinking. Now, we have two renegade cops, armed to the teeth, and enough dead people to start a town. That dime's kind of thin right about now."

"Interesting, isn't it, that Roberts held out that information about his nephew. Do you suppose he was planning to do Jerome in anyway?"

"That thought keeps rambling around. Becky'll be here a little later. She might have some ideas. That blood in the salon and the blood on Jennifer's car was from both the Tichners?"

"That's right. Jennifer and Jerome were both in the salon along with that third person, and that third person didn't do any bleeding."

"Okay, ride with me here for just a minute. If Jerome ran to his salon to feel safe, who killed Deputy Edwards? Jennifer? Or Jerome? And if it was Jennifer, how the hell did she do that without either George Andrus or Barbara Mingus seeing or hearing anything?"

"And, I keep adding things to this, don't I, and if Roberts was going to Jerome's to either kill or abduct him, why did he go to the salon? Why did Jennifer go to the salon? Why didn't Andrus or Mingus see or hear anything?"

"I can answer that, Sheriff." Barbara Mingus was standing in the open doorway. "We weren't able to hear anything because we were having an intense conversation. We were discussing how much in love we are with each other."

Mingus knew they had made a fatal mistake, that it might even cost her career. "Indiscriminate? Yes, but we simply couldn't control our emotions. Anything could have happened on that property, and we wouldn't have known it."

Dr. Darling and Sheriff Perkins just stared straight ahead. Complications of what was said were at the very heart of the current investigation, and now, compromised.

"You and George—?" was as far as Perkins got.

"Yes, Sheriff, me and George. This is a very embarrassing thing to say, as you can imagine, but I had to come and tell you. I don't know exactly what may have happened during the time of, well, of our indiscretion, but, Jesus, Claude, I don't know what to say."

"Best right now, Barbara, not to say anything. If you do remember possibly hearing people screaming in or near the garage, or others running from this grisly murder scene, please inform me right away." He was as cold-blooded as anyone had ever seen him, and he waved his hand, dismissing the attorney. A grim look crossed his face, and he felt the entire burden of Sandesta County on his shoulders. "An indiscretion? A man dead, two others probably either dead or being held hostage, and she calls it an indiscretion?

"Well, if that doesn't just about put a foot of shit frosting on my fucking cake. Has this whole county gone tits-up crazy, Doc? Such a simple thing, you know, use your search warrant to discover crime scene evidence, look for suspect Jerome Tichner, and above all, protect the crime scene.

"Oh, hell no, I won't do that, our skinny little DA says, I'd much rather bang the primary suspect's attorney. It's far more fun to do that than know that a deputy is being slaughtered, that suspects from all the murders are just slipping on and off the property, or that a rogue cop from another jurisdiction is lurking about.

"What the fuck is the matter with that man?" His tirade was getting a good head of steam when Deputy Peters stuck his head in the door.

"They've got Swicker cornered down by the river, Sheriff."

"I'm on my way." He grabbed his uniform hat and headed for the door. "At least this part of the morning hasn't fallen on our heads. Ride with me, Doc? We might need a sane voice."

"I wouldn't miss this. George Andrus neglected his primary job in order to get in bed with Barbara Mingus?" As soon as he said it, he realized that Peters was still standing there. Now the whole courthouse would know in less than five minutes.

245

***

Becky Martinez was about an hour away from Sandesta when she got the word that former Sergeant of Detectives Ken Swicker was holed up along the Sandesta River, and was being talked to by Sheriff Claude Perkins. Tension gnarled her fingers around the steering wheel, and she tried to project her feelings, her alarm to Perkins. "Claude, baby, you be careful. That man is insane and will not come out without pain. Use all your skills, cowboy." She was well above the speed limit by now, but with her special Attorney General license plates no cop in his right mind would pull her over. "Come on, Claude, be really cool."

She was racing down the Interstate, talking to herself the whole way. Perkins was talking too, but his comments were directed at Ken Swicker. "Sergeant Swicker, this is Claude Perkins. Let's let this end now, Ken. As you're aware, the Sandesta County Sheriff's Department has you surrounded, with officers on both sides of the river, and up and downstream from where you are." He tried to let Swicker feel important, which was so important to him all his life, and at the same time make him understand there was no way out.

Perkins was on one side of the river, Swicker on the other, both somewhat shielded by willows and other streamside vegetation. Large rocks, more ornamental than functional had been placed along the banks, and both men were using those for added protection. Springtime sunshine warmed the air, gentle breezes brought the aroma of flowers wafting about, but the possible stench of death hung heavy in the atmosphere.

"Put your weapon down, Ken. Just put it down and walk out slowly. No one wants to see any more deputies die, particularly one who needs help. I mean you, Ken. Come out and let us end this now." Dr. Darling motioned that Perkins might also let Swicker know he was there.

"If you'd like to talk to someone other than me, Sergeant Swicker, Dr. Darling is here." A volley of shots rang out from the bushes and rocks where Swicker was holed up, putting everyone face down in the mud immediately. Perkins motioned for two of his deputies to fire tear gas canisters into the bushes. He had already made his plans, and also sent a deputy close enough to fire a noise grenade, one that would stun anyone close when it fired.

Perkins watched as two tear gas grenades arched through the air and exploded at Swicker's feet. They were followed immediately by the stun grenade, and several officers carefully moved closer. Swicker came out from the bushes wearing a gas mask and firing two semi- auto service weapons. One round clipped Perkins on his left arm, but the sheriff got off two quick shots, one through Swicker's neck, the other into a Kevlar bullet proof vest. Swicker was dead before he hit the ground.

"I didn't want it to end this way, Ken. I'm sorry," Perkins said as he stepped out from behind the bushes, directly across the river from the dead former sergeant. "Doc, can you put something on this? That round went right through my arm, I think. Damn, it hurts." Blood was streaming down his bare arm from the entry and exit wounds, about two inches below his elbow.

"You're pretty lucky, Claude. No bones broken or anything. We'll patch you up quick." He already had his kit out, and deputies were coming over to make sure their new boss was okay. In the middle of all the excitement, a state car slid to a stop and one long-legged, agitated, AG investigator sprinted to the sheriff's side.

***

Hours of reports to write, hours of interviews with the press, and more hours making sure the murder investigations were continuing, got in the way of a welcome back for Becky. "I hope we can spend most of the weekend just being together, but I think we both know that isn't going to happen.

"This is a hard thing to say, but I'm relieved that the Ken Swicker episode is finally over, even if it did end badly. The whole thing was interfering with the real investigations. Now, with other problems, Swicker would have been a serious problem. If you pour another little glass of that wine, I'll bring you up to date, and you won't believe what you hear."

"If you're talking about George and Barbara, it's the first thing I heard when I got to the courthouse today. At any other time, in any other circumstances, it would be so sweet, but what the hell do we do about it, Claude?"

"There isn't a damn thing I can do about it. The District Attorney doesn't work for me. In the long run, I'm to blame. I was so short-handed, I asked him to do what a deputy should have been assigned to do. I am amazed at what they did, though. I mean that. I'm amazed, shocked."

"Well, at least we're aware he isn't a racist." They drank some wine, pulled the covers up and let nature take its course. "How long has it been since you were on your ranch?"

"Last summer I made one trip. That's all. About three days. I missed all the holidays, most of the haying season, deer season. Everything last year was missed."

"Will you take me for the haying season this year?"

"We get three, and if we're really lucky, four cuttings, so I think we can make at least one of those. Why haying? Not calving? Or winter roundup?"

"Haying. When I was a little girl, we visited a farm and the farmer had just cut tall grass. I love that smell. You smell like fresh cut hay, Claude, did you know that? Fresh cut hay, the aroma of earth, rock, rain. That's you, Father Nature."

Saturday morning came too soon, arriving on the sound of an upset telephone operator. "Sheriff Perkins, Sara

Lane just called on a landline, not the radio, and wants you to call her on her cell phone. She said it was urgent. Do you need the number?"

"No, I have it, thanks." A gentle prod brought Becky awake, and he told her about the call as he was dialing Lane. Becky headed downstairs to make coffee while Perkins talked with his Lieutenant of Detectives.

"I'm at the old Baldwin farm, Sheriff. About five miles north of town. I'm in a stand of trees about half a mile from the farm house. The Baldwin family just moved out one day and abandoned the place. Anyway, there's a car in front of the barn, and I think it matches the car that Jim Roberts drove."

"Don't make any kind of move, Sara. I'll mobilize some deputies and be there as quick as possible. No radios under any circumstances. If it's Roberts, he'll be listening. Good work, Sara. Stay low and if anything changes before I get there, call me immediately." He dressed as he was calling the office and getting two patrol units on the way and assigning other units to cover the entire perimeter of the old farm. He pulled most of his patrol units, all the detectives, and even some reserve officers into duty.

"Make sure everyone understands, no radios. I don't want to spook this situation. If it's Roberts, he might have two hostages. Just come close to the old farm, but not close enough to be seen. Set up a command at that little intersection where the three roads come together. I'll meet you there." He and Becky headed out in his car, and she force-fed him coffee. "My damn arm really hurts. What the hell did you do to me last night, woman?"

"A crybaby cowboy. That's a new one." She hadn't had time to put a new bandage on Perkins's arm and could see fresh blood. "When we stop, I'll redress that. You probably should be in the hospital, you know."

"They call this a flesh wound. Nobody ever told me the damn thing would hurt this much. No hospitals, Becky, that's where you go to die. I'm not ready." He was trying to chuckle, but it wouldn't come out right.

"How much do you know about Roberts? Is he going to overreact like Swicker, or will he be one who can be talked out of this situation?"

"I don't know much, I'm afraid. I also don't know how close we'll be able to get. It's been a long time since I've been to that farm. Sara Lane will have a good picture of the lay of the land when we get there. I remember reading that you are a fine hostage negotiator. Are you up to this?"

"It's been a while, but you don't lose that ability. Will Sara be able to determine where Roberts might be holed up on the place?

"In fact, why don't you call her right now and see if she can direct us to her." He handed the phone to Becky and she dialed Lane's number.

"Hello, Sheriff Perkins. This is Detective Roberts. Your little girl lieutenant isn't very bright, is she? Anyway, she'll die right along with the evil pedophile if you come anywhere near this place." And the line went dead.

Chapter Twenty-Four
Saturday, May 23

B ecky was shaking—part anger, part fear—as she handed the phone back to Perkins and outlined what Roberts had just said. "He's mad, Claude, fucking insane." Perkins sat very still for just a moment, the wisdom that comes from many years as a cop, coming together as a plan of action. Becky saw many emotions move across his rugged face, his eyes closing and opening, slowly, and he grabbed the radio mic.

"All units, this is Sandesta One. Go to your prearranged positions and stay put until ordered to move. This is a priority one message. All units, we have a hostage situation at the old Baldwin farm on the northern outskirts of town. Let me repeat, we have a hostage situation at the Baldwin farm. Mobilize the SWAT unit and medical units immediately.

"All radio traffic from now on must be priority one only. Sandesta One clear." Claude Perkins looked over at Becky as he pulled into the dirt lane that served as a driveway into the Baldwin farm, the driveway that intersected three roads. "We will save Sara, Becky. We will. I don't really mean this, but I'm going to say it. If we have to sacrifice anyone during this operation, let it be Roberts or either of the Tichners." She squeezed his hand as they left the car and began setting up a headquarters.

"We have a big plus on our side, Claude. We have a direct phone link with Roberts. What we have to do is establish some kind of willingness to negotiate on his part. That's always the hardest." She sat down with the phone. Members of the SWAT unit were setting up their office of sorts.

Dr. Darling and Stan Lyons were huddled with a few of the deputies watching as people moved about, seemingly in an orderly manner. "Perkins is good," Lyons muttered to himself.

"Here's the latest map of the place, Sheriff. I got this from the county assessor, so it should be accurate." Perkins looked over the papers spread out in front of him. "That bastard could be in any of four buildings, or even in one of the ravines that seem to border most of the place." Perkins agreed with Sergeant Towers entirely and called Stan Lyons over to the table.

"Stan, are you strong enough to take command of the SWAT operation?"

"I can do that, and I have something else I brought along. These are citizen band radios that I use when a bunch of us are out hunting. Short range, for sure, but if each SWAT units had one, I could coordinate all the efforts, and Roberts wouldn't be listening in." Combat experience along with a quarter century of police work in his memory, and Lyons was ready.

"Damn good, Stan, damn good. Sergeant Towers, help Sheriff Lyons distribute these, and get these men dispersed."

Lyons took command immediately. "I want some of your men in every one of those ravines, Sergeant. Get them moving right now, and remember, don't engage Roberts unless he engages first. Stay away from him. State's Attorney Martinez is going to establish a com link with him and try to talk him out." There wasn't a single member of his old department that cared one way or the other whether the 'old man' was gay or not.

"What I want your men to do is see if they can find out where he is in there. Remember, he has three hostages, and one of them is one of our own, so use all your skills." Sergeant Towers sent his men into the field and cautioned each group to stay off their police radios except in the event

252

of emergency, and use the ones Lyons had brought. Becky and Perkins continued looking at the map.

"House or barn would be my guess, Claude. The equipment shed wouldn't be easy to defend, and neither would the garage. House has the most windows, and access to things like water and possibly even food."

"I've already cut off the electricity and gas, and since the place is on a well, they don't have any water now, unless Roberts stored some. Let's see if we can raise the prick, Beck. He knows we're here— let's talk to him." She was already dialing Sara Lane's cell number.

"So, Sheriff, are you coming in, guns blazing? Wild west show and all?"

"Hello, Detective Roberts, this is State Attorney General Investigator Elizabeth Martinez. As you are already aware, we do have a sizable force surrounding you, but to answer your question, no, we don't intend to come in guns blazing. You're in a lot of trouble right now, and we want to minimize that. So far, no one's been hurt, and that's a big thing.

"What can we do to help you make the right decision? There's no reason for anyone to get hurt, and no reason for you to continue this situation."

"I heard you've already screwed half the Sandesta force, and now you want me, eh? Well, little bitch, come get me, because that's the only way I'm coming out. I have that bastard pedophile here, ready to hang. He has a rope around his neck, he's standing on a chair and there's a rope tied to it. The end of that rope is tied to Lieutenant Lane, and all I have to do is knock her on her ass and that fucker dies. And Lane would be my ticket out of here, so you better get ready for my demands. Do you understand, state bitch?" Becky was breathing hard, controlling her emotions, and Claude Perkins was ready to storm the fort. She hit the mute key on the phone.

"I'm almost sure he's in the barn, Claude. I heard

noises like shuffling feet in hay or something like that, and to tie a rope to a ceiling isn't easy, but to a beam in the barn would be." She unmuted. "Roberts, there's no reason for anyone to die. We have more than enough evidence to convict Jerome Tichner of the murders of those children, and the attack on the boy in your county. Let the judicial process take care of this. He will be found guilty, you have to know that."

"He'll spend the rest of his life being coddled in some prison while the victim's relatives will suffer their loss. No way, Martinez. This bastard dies, and I mean today.

"Now, I want you to get me a helicopter and one million dollars in unmarked currency, and I want it here in less than one hour, because in just one hour, Jerome Tichner is dead. If there's a copter here, with the money, and no funny stuff, the bitch cop lives."

"I can't make that decision, Roberts. I'll pass along your demands, but you should know, with your fine background as a detective, that these kinds of demands are rarely honored. You don't have to die. Let these people go, and walk out of that barn right now." She specifically mentioned the barn to see if there was any response.

"You think you're pretty smart figuring out where I am, don't you?" Becky looked over to Perkins who immediately got on Lyons's radio and sent word to his SWAT units to concentrate their activities on the barn. He gave a big positive shake of his fist to Becky.

"You just get that helicopter and that money. First Tichner, then your fine little split tail lieutenant, then the old bitch. Got that? Don't play cop games with me, just do as I say." And the phone went dead.

"This guy hasn't lost his mind, Claude. He thinks he can win this. His plan has lots of flaws, but not in his mind. He has to know he can't get away, his demands are just a ploy. He doesn't care if he lives or not. He only cares that

Tichner dies. He doesn't want the chopper or the million bucks."

"I know. He intends to kill them all, and then himself. He knows that because of Sara Lane, we're not going to storm the barn. She is one of our own, and more valuable to us than either of the Tichner's. If we can get close, we'll get one shot, and one shot only. If it isn't a clean kill, he will shoot, trip, or hit Sara, she will fall and jerk the chair out from under Tichner.

-"One thing, though, at least we know that all three hostages are alive. The only good thing on my mind right now, he has had to listen to Jennifer Tichner all this time. I bet she's given him an earful." It was the only smile he could conjure.

Sergeant Towers and his squad of three others were crawling on their bellies toward the rear of the barn. Each was in combat camo, faces marked with black, brown, and green paint, each going through the same maneuvers used in training. The only difference was that there were live rounds in their high powered rifles. These weren't your standard assault rifles; rather, the type that would be used for hunting big game, powerful sighting scopes in place. Using hand signals, he sent one man to get as close to the front as possible, and another to the far side. Each of the four men were crack marksmen, but only Towers had killed before, and that was years ago at the end of the Vietnam war. Each of the four men knew they might have to kill today. Several had been on the scene when Sheriff Perkins killed Ken Swicker, and now, they might be called on to kill a cop as well. It wasn't a good feeling.

They saw Jennifer first. She was the closest to them, and Roberts had tied her to one of the interior barn posts. For once, she was silent, avidly watching the scene before her.

Sara Lane never took her eyes off Jim Roberts, never gave the slightest indication she was terrified. Her hands were in handcuffs behind her back, and tied to the cuffs was a rope that led to the chair on which Jerome Tichner teetered. His hands were tied behind his back, and a noose draped his neck. He was sobbing, crying like a baby, ready to fall off that chair at any moment. Roberts prodded him once in a while, but wouldn't let him fall. "You'll die when I say so, you baby fucking bastard. You'll slowly choke to death, your feet not quite touching the floor, the fall not far enough to break your fucking neck. You'll die, murderer, when I say so." Sara Lane kept staring at him.

"You know you're going up against the best two lawmen in the country, don't you? Actually three, Roberts. Sheriff Perkins, Sheriff Lyons, and Investigator Martinez. You are the dead man. You just don't know it yet." Her prods had come right from the minute he had surprised her by coming up behind her from a ravine.

"You might have bested me, Roberts, but you are a dead man."

"Shut up, dyke bitch. Shut up." He came up next to her and slapped her across the face with the back of a big hand, his ring bringing blood, but wouldn't let her fall and choke Tichner. With blood streaming from her lips, she spit full in his face and he almost lost it. He pulled his service revolver and put it right next to her head, cocked it and almost pulled the trigger. As he pulled back, she caught just a glimpse of a man covered in camo, just outside a side window. He was gone that fast, but she knew there were more of them outside. The SWAT units always worked in teams of four.

"You've been a cop for a long time, Roberts, you must know what's happening right now. Maybe you're not a very good cop and that's why you think you can get away with this. Special Weapons And Tactics. Do you know what that means? Your head is already filling the scope of a Sandesta sharpshooter, that's what it means.

"You're pathetic. You're not qualified to be called detective. Any two-bit drunk could do a better job of police work than you. Look at you. Going to hold off the entire Sandesta County Police force?"

He hit her full in the mouth once, then slammed a fist into her nose and eye, then caught her before she fell, and she put a knee in his groin, then used her head to bash his. He staggered back and she rushed toward Tichner, fell on her knees and let his body fall on her, not the barn floor. One shot rang out and Roberts fell to the ground, half his head splattering all over the barn.

Sergeant Towers cut Tichner free and got the cuffs off Lane. "How the hell did you know we were here, Lieutenant?"

"I saw you through that window, Sergeant. But Roberts was looking the other way. I knew I had to get him angry enough to be a target, and he was. I'm going to need dental surgery, I think. Fucker throws a mean left cross."

"You throw a mean knee, Sara. That trick of falling on your knees under Tichner saved his life, you know." Between Tichner's crying, SWAT team members streaming in along with half the Sandesta Sheriff Department, one other voice screamed loudest.

Jennifer Tichner was incensed that her son did not die. "You bitch!" she screamed, over and over, at Lane. "You should have let him die! That pervert should be dead! You should have let him die!" Lane cut her loose as the SWAT unit scrambled in.

It took two of the burley men to subdue and control the woman, and to get her out of the area.

Chapter Twenty-Five
Monday, May 25—Tuesday, May 26

Sheriff Perkins was seated at the head of the table in the courthouse conference room with George Andrus, Becky Martinez, Stan Lyons, Sara Lane, Hank Towers, and Tim Darling gathered around the well-worn courthouse artifact. This wasn't going to be easy, he knew, but it had to be done, but he knew there would be an upside to the meeting. His brows were knitted as he looked up and down the table. Andrus appeared perplexed, maybe embarrassed and the new sheriff knew he should be because of his actions at Tichner's residence. Lyons and Towers, professional cops for decades, showed no emotion, while Sara Lane, still trying to accept her lieutenant's rank, sat with two beautiful shiners and a fat lip, thanks to Jim Roberts. She told Porter earlier, "Just that good old badge of courage, and son of a bitch, it hurts." These are good people, Perkins was thinking. but he was also aware that he didn't have the confidence of all of them, in particular the district attorney.

"Some news before we begin. I've been informed this morning that due to some personal indiscretions, Barbara Mingus has withdrawn as Jerome Tichner's attorney. She has brought in another firm, and I have to tell you, at her own expense. On this same subject of personal indiscretions, the State Attorney General's Office has made a decision to prosecute these cases due to Sandesta County District Attorney George Andrus's personal relationship with Barbara Mingus. A team of prosecuting attorneys will arrive sometime today from the capital and will coordinate their efforts with Special Agent Elizabeth Martinez." Andrus jumped to his feet, slamming his hand onto the table. For a small man, there was considerable force behind it, indicating his anger.

"You like this, don't you Claude. Humiliating me in front of these people. Giving homosexuals special privileges in your department, and now, forcing me to just sit back and watch. I hope you fry, Sheriff Perkins. I hope you fry." He stormed out of the conference room.

"I think I better go with him, Claude. Just to make sure he doesn't do anything rash."

"That's a good idea, Doc. I hope everyone realizes I wasn't trying to humiliate Mr. Andrus in any particular way. He did a pretty good job of that without my help. I won't come right out and say that his inopportune time to make love to his girl friend had a direct connection to Deputy Edwards death in Tichner's garage, but the timing might make that conclusion readily available." His point made, Perkins knew he had to get on with the meeting, not give opportunity for discussion of Andrus's conduct, or his references to those in the room who are gay. It dawned on him that he had made quite a transition from deputy to sheriff, and had the political savvy to carry it off. He liked that, and he was going to enjoy the next few minutes.

"I do have some good news, however, and all of you are part of it." He was smiling as he looked up and down the long conference table. "Each of you is to be commended on your efforts in ending the hostage situation at the Baldwin farm. Stan, the deployment of those civilian type radios was brilliant, and Sergeant Towers, your immediate action to end the problem will be a big factor in your personnel folder. Sara, Lieutenant Lane, your recognition of the fact the SWAT teams were in position, and forcing Roberts to only concentrate on you, at great physical risk to yourself, allowed this to come to an end." He wanted to comment on the black eyes, but just didn't know how without seeming to humiliate her. Just not the time for that good old boy humor of his. He had consulted with Stan Lyons and found out the department did have commendation awards, and took the extra minutes to hand them out to each person. "For service above the norm, people. You all deserve more, but it's all I have at my disposal. Raises? Damn me. I guess not." His humor popped through anyway.

"We still have a big job ahead of us. Between Ken Swicker and Jim Roberts, we have been distracted from our primary mission, that of solving the murders of Florida and Sandi Justus, and the murder of Deputy Edwards. What we did over the weekend is save the lives of our prime suspects, and it's time to once again focus on them. I think we all agree that one or the other of the Tichners is probably our murderer."

Perkins looked around the table, and all were indicating they agreed with him. He also realized one more time just how many big changes had taken place in his life, in his police department, in the lives of so many people. Just a few weeks ago he was a detective investigator, now he's sheriff, Sara was a deputy serving in the communications department, now his lieutenant of detectives, Stan Lyons was retired, coming out of the closet and back as his number two, at least for a while, and Becky Martinez was going to be his, what? Wife, girlfriend? It occurred to him they hadn't even talked about that. Well except for that one time when Becky popped off about marriage. "Marriage? Me?" His head was swimming, his arm hurt like hell, and he knew he had to continue.

"Becky, when we get through here, and before your team of prosecutors get here, I need a few minutes alone with you." He had that cockeyed smile playing across his face again, and Becky was seen to blush for the first time amongst these people.

"Nothing indiscreet, I hope." Sara Lane and the rest of the table broke into laughter, probably as much from the release of tension as from what Becky had said.

"Back to our murder investigations, folks." Perkins too was blushing, and Dr. Darling picked that moment to come back into the room.

"Bad timing?"

"No, Doc, just a little humor. We're just getting started on updating where we are as far as the murders of the Justus women, the death of Deputy Edwards, and the deaths of the two children whose remains were found at Jerome Tichner's residence.

"Do you have anything to add to what we already know?"

"I think I might. We have recovered a pair of canvas shoes—you call them tennie runners—that have several different types of blood on them. And, I now have a beer can opener with blood on it. This is the breakthrough that you were looking for, I think, Claude." He handed a report that was several pages long to Perkins, and distributed copies of the report to the rest of the group.

"Based on this, I think we need to call a couple of people in for questioning. Right now, Jerome Tichner is being held in the county facility on a no bail hold for the murder of the two missing children, and there's a hold on him from Johnson County for child molesting charges. He's not going anywhere soon." Perkins had a smile on his face as he continued. "I think we're getting close now, people. We can't interview Jerome until his new attorney is here, but there aren't any charges filed against his mother, and I think we would do very well by ourselves to ask her to come in for a couple of questions." Becky looked around the table, fidgeting actually, and finally spoke up.

"Claude, you have to be very careful here. If she's a suspect, and you question her without telling her she's a suspect, you could destroy the case."

"I couldn't agree more. But if she thinks we're talking about Jerome when we ask certain questions, she could let us know the truth about who killed whom. I'm not convinced she's the guilty one, but I also can't say I think Jerome is responsible. The one thing I think we can all agree on, Jerome has killed before, and could very well be our man. There is a belief that the first killing is the hardest, and that following murders are easier to commit.

"On the other hand, his mother is a basket case when it comes to recognizing reality. They are a pair, and we know they hate each other. By being very cautious with Jennifer, we could find out what really happened. I'm still under the opinion the voice that called in Sandi Justus's murder was a woman. Dr. Darling's report here, and blood samples to back up the words, could bring this thing to an end, finally." A thought crossed his mind as he said that. "Doc, is it possible to find something inside one of those bloody shoes that might point a finger at whoever was wearing them?"

"We are still investigating that, Sheriff. Anything from a broken toenail to a shred of skin would give us a possible identification, but so far, nada."

He asked Sara Lane and Sergeant Towers to find Jennifer Tichner in the morning and bring her in to be questioned. "With the prosecutors coming in this afternoon, and briefings and meetings scheduled all day, let's put tomorrow aside to talk to Jennifer. She won't be going anywhere with her car being impounded. It wouldn't hurt, Sara, to put a watch on her, though." With that everyone gathered their notes and started leaving the room. Dr. Darling, Stan Lyons, and Becky held back in order to walk out with Perkins.

"George had his letter of resignation already written, Claude. He delivered it to the County Clerk as soon as he left the conference room. It's a big loss to the county."

"It is, Doc., but it won't be the end of life as we know it. It's just a shame that he's allowing his prejudice to rule his life. Emotions that close to the surface are rarely found in attorneys. I wonder if there isn't something in his background that might answer these questions."

"You know, until I went up to the state capital and talked with the chief of police there, I was as ignorant of what it meant to be a homosexual as George seems to be about the question." Stan Lyons's face was drawn and tired. His shoulder slumped as he continued, "I knew I was gay, but I had no idea what it meant. I think if George had an ugly encounter with a gay person, maybe when he was very young, it may be clouding his thinking. Unfortunately, this isn't something we can do anything about. There is a large gulf separating the gay population from the straight, and that gulf needs to be bridged, and can be through such simple measures as education."

"Have you found your next calling, Stan?"

"You have helped me so much, Tim, it may be that I have. Being gay is not criminal. Criminal action is, whether we're talking about stalkers, pedophiles, rapists, molesters, people who take advantage of others. Yes, maybe I have found some way to project the truth." Contemplative as always, Lyons was actually feeling good about what was happening, with his life, and with the sheriff's office. If he left today, he was thinking, he would be leaving his old department in good hands. He liked everything he saw in Claude Perkins.

"When this is all over, Sheriff Perkins, sir, I will respectfully request that I be allowed to ride off into the gathering shadows of my old age." Perkins stood just a bit taller at those words.

"Depends on whether we have more multiple murders around here, Stan."

It was a short drive back to Perkins's apartment, and he was surprised at how long it was taking him to get there. He had worked his way through five or six scenarios, ways of asking Becky to be his wife. *My God,* he was thinking, *it shouldn't be this hard. I love her. She loves me. What's hard?* But he knew what was hard. He'd never even told anyone before in his life, except his mother of course, that he loved them. *How the hell do you do that? What the hell am I going to say?* He looked across the front seat and found Becky looking back at him, smiling that evil smile he was beginning to enjoy.

"Are you going to drive around the block several more times, or just pull in and park somewhere?" He hadn't even realized what he'd been doing.

"Just looking around the neighborhood." And then the two of them broke into fits of laughter and giggles. Cutting through the crap and relieving the tension was one of Becky's high points.

"You're cute when you get caught, do you know that?" He parked the car and they went inside, she continuing to prod her big cowboy. "Indiscretion? You're very special, Sheriff Perkins. One of a kind. Should we wait until we get to the ranch in Nevada to get married, or just get it over with right away?"

He just stood there, grinning, wringing his hands, unable to say a word.

***

"Those guys you brought in are damned sharp, Becky. I think they got a full grasp of the cases, even of the problems we've been facing in the department. Losing George Andrus is not a good thing, but the cases against Jerome Tichner are going to hold up well. We need to put the same kind of end to the Justus murders." It was just after six on Tuesday morning and beads of perspiration still danced across his forehead, and a wonderful feeling of satisfaction filled his body. "Isn't this just a piece of cake? I make love to the most charming woman I've had the pleasure of knowing and loving, and I want to talk about murder and mayhem. You need to smack me once in awhile, pretty girl."

Her arms and legs were wrapped around his big

frame and her head was buried in his shoulder. "Your arm is bleeding again, cowboy. If you promise to love me like this for a long time, I'll patch it up for you."

"It's against the law, you know."

"What's against the law?"

"Bribery. Jesus, what do they teach attorney general investigators?" He snuggled down with her and if the phone hadn't put up a squawk, they would probably have been late for the interrogation of Jennifer Tichner. "Perkins."

"Wake-up call, Sheriff. Just as you ordered."

"Thanks, Porter. Anything of any consequence overnight?"

"All quiet on the Sandesta front, Claude. Uh, Sheriff. Sorry."

"No problem. Thanks again." He tried untangling his arms and legs and Becky fought back just as hard. "Damn you're strong, girl."

"I'm a crime fightin' witch, cowboy, and don't you forget it."

***

Jennifer Tichner was frowzy. There was no better way to describe the woman, and this morning her hair, some white, some black, some even red from a mismanaged dye job, was in complete disarray. Sara Lane couldn't understand how someone could go out in public looking that way. She told Sergeant Towers what she had found after going into Tichner's home. "There was dirty everything. Dishes, clothing, carpets, even the furniture was filthy. This woman simply doesn't care. I had to get out of there. I should have asked you to go in and get her. And her language. She called me every name you can think of, primarily because I had saved Jerome's life Saturday. Amazing, too, she never even said thank you for saving her fat ass."

It had been quite a scene at the residence when the

patrol car pulled up. Jennifer was in her robe—at least according to her she was in her robe. There was more of her out of the robe than in, and when she recognized Lane, she started screaming obscenities. "You bitch! Why did you save that child killer? Why didn't you let that child fucking monster die? What do you want with me? You bitch, you should have let him die. He deserves to die a thousand times and you had to go and save his filthy ass." She stormed toward the house, but Lane was able to get there at the same time.

"It's up to a court to make those kinds of decisions, Ms. Tichner. I'm here to ask you to come down to the courthouse for a few questions, mostly regarding your son and some of his activities. Will you do that for us? We think he's guilty of some very serious crimes, but we need to ask you about some of his activities." The two women stood on the porch looking into each other's eyes, complete contrasts in style. Lieutenant Lane in perfect spit and polish from black leather boots to a uniform cap at just the right jaunty angle. She was just as tough as she looked, and sported two black eyes from her head butting episode and punch in the face, to prove it.

Jennifer was just as tough, as she had proved in a knock down drag out battle with Sandi Justus, and despite her comical bath robe and filthy slippers, she had her chin jutted out and her eyes sparkled with defiance. Lane was wondering if the old broad was going to take a poke at her. "No way, bitch. No way I'll come with you. Right now, I'd do anything to get that bastard put away, burned to death in an electric chair that isn't working right, suffocating from fumes coming from his own bile, but I'll be damned if I'll come with you. That man should be dead and you saved his filthy ass, and now you can't win without me? Well, suffer bitch, 'cause I'm not helping you at all." She walked into her living room, kicking clothes and dishes aside. Lane followed, and stood, slightly inside the open front door, wishing she was back out on the porch.

"It's true, Ms. Tichner, we do need your help. You want your son found guilty of these crimes? Then come help us. You know him better than anyone, and indeed, we do need your help."

Jennifer Tichner flew into a rage, whirling on Lane. "What are you saying, you bitch? Are you saying I'm a bad mother? What do you mean I know him better than anyone? Are you saying because of me he's a child-fucking bastard? You get out of my house right now. Get out!" She dashed into the kitchen and returned with a beer can opener in her hand, a church key just like the one that killed the Justus women and Deputy Edwards.

Lane retreated, watched as Jennifer stalked, cat-like, can opener slashing the air, threatening, and the mind of the well-trained cop went into action. Just a few days ago her life had been threatened, and it was quick thinking that got her out of it. She danced out of the way of a series of vicious slashes, reached up to her radio microphone clipped to her uniform blouse and held the key down.

"Stay back, Jennifer. You're under arrest. Put the weapon down now." She released the mic button, hoping like hell that Sergeant Towers picked up the message. "Jennifer, I don't want to have to hurt you, but I will. Put the weapon down." Tichner leaped at the detective, slashing, snarling like an animal, screaming "Bitch, bitch, bitch!" The church key slashed, Sara ducked out of the way but couldn't get her hands on the woman.

She attacked again, knocked tables over, scattering beer cans and ashtrays, smashed lamps, as she tried to kill Lieutenant Lane, who was able to avoid the vicious weapon.

"Put the weapon down, Jennifer. I won't say it again." She pulled her service weapon, a 9mm semi-automatic pistol and aimed it at Tichner. "Put it down, now." Jennifer Tichner was alone in her mind. Only the vision of Sara Lane saving her son, Jerome could be seen, and she was going to kill that vision.

A single shot rang out and Jennifer Tichner fell to the floor, the impact of the bullet hitting her arm knocking her backwards. Lane jumped on her, wrenched the beer can opener free, and then attempted to stop the bleeding. Towers slammed through the front door, and Lane heard him calling dispatch for an ambulance. Jennifer Tichner was still screaming, thrashing, kicking, but wasn't going anywhere. A well-trained cop with a pair of black eyes was sitting on top of her, smiling.

Chapter Twenty-Six
Tuesday, May 26

C laude Perkins knew immediately that the last days of spring were going to be hot and humid in Sandesta County, with only sporadic breezes along the river. Closer to the coast, mornings were much more enjoyable, with wisps of fog, sea winds drifting across the dunes, but not inland. Perkins's uniform shirt was already stained with perspiration and it wasn't even eight o'clock. His mind drifted back to days on the ranch, hot yes, but very dry, the wind crackling like a fire as it braced the sage and rabbit brush. Rain fell seldom, and the lower valley was often filled with towering dust devils. Just a quick ride and you were in the Santa Rosa Mountains and brisk air. A man can work in dry heat for hours, but not heat like this, making one feel as if he was trying to work his way out of a sauna. Sheriff Perkins would be changing his uniform shirt several times this particular day.

Becky had spent a fruitless half hour trying to convince the new sheriff that he should probably wear just regular civilian type clothes. She had her mind on a summer weight, light and airy type. "Most police agency heads wear suits, Claude. Do you even have one?"

"One. For funerals and such. No, Becky my love, I'm pretty damned proud of this department and I think I should represent it by wearing my uniform. Dignity and all that crap. What I miss isn't suits and ties and things like that. I'd love to put on some well-worn jeans, a western style shirt, and my old black leather vest. Trade in that county car for a good cow pony, and bust through some sage with shotgun chaps all scratched and worn. Now that's how a sheriff should dress." She gave up and they headed for the courthouse.

"I'm going to sit in on this talk with Jennifer Tichner." They had discussed whether Becky should be in on the questioning without reaching any answer. Martinez just gave her answer. "No matter what, it can never be discussed as an interrogation. Just some questions about Jerome. Agree?"

"All the way. If we do it in the conference room instead of one of the interrogation rooms, will we be able to record it?"

"No, not with those hard walls, but we can have a stenographer present. And, again, for our protection, Jennifer has to know this. Nothing hidden, no way anything can be thrown in our face once we get to trial. One of the people from my capital city office is a court stenographer in a previous life, and she's going to do the honors.

"I still think Jerome's our man, but it will be interesting to see what we get from his mother. They are a family."

"Tim Darling says the blood on those shoes is from Edwards, Roberts, Jerome, and Jennifer. Doesn't tell us one damn thing other than what we already know, that all of them were in some kind of physical altercation amongst themselves, or even separately. The shoes were found in Jennifer's car, but the blood on the doors of the car are from her, Jerome, and Roberts. Blind alleys, Becky. Whoever was wearing the shoes killed Edwards. That's the only conclusion I can draw."

"And that could have been any of the three. I agree. No. Wait, Claude, it all but rules out Roberts killing Edwards. He could never get his feet in those shoes, so we're back to square one. Jennifer or Jerome?"

They spent the next several minutes outlining how they would question Jennifer and had a pretty good plan as they arrived at the court house. Perkins headed for his office first while Becky met with her attorney general team.

Dr. Darling was already in the sheriff's office, waiting. "Of all the people to call me, Claude, Barbara Mingus called this morning. She thinks that Jerome Tichner might be contemplating suicide."

Perkins picked up the phone and called the jailer. "Put Tichner on a twenty-four hour suicide watch, and that means somebody actually watching. I have reason to believe he may want to try to do himself in." He motioned the coroner to sit down, and wondered why Mingus would call him.

"You've been on this case from the first minutes, Doc. Am I missing anything? No matter how small, some details are important, and I don't want my first case as sheriff to get laughed out of court."

Darling smiled at his new boss. "No way, Claude. The blood and cloth on that beer can opener belonged to Florida. That's the one you found in the river. No blood from Sandi Justus or from Deputy Edwards of course, and we don't have any other opener with blood on it. Sorry, but your crime lab people say no prints of any kind. I thought we had something there, but it turns out, it was one of the weapons used to maim Florida.

"I can't think of anything you've not discussed with all of us, Claude. Like you, I'm torn between the two Tichner's, but there is always the possibility that there might be someone we don't know about."

"Don't even go there, Doc. We have beer can openers at both their homes, and Jerome's business, both wear the kinds of shoes worn around all three of the murders, even a pair with lots of blood, and a voice on the telephone that could belong to either.

"Did Mingus say anything else? Did she say anything about who Jerome's new attorney might be?"

"I wondered for some time why she called me, but I think probably George had her call me instead of you. They are even tighter now than before, and he doesn't have good

271

thoughts concerning you. She said the AG's people would be contacted as soon as the attorney was ready to talk to Tichner, but didn't say who it would be."

"That would be the proper thing to do. Between Swicker, Harris Fletcher, and now George Andrus, we're lucky to even have a case. Will you sit in with us when we talk with Jennifer Tichner?"

"I don't think that would be quite right. You have notes and reports on everything I've done, and I think we'll be better off not to have too many people in there. Don't want to scare the old hag. I will be in the lab, though, if you need me."

"Thanks, Doc. Here's a copy of the list of questions that Becky and I drew up coming in this morning. Sorry it's in pen, but look it over and see if there's anything we may have missed. Remember, this is supposed to be just a session to get some answers about Jerome. The questions are only slightly loaded." There was a chuckle to that, but his eyes also testified to the seriousness of the meeting.

"You can't put words into Jerome's mouth, but you might ask how it is they both have the exact same canvas shoes. And, of course how her car came to be at the beauty shop. Maybe not, though."

"That one's off limits, Doc. We're hoping she will just pop off with it. You know, chasing the little bastard. It could be that's how Roberts found them together as well." He was about to go on, but his intercom rang.

"Sheriff, reporter Nancy Carrington is on the line. About Jennifer Tichner."

"Thanks, Lori, I'll take it." He motioned to Dr. Darling to stay and listen, and he turned the speaker phone on. "Good morning, Nancy. What can I do for you?"

"Good morning, Sheriff. I understand you've brought Jennifer Tichner in for questioning. Is that true?"

"No, Nancy, we have not brought Ms. Tichner in for anything." He glanced at Darling who smiled slightly.

"She is in the courthouse, isn't she?"

"We've asked her to come in, Nancy. But she'll be coming in of her own volition. She will not be brought in; everything is purely voluntary. Anything else while you have me?"

"Just one thing, Sheriff. Swicker's funeral is scheduled for day after tomorrow. Is your department planning anything special for it?"

"Ken Swicker was a good cop, Nancy, but he had psychological and physical problems that he wouldn't address and those led, ultimately, to his death. He embarrassed this department by his actions, and was running from felony charges when he died. The Sandesta County Sheriff Department will not participate in the funeral in any official capacity. Swicker had many friends in the department and in the county and of course, many plan to attend.

"I'm afraid, Nancy, I must leave now. Meetings and such, you understand. Please don't hesitate to call with questions. Unlike the previous administration, I welcome a chance to let our county residents know what their sheriff's department is doing. Bye, bye." She said her goodbyes, and Dr. Darling let Perkins know he did very well.

"You might make a politician yet, Claude."

"You can go straight to hell for that comment Doc." But he was smiling when he said it. "Gotta get to the Tichner session, Doc. See you afterward. Becky has a stenographer who will make all the notes available." The intercom rang again, and it was Sara Lane. "Come right in Lieutenant, come right in." Perkins was exuberant about being able to talk with Jennifer Tichner, had even told Becky he felt this session could very well break the case.

The smile of anticipation left his face immediately. "Sara, my God, what the hell happened?" Lane stood in the doorway, her uniform covered in blood—not hers—her blouse torn, and her face looked more serious than Perkins

273

had ever seen.

"Ms. Tichner attacked me with a beer can opener, Sheriff. A beer can opener." She said that the second time for its guaranteed reaction. Perkins knew Jennifer Tichner was slightly off center, knew she had church key beer can openers, but this is the first time he knew she would use one as a weapon. "She refused to put the weapon down or stop the attack. I was forced to shoot her. She's going to live, and she's in the hospital now. I've arranged for a deputy to stand guard.

"It took both Sergeant Towers and myself to subdue that woman, even after she'd been shot. I've never seen anyone as far out of control as she was, Sheriff. Her eyes weren't focused, she was screaming and snarling like an animal, and if she had gotten near me with that can opener, I'd be dead right now."

Perkins just sat back, took about three big gulps of air and tried to calm himself and his lieutenant down. "Are you injured, Sara?"

"I don't know why, but no. She kicked chairs, broke lamps, swung at me with that church key, caught my blouse once, but somehow, didn't actually hit me. She is as mad as they come, Claude. She blames me for letting Jerome live following the hostage situation, and said that I was forcing her to prove to the town that she was a bad mother by asking her to come down here. It was then she just plain old fashioned went tits up.

"Sorry for using that language, but I don't know how else to explain the change that happened. She just blew up, Sheriff. Just blew up."

"Are you able to write your report, Sara?" He knew he had a stenographer at the ready, and if Lane wasn't composed enough to write it up, at least she could tell in her own words what happened, and the report could come later.

"I'm okay. Hell, Sheriff, all I wanted was a little

patrol time. You didn't have to start a war on my account. Taken prisoner, almost knocked off by a loony tunes detective, and now, almost sliced to shreds by an out of control murder suspect. Those days of being in the communications room and making coffee are starting to look just a little better." It was hard for both of them to laugh, but they knew they had to, had to get it out of their system.

"Just wait till those AG boys and girls hear this story. They think we've been making up half these stories as it is. Go get cleaned up, Sara, and get your report written and in to me as soon as you can. You know, also, that because you used your weapon in the line of duty, I have to put you on paid administrative leave. All that means at this time is, take a couple of days off, let your eyes heal, and get your nerves straightened out.

"Becky will have to conduct an official investigation, and you will be asked a thousand questions, but you might very well be the person breaking this case wide open. It's not the best thing to say right now, but I'm kinda glad that woman attacked you in the manner she did. I want Dr. Darling to draw some psychological conclusions from your attack. It sounds so much like what happened to the Justus women, and to Edwards.

"Keep me posted on anything that you can think of regarding this morning, Sara, and don't worry about anything. No cop could have done a better job." They were both smiling, he wanted to give her a hug, knew he couldn't, and offered a big right hand for shaking.

***

Within the hour Perkins finally had time to sit at his desk and enjoy a conversation with Becky. She started the conversation. "Think of it this way, Claude. You have both suspects in one form of custody or another. Neither is going anywhere, and as soon as a lawyer is produced for Jerome you can start your interrogations. In the meantime, Jennifer

275

is being held for attempted murder, and you can interrogate her as soon as she has been read her rights. I don't know if she's smart enough to know she can have an attorney present. In fact, she's so smug, she may feel she won't need one.

"I really do feel the end of this piece of shit coming up. I feel an indiscretion coming on, Sheriff. Big boy. Cowboy."

Chapter Twenty-Seven
Monday, June 1

"Is there anything else we need before we go into court this morning? Anything at all? This will be a preliminary hearing, so there will be testimony, but not long and detailed as a regular trial might be." Becky Martinez, along with being the chief investigating prosecutor in the state Attorney General's office, was also still responsible for the activities in the Sandesta Sheriff's department, even though she and the AG both agreed that Claude Perkins was the Sheriff. The days of Harris Fletcher were over, and the chaos brought on by Ken Swicker had subsided, mostly. There were still court dates dealing with Swicker beating the hell out of George Andrus, and a civil suit pending from Sara Lane, but with Swicker dead and Lane reinstated to duty, that issue might also be off the docket.

"Jerome's new lawyer is a New York dude, so he just might try something stupid thinking the rural types wouldn't understand. I've got my absolute best courtroom attorney prosecuting, and he does have help from me and two other fine attorneys."

"I'm only worried about one thing, Ms. Martinez." Sara Lane's eyes had subsided to brilliant purple from the deep almost black of last week, and the cuts on her cheek and arm, still bandaged. gave her the look of a combat veteran. In other words, she looked a frightful mess. Deputy Porter had made that comment earlier this morning, but it wasn't her looks she was concerned about. "Do you think it's safe to bring Jennifer Tichner into the same court room with Jerome?"

"I agree with you, Sara, but we need her testimony

about Jerome and his proclivities toward children. Remember, this is the case of the two children whose body parts we found buried in his yard, not the cases of the Justus women, although his dealings with Florida Justus will be a part of the testimony." Becky's mind went back to the interview one of her prosecutors had with Jennifer the day after she was admitted to the hospital suffering from Sara Lane's well placed pistol shot. The report had circulated throughout the courthouse.

There were two telling paragraphs in the report. "If this woman is to ever be charged with a crime, regardless of the severity of the crime, I seriously doubt there could be a successful prosecution in any court." The report detailed the complete mental state of Jennifer Tichner simply by stating, "This woman is mentally unbalanced and desperately needs treatment, and I feel that to safeguard the general population, Jennifer Tichner needs to be confined. She is a danger to herself and all others around her. At one point in the interview of May 28, she attempted to attack, not only me, but a nurse provided by the hospital. She came at us with a plastic knife she apparently kept following her dinner the night before. It's only because I'm fairly large and strong, and the fact the nurse had a syringe of sedative available, that neither one of us was injured."

Again, the details about finding every thought or comment to be a slur against her being a good mother, every opportunity that came up there was a challenge from her to do bodily harm, not only to her son, but to the interrogator for even asking the question.

The capper in the report, however, was this: "After my second meeting with subject Tichner, she spent most of the hour attempting to seduce me. At one point, a nurse who was standing by with sedatives, just in case subject got out of control again, had to leave the room because of uncontrolled laughter. I called it childish giggles and demanded she return. Subject Tichner pulled the sheets down at one point and exposed herself, demanding that I take advantage of the situation.

"It was at that point that I concluded the interview and returned to the courthouse to write my final report. This subject's mental capacity is such that she will never face the reality of a courtroom."

***

"To answer your question fully Sara, Ms. Tichner will be in restraints and will be attended by one or two of Sheriff Perkins's jailers. I agree with you, the potential for violence is very high, but the judge will not allow for video examinations or testimony. He's a stickler for having those testifying actually be in his courtroom, and we need her testimony. If she behaves as most of us think she will, the judge will have to be the one to hold her in contempt and be dismissed from the proceedings. I really hope that doesn't happen, but it is something we have to think about.

"Doctor Darling, I'm sure I don't even have to ask this, but is your testimony clear in your mind?"

"Absolutely, Ms. Martinez. The findings of the forensic investigation are very clear, and I'll be comfortable testifying. But, I have to admit, I'm not pleased with having both the mother and son in the court room at the same time. But, like you said, I think we do need her testimony."

"Thanks, Doctor. I think that's it, folks. Let's go have our day in court and start Jerome Tichner on his journey to the death chamber." Her eyes were narrowed and almost angry as she said this and Claude Perkins was reminded again what a fine investigator and prosecutor she was.

Jerome Tichner was flanked by two attorneys, Thomas G. Harrington was lead, sitting to Tichner's right, and James Caughlin, more investigator than attorney, sat along the rail, to his left and slightly behind Tichner. Harrington was a small man, thin with almost no shoulders.

279

His face was like that of a hound being punished, and his hair, what there was of it, flew in every direction, no one strand more than two inches in length. Despite his almost comic appearance, his reputation was that of one of the East Coast's finest criminal defense attorneys. Caughlin, on the other hand, a former Chicago police officer, was huge. After fifteen years on the streets of the windy city, he went back to school, got his law degree, and became a partner in Harrington's firm. Harrington was pasty white, frail almost, and tense, while Caughlin, a black man from the streets of Chicago, looked for all the world like a pumped up recently released prison inmate. They presented a picture of extreme contrast in the courtroom.

Becky and two representatives from the capital sat at the prosecution desk, while Sheriff Perkins and Lieutenant Lane sat in the spectator's section of the courtroom. The courtroom came alive when two deputies entered with Jennifer Tichner between them, all eyes on who the press had been describing as the mad woman of the case, the mother of the child molesting killer. It was obvious she simply didn't give a damn what she looked like. Her prison jumpsuit was only partially zipped up; her hair was just a matted mop, probably hadn't seen a comb or brush for weeks, and she was wearing no makeup of any kind. Sara Lane was amazed that she only had handcuffs on. She was not restrained as earlier described.

"Sheriff, look. She's not fully restrained. Why?"

"I don't know, Sara." He got up to talk with the deputies when the judge entered and the courtroom was called to order. He never got a chance to ask the question before Jennifer was seated in the witnesses section and off limits to anyone in the court room except the two deputies.

The hearing judge was Geraldo Torres, a native of Sandesta County who'd won every judicial election he's faced in the last twenty-five years. "Tough but fair" described him, and he was very aware of the potential for trouble in today's hearing. Since his first day in office, there was a rumor that Torres kept a loaded service revolver in a drawer on his bench, and most in the courtroom were aware of the rumor. No one knew for sure, though. Torres always felt that was to his benefit.

"Let's get this underway, shall we? There are several charges brought against Mr. Tichner, but I want to hear testimony dealing with the bodies of two children allegedly found on Mr. Tichner's property." He called on the state to present its case, reminding all that this was only a preliminary hearing to find out if there was enough evidence to hold Jerome Tichner for trial. A confession from Tichner was read first.

"Your Honor, this is the confession of Jerome Tichner, made to the Sandesta County Sheriff, Claude Perkins, and witnessed by Mr. Tichner's attorney, Thomas G. Harrington. This is the printed version, and we have the confession on audio and video tape as well. The defendant was being questioned about those children whose bodies are the subject of this hearing, but he also, and at his own volition, brought up other subjects. They must be considered along with this confession." The paper was given to the judge who read the transcript aloud.

"That little boy in Johnson County. Is he okay? He was so pretty. I didn't want to hurt him, but he kept fighting me. I accidentally hurt a little boy once, and a little girl. I gave then excellent burials, Sheriff. I really did, but then some dogs got in my yard and uncovered them again. I spread the pieces of those children around so the dogs wouldn't be able to find them again.

"I never wanted to kill anyone. I didn't mean to hurt them. I just wanted them to know I loved them, and I wanted them to love me." By the end of the reading, the judge was choking back tears, emotion staining what should have been a stern judicial face, and Jerome Tichner was sobbing at the defense table.

"Is there more, Ms. Martinez?" He knew there would be, but he didn't really think it was necessary. The confession alone should be enough to bind Tichner over for trial. "Before you answer, let me direct a quick question to Mr. Harrington. You allowed your client to give this confession? You didn't try to silence him in any way?"

Harrington stood up and approached the bench. Becky Martinez immediately joined him. "He made those comments before anyone even realized he was going to do it. I had implored him to let me do the talking during the interview, but he just jumped right in and confessed. I feel terrible about it, but it was his decision.

"I already know your next question, and yes, I feel we can still give an adequate defense. I feel he is psychologically unfit to stand trial, and if you bind him over for trial, I will immediately ask for psychological evaluation."

"I understand. Ms. Martinez, do you have anything to add?"

"No, Your Honor. The defendant did confess and in order to continue this hearing, I feel we need to hear from his mother."

"Very well, then, call your witness."

"Yes, Your Honor. We call Jennifer Tichner." There was a tenseness in her voice and demeanor, and Claude Perkins immediately picked it up. He had been watching Jennifer during the reading of the confession and the interlude of attorneys at the judge's bench, and could see her anger boiling close to the surface.

"Be ready for anything, Sara. We can't have our guns in the courtroom, but I hope you have that little sap of yours." He was very pleased when she patted her purse and smiled at him. "I feel naked without that damn pistol on my hip. Let's just be like a pair of cats, here. One false move and she's pinned and helpless, okay?"

"We make a pretty good team, Sheriff. Except I'm

the one that always gets beat up." They both smiled hard, tight smiles, and were tensed for anything that might come about. Jennifer was escorted to the rail, but the deputies had to stand there while she walked to the witness stand. She was glaring in the direction of her son, but didn't make any kind of move toward him. Her swearing in was handled in an official manner, and she settled into her chair. She offered a big smile to the judge, crossed her legs in what she assumed would be a provocative manner, but was more obscene than anything, and then glowered at Jerome.

The swearing in went without complication, and Becky began by having Jennifer state her age, her relationship to the defendant, and then asked the big question. "You raised Jerome Tichner in a loving home, Ms. Tichner?"

"I'm a good mother. I'm the best mother in this whole community, and anyone who says otherwise is a liar. That little bastard is evil, and it isn't my fault. I've given him nothing but love and kindness all my life, and all he's ever done is try to destroy me, and humiliate me before the whole world." The judge was trying to get her back on track, and she shushed him, stood up and directed an attack at Jerome, despite the demand for order from the bench.

"Those cops showed you pictures of your little dipsy Florida, didn't they? That's what you're going to look like when I get through with you. I'm gonna rip your filthy body to shreds and feed it to the dogs, just as you did those other children. You're vile and evil, Jerome, and that little girl was the nicest little person I ever met, and you ruined her. You and her horrible mother. You fucked her and her mother beat her constantly."

Jennifer's anger had her shaking as she spoke, her words coming at a machine gun tattoo, her fist was balled as if to reach out and strike her son. The tension in the courtroom was palpable as she continued.

"God, Jerome, I tried to tell her how wrong she was

to be with you. I tried to tell her what a horrible person you are, and all she could say was she loved you. Do you know how that made me feel, you child molesting bastard? Do you? She was so sweet, but she had to die, she had to die, Jerome. She had to die because that was the only way I could keep her away from you and her mother."

Jerome had endured this kind of vocal wrath from his mother all his life, and just sat with his head bent, until that last sentence. He immediately sat straight up when he realized what Jennifer had just said. *She killed them* screamed through his mind, suddenly fully alert.

"She died and her mother died, Jerome, and you're next. You're gonna die now, Jerome, now, and I'm going to destroy you so bad nobody will be able to recognize your evil body." She leaped from the witness box, covered the twelve feet to the defendant in under a second, and pounced on Jerome before anyone could stop her. She had her son's head in her manacled hands, and with a massive twist of her entire body, she wrenched his neck. He was dead in that instant, and before the deputies, before Becky Martinez, before Sheriff Perkins or Lieutenant Lane could reach her, she was bashing his lifeless head on the table.

It took the combined efforts of everyone involved to get the situation back under control. Perkins had the jailers take Tichner to the court's holding cell, and the judge finally got back in control.

"Before I conclude this hearing, I want everyone to understand something. It was me and me alone who is responsible for what happened here. Sheriff Perkins, I know you ordered your jail staff to bring Ms. Tichner in under full restraint. I'm the one who said simple handcuffs should be enough. It's very obvious I was wrong, and what that might mean to my own future, I'm not able to say, but it is important for everyone here to recognize my fault in this."

There was a hushed silence, a quiet shuffling of feet

as the judge made these comments. The crowd just watched, horrified, as a man was murdered, and now the judge admitting fault. He continued.

"This hearing has also obviously been concluded. Charges for the murders of Florida and Sandi Justus must be filed against Ms. Tichner. The clerk will make all the papers available to you, Ms. Martinez. If there's nothing further, this hearing is over."

***

"You wipe that smirk off your face right this minute, Sheriff Perkins." Perkins, Martinez, Dr. Darling, and Sara Lane were all in the sheriff's inner office, and the sheriff was leaned back in his chair, Cheshire Cat written all over his face.

"Sorry, Becky, but I've been saying for a long time, it was Jennifer. When you write up your charges, make damn sure you include the murder of Deputy Edwards.

"We've been through a lot in a short period of time, folks, and it ain't over until it's over, in the words of Yogi. I do believe it's over. I think it's time for a bit of indiscretion." He pulled her close and they kissed passionately. The room erupted with applause. Perkins and Martinez joined hands and walked from his office, out the big front doors of the courthouse, and to his car.

"Can you get away for a week or two? There's a little ranch out in Nevada you need to be acquainted with."

"My people are already on their job, and we only have a day or two of paperwork between us. Fly or drive, cowboy?"

"I'll ask my brother to pick us up in Reno, and I'll make the flight reservations as soon as we walk in the door."

"You can do all that just a while after we walk in the door, hot shot. Indiscretions always come first. It's a rule, you know. Code of the West, and all that."

About the Author:

I've had a wonderful and varied time along this bumpy highway called life. I spent my early years in Santa Cruz, California, swimming, fishing, and wallowing in the splendor of redwoods, the Monterey Bay, and a loving family. Then, my four years of high school were spent living on the Island of Guam. That was back in the early 1950s.

My beautiful wife Patty and I live on a small hobby farm about twenty miles north of Reno, Nevada, sharing space with a couple of fine horses, a flock of egg-producing chickens, and some breeding rabbits. You're always welcome to visit. I need help cleaning those corrals.

Social Media Links:

Facebook: https://www.facebook.com/johnny.gunn.31

Blog: http://johnny-gunn.blogspot.com/

Twitter: https://twitter.com/johnnygunn11

Other Books by Johnny Gunn

Paradise Challenged

Thornton Holiday is a murderer and a bank robber. He's a man with a plan—a plan to create an outlaw haven in the New Mexico community of Plainsville. The village is overrun with the meanest outlaws in the west and fights back with the help of a fourteen-year-old boy who demands to be considered a man.

http://bookgoodies.com/a/B015QFSMAS

Jacob Chance, U.S. Marshal

Land law, water rights, deeds of ownership? Boring. Unless of course, people are shooting at you because of them. The Civil War has disrupted thousands of lives, including that of Sarah Jackson, whose husband was killed for not joining the Confederate Army in Georgia. Sarah and her daughter flee to Nevada Territory and are eligible for homestead rights. After claiming her one hundred sixty acres in the lush Golden Valley, her world crumbles again.

Banker Preston Miller claims he owns the entire Golden Valley and all the water in the Good Hope River. Jackson cries foul in a letter to the U.S. Attorney in San Francisco, and Jacob Chance, U.S. Marshal rides to Preston, Nevada Territory to "settle this little land dispute."

He finds many in the town fear for their lives and livelihood, but it takes just a few shots from big guns to convince them to back the marshal. Lives are lost, buildings are burned, the town itself is in jeopardy, and the

U.S. Marshal finds himself up against an army. Anarchy is the rule in the Golden Valley.

Fighting the bad guys is hard enough, he also finds himself fascinated by the daughter of one of the ranchers whose property he is trying to save. Will the town survive? Will the ranches survive? Is romance in the air? All the answers are inside these covers.

http://bookgoodies.com/a/B00XWBQ0OO